IN THE FOREST
OF THE
LOST AND FOUND

By

K.D. Van Brunt

ISBN 978-0-9913747-3-1

Published by Ars Fabula LLC
ArsFabulaLLC@gmail.com

Visit www.kdvanbrunt.com

IN THE FOREST

OF THE

LOST AND FOUND

TABLE OF CONTENTS

PART I

"To find the light, search the darkness"
—Brigita Păcurariu

CHAPTER ONE

Scarsdale, New York

The black Mercedes sedan lurched to a stop in front of Scarsdale High School two feet away from me, but when I tried to open the passenger's side door to enter, the handle wouldn't budge. The door was locked. I rapped two knuckles on the tinted window glass, and the lock clicked open. Frederick, our driver, should have greeted me with a disinterested nod, but instead my mother gave me a quick waggle of her fingers in greeting. She had her phone plastered to her ear talking rapidly to someone.

"Okay, call me tomorrow," Mom said. "I have to run. Allie is here." She dropped her phone haphazardly into the cup holder and smiled warmly at me. "How was lacrosse practice?"

"Fine. I'm starved."

"We have to make a slight detour. Grace needs a ride home from Sasha's house."

My mouth fell open in shock, and after two gulps, I asked, "But I thought she was grounded?"

"She is. She was supposed to come straight home."

"Well, what are you going to do about it?" I demanded.

"It's between her and me. You stay out of it."

With an exasperated sigh, I slumped in the front passenger seat and shook my head. Grace was a grade behind me, but my parents let her get away with just about everything—up to, and including, her latest stunt: shoplifting Q-tips from a drug store. Attempted shoplifting. She got caught. Her purse had over a hundred dollars in it; she could have bought thirty packs of the things.

The theft was a prank, a joke among her friends. The store didn't bother calling the police, and Mom barely gave her a slap on the wrist. If I had done it, I probably would have gone to jail and received a felony conviction.

Mom and I didn't speak further during the ten-minute drive to Sasha's house. Since Mom listened to a radio channel playing nothing but smarmy, lame-ass nineties songs, I inserted my earbuds and scrolled through my phone until I found my favorite playlist. As the first song began, a text dinged from Olivia, my best friend, confirming all the rumors around school today that her ex-boyfriend, Evan, had indeed hooked up with Victoria. My thumbs hurriedly texted a message back.

Me: ***Sleepover at my house Friday? Chocolate party?***

Olivia: ***Yes!***

With a couple clicks on the volume button, the song by Slimy Eel became almost loud enough to drown out my annoyance over having to pick up Grace. Almost. When we reached Sasha's house and pulled to a stop in front of a stone walkway, where Grace was supposed to be waiting for us, she was MIA. Of course, she was. Even Mom clucked her tongue in frustration.

"Hop out and get Grace," Mom said. "Say hello to Mrs. Heller for me."

"We should just leave and let her walk home."

"Allie, be nice. Let me deal with her."

Mom punched on the car's hazard lights as I jumped out and jogged toward the house, which was actually a mansion—not quite as opulent as our mansion but close. The air around me had the distinctive, pungent smell of newly mown grass and overturned earth. Their lawn company must have come earlier. Not sure why I noticed this.

Once on the porch, I tapped the electronic doorbell and stepped back to wait. The late-afternoon autumn sun glinted orange off the home's front windows.

The Hellers had a very distinctive doorbell chime—a bugle sounding reveille. As soon as the horn noise ended, the ensuing calm was quickly replaced by the blaring noise of an approaching emergency siren. The scream of a revving engine accompanied the alarm. The chaotic noise sounded like the roar of a prehistoric monster rampaging through the streets.

Instinctively, I swiveled my head around to gaze down the street at what was going on. The shrill squeal of tires negotiating a turn at a high rate of speed tore through the air, and I flinched. At the end of the long block, a black Mustang with darkened windows barreled down the street in our direction, its engine roaring with angry growls. Flashing lights from a pursuing police car came into view a few car lengths behind it.

At the speed the Mustang raced along, no way could it make the approaching turn and avoid hitting our car.

Once I realized what was happening, I had less than a microsecond to react. Even if I could have slowed down time, what could I have done? Nothing. I did the only thing I could—I screamed. The Mustang plowed into the back of Mom's car with a thunderous boom, shoving her car forward twenty yards and utterly annihilating the trunk and back seat, as an explosion of glass and metal parts rocketed into the air. Our car was pushed directly into the path of a delivery truck traveling fast the other direction, and my stomach twisted as the head-on collision unfolded in front of me. With a sickening screech of crunching steel, our Mercedes was reduced to a giant accordion in half a nanosecond.

"Mom!"

Without even thinking about what I was doing, I raced toward our car with raw, panicked screams ripping out of my lungs. The cloying, sweet smell of gasoline slammed into my nose. Moments later, the smashed and twisted wreckage of our vehicle, the lump of metal with my mother in it, exploded in a ball of fire that rose high into the air. The heat from the inferno forced me to stop yards away and shield my face with my arm. I tried to inch forward, but the searing-hot air stopped me dead in my tracks.

"Mom!"

I sank to my knees on the walkway, screaming incoherent words, while ash and smoke swirled all around me. I choked on the black soot that filled the air and my lungs.

My world ended that afternoon, and I died on that sidewalk.

CHAPTER TWO

Four years later

June 22

"Allie, breakfast is being served!" Brooke, my stepmother, yelled from the downstairs landing.

"Coming!"

With a groan, I unwrapped myself from the blankets tangled about me and sat up in bed, placing my bare feet on the cool parquet floor. I surrendered to a yawn before heading off to the bathroom, where I stared at my reflection in the mirror, debating whether to use a brush or my fingers on my caramel-brown hair.

No time for the brush. Brooke was a stickler about everyone sitting down to breakfast together on time so she could feel like we were all one happy family. How adorable.

I slipped into a pair of baggy sweats and wiggled into a Yankees hoodie. I had plans for the day, and they involved spending as little time with my family as possible. Although I had graduated from Phillips Exeter Academy last Friday, five days after I turned eighteen, I didn't plan on spending much time at home over the summer.

"Good morning," Brooke declared in a chirpy voice when I entered our formal dining room. "Welcome home, dear."

"Yeah, whatever," I murmured.

So, meet my dysfunctional family. In Rudolph the Red-nosed Reindeer Christmas special terms, my house was the island of misfit toys. Everyone here was a complete loser. Except me. I was the only normal person in this place . . . Well, possibly Dad, too, on his good days.

"You look so gorgeous," Brooke went on, upshifting into her suck-up voice.

"Don't start," I snapped.

I wasn't gorgeous. I had morning hair, morning face, morning armpits, and morning splotchy skin. Brooke, on the other hand, looked like she was about to pose for the cover of Elle.

Yes, family member number one was my stepmother, Brooke. I didn't dislike Brooke; dislike would require more emotional involvement than I could muster. What I felt toward her was indifference; as long as she left me alone, which she generally did, I ignored her. She reminded me of an attractive knickknack—place it on a shelf somewhere and keep it dusted.

Okay, Brooke really did love Dad, I'll give her some bonus points for that. But at the end of the day, she was a stranger to me. She would always be an outsider. Of course, it didn't help that she was only twenty-nine, young enough to be my older sister.

Brooke and Dad met on the set of Dad's movie, The Broken Maze, in which she was one of the leads. I had a three-line role as a girl in a flashback, by the way. Huzzah!

Anyway, the entire time we were on location, I had zero clue that Dad and Brooke were hooking up until I saw the juicy headlines splashed across the front page of a grocery store tabloid right before the wrap party. Surprised didn't quite capture my reaction—I grabbed the one-inch pile of papers and flung them across the floor.

Seated at the table to Brooke's right was family member number two: my seventeen-year-old sister, Grace the disgrace. She killed my mother, so I hated her. She was also an impetuous idiot, who had been expelled twice from the private school she attended. Dad owed the school a modest mortgage payment every month to put up with Grace's antics and help with her dyslexia. My pathetic little sister was definitely a broken toy all right.

Finally, seated to Brooke's left was family member number three: my thirteen-year-old brother Nick. I tried to watch out for Nick, but he was high maintenance. One minute he was totally normal. The next? Well, he might fall writhing to the floor. He had what our doctor called "episodes," which was the polite way of saying he had epilepsy. An unusual case of it, the dude explained, as if that should make us feel more special. So, Nick was homeschooled by a tutor.

Nobody knew for sure what triggered Nick's episodes. They just came out of the blue like heat lightning. Consequently, whenever he left the house, other than to play in the backyard, it was always an adventure. Would he do fine? Or would he collapse on the floor?

"What time did you get in last night?" Nick asked me.

"Midnight," I replied. "The idiot driver couldn't find Scarsdale.

He took a wrong turn, and we ended up going over the Tappan Zee Bridge. Where's Frederick, Brooke?"

"Bereavement leave," Grace answered. "Brother died. Antwan is filling in until he's back. Be nice to him. He doesn't know the area as well as Frederick, and you probably made him nervous with that scowl of yours."

"Grace," I said, "do the world a favor and swallow your tongue."

"Allie," Brooke protested. "Can you please not fight with your sister at the breakfast table?"

"That'll be a first," Nick muttered.

Nick sounded perfectly normal this morning. Good.

I started to tease Nick about his unkempt hair, but I swallowed the words when he popped the white cap off of an amber-colored prescription bottle, fingered out a white-and-green capsule, and tossed it in his mouth. Then, he chased it down with a gulp of orange juice. I pointed at the bottle and wiggled my finger for him to give it to me. He lobbed it over to me in a high, lazy arc, as if he was shooting a hook shot. I caught it and glanced at the label, squelching a snarl that tried to rip out of me. Nick didn't take drugs; we had already tried them all, and they were worse than the disease. So, what the hell?

Deal with it later.

I pitched the pills back to him as I rose to my feet to get my food.

Grace whispered something under her breath while I made my way over to the sideboard, where our cook, Patty, had breakfast laid out. Her assistant, Andrea, who wore her black hair in a tight bun, wasn't much older than I was. She stood at the ready to serve me, trying to smile pleasantly, but I seriously intimidated the poor girl. Some of our servants had been with us forever, but we tended to lose kitchen staff when I was home.

Yeah, so I was even more high maintenance than Nick. We were rich, lived in a mansion, and had 1.2 servants per person. I was the quintessential entitled white chick.

Anyhow, sighing from an incredibly bad night's sleep, I scanned the breakfast offerings laid out in front of me—meats, fruit, potatoes, eggs benedict, drinks and . . . it was missing.

"Good morning, Miss Alyssa," Andrea said. "What can I get you?"

She had a china plate in one hand and a serving spoon in the other, poised to dish me up whatever I wanted and take my plate to the table for me. When I frowned at the spread, she pointed to a mount of scrambled eggs. This made me angry, but I bit my lip, relying on the pain to hold back my urge to dump the entire warming tray of eggs on her head.

"Andrea," I said calmly, "where's my granola? And what about grapefruit juice?"

Andrea's face blanched. Clearly, she had forgotten my hissy fit the last time I was home for breakfast.

"Sorry, Miss Alyssa. One moment." She scurried out of the room.

"What's with all this stuff?" I asked Brooke. "You know I don't eat this garbage."

Brooke surrendered to a heavy sigh. "I wasn't sure what you're eating nowadays, hun, so Patty made a little of everything. Besides, you're not the only one eating, you know. Some of us like eggs and bacon."

"I've only been gone five months," I replied. "You think I might suddenly start eating swine flesh?"

"Too bad you couldn't have been gone longer," Grace quipped.

"Bacon is gooood," Nick drawled.

I shot him a grin, even though bacon was not good. I was vegan, but I didn't take offense that Nick—and the rest of my family, for that matter—didn't share my diet. As long as people remembered to provide stuff I could eat, I was fine with whatever muck they wanted.

"Come on," Grace said. "Why not try one little piece of bacon, or how about a sausage link? You used to like them before vegan became trendy, remember?"

"Grace, I'd rather walk into a public restroom and lick the tiles beneath the men's urinal than eat that crap."

"Allie!" Brooke yelled. "Watch your mouth!"

"That is the grossest thing I have ever heard," Nick said, nodding his head as if in admiration.

Andrea returned before I could respond, carrying a tray of my ingredients. She prepared a bowl under my directions, layering granola, strawberries, and blueberries and dousing it all with soy milk. Taking a seat at the table as far from Grace as possible, I began to eat slowly and methodically. Andrea quickly fetched me a cup of coffee and poured in a generous splash of almond milk. At least she got that right.

No one spoke to me while I ate although Nick stared at me as if waiting for me to do something entertaining. I was almost finished with my food when Kate, our housekeeper, tried to slink past us into the kitchen. She was a plump woman just south of sixty, and she had been with my family since my earliest memories. Still, I'd had my issues with her over the years, particularly when she used to rearrange the stuff in my room under the guise of cleaning up. When I was in eighth grade, I lost my temper and yelled at her after she accidentally-on-purpose threw out my black lipstick. Still, Mom had loved her, so I tried to cut her some slack, but enough was enough.

"Kate," I said in a commanding voice. This drew her up short.

"Yes, ma'am?"

"There was garbage in my bed last night," I replied. "Garbage. What the hell?"

A mortified expression slid over her face and her mouth fell open. "I'm sure I don't know what you are talking about, ma'am."

"A long piece of plastic wrap under my pillow." The anger from last night returned. "This is housekeeping 101. Beds are not trash cans. If—"

My indignant rant was interrupted by Nick guffawing in laughter, his hand held over his lips to keep his mouthful of food from blasting out.

"It wasn't plastic," he said in between gasps of laughter. "I found a snakeskin in the rose garden. I thought it would be a funny way to welcome you home."

He resumed his belly laughs, triggering chortles from Grace and an "isn't he sweet" smile from Brooke. My body immediately shivered in utter and total revulsion. I touched the dead, desiccated skin of a snake? OMFG. On impulse, I grabbed a blueberry out of my bowl and tossed it at Nick, who didn't duck quick enough, and it bonked him on the nose.

And just like that it was a Baylor family food fight.

Nick and I lobbed fruit, bacon, toast, and other bits of food at each other. Brooke sat there with her mouth open in shock while Grace leaned back in her chair, crossed her arms over her chest, and watched us go at it with an amused grin on her face.

I couldn't help laughing at Nick and even chuckling a little at Brooke's shocked O-mouth, but Nick and I soon regained our decorum and agreed on a cease-fire.

"We're not animals!" Brooke shouted. "And this isn't a barn-yard. What is wrong with you two?"

I ignored her as per usual and finally broached the obvious question, noticing for the first time his vacant seat. "Where's Dad?"

"Geneva," Nick answered.

"London," Grace corrected. "He'll be in Geneva starting to-morrow to reshoot scenes."

"London?" I blurted out. "What about this trip?"

Brooke's shoulders slumped. She took a deep breath before glancing at both Grace and Nick in turn as if casting about for their moral support. And then I knew.

"He's not coming," I said. "After practically twisting my arm out of its socket to persuade me to go on this trip, Dad isn't even coming. That's just effing great!"

"Allie," Brooke soothed. "He couldn't help it. The ending fell apart in editing, so they have to do a bunch of last-minute reshoots."

"Reshoots," I repeated. "Right."

Grace added, "Dad said they were over budget, out of time, and . . . what was the other thing?"

"The rough cut sucked," Nick said, smiling.

"So what?" I said to no one in particular.

"He *is* the director," Grace said in a "well, duh" tone.

"He *is* the director," I repeated, mocking her by speaking in a whiny, falsetto voice.

"How would you like mace in the face?" Grace replied.

"Please try. That way killing you would be self-defense."

"Congratulations, Allie," Brooke said icily. "It took you less than five minutes to ruin everyone's breakfast."

Tossing my napkin on the table, appetite gone, I rose to leave. The only reason I was even here was to talk to Dad—the great Paul Baylor, winner of last year's best director Oscar and fabulously wealthy movie mogul. And I didn't want to talk to him because I craved conversation with him. I had plans, and I had to tell him about them. It wasn't that I was seeking his permission exactly, but I did need his approval. He held the purse strings after all. And while I was used to him giving me almost anything I asked for, I was about to escalate the daddy-spoils-his-daughter routine to a whole new level.

"He's very sorry, dear," Brooke said, as if this lame apology helped at all, particularly filtered through her too-much-lipstick mouth.

A flush of anger surged inside me. "So, I pushed my summer study program at the Sorbonne back a month for this trip and now it's canceled?"

"What do you care if it's canceled?" Grace sniffed. "You didn't even want to go in the first place,"

"And you did?" I countered.

None of us were particularly enthusiastic about this vacation, but Dad had insisted. He never stopped talking about the great trip he had with his father when he was young, before he made his first movie and rocketed to wunderkind status. He and his dad flew into a remote Canadian lake by float plane and stayed a week in a cabin—fishing, hiking, canoeing, and . . . bonding. He wanted to recreate that same experience with us.

My reaction when he first pitched the idea to me? Please, pass me an emesis bag.

Instead, I suggested we jet to a nice five-star resort somewhere with a sauna and a pool . . . and separate rooms for each of us kids. He nixed the idea. I think Brooke was actually on my side on this one.

Instead, Dad wanted to disappear in the wilderness for a week, totally cut off from civilization. We would live life the way pioneers lived a couple hundred years ago without the distractions and stresses of modern-day life. So, no phones, no neighbors, no internet, no cars, no restaurants, no shopping, etcetera. The list of horrors went on and on and on.

"Isn't this dangerous?" I asked him when he first pitched his idea to me. "What if something happens out there?"

"We radio for help," he said, "and wait for a plane to fly us out."

"Are you serious? What about Nick?"

"Nick loves camping," Dad replied. "He'll be fine. We'll all be fine, Allie."

So said the captain of the Titanic, I'm sure.

In the end, after Dad gravely explained how much this meant to him, I agreed to go on this Lewis and Clarke wilderness expedition, but only because he and I needed to have a heart-to-heart talk. Apparently, the only way that was going to happen any time soon was for me to agree to tag along on this stupid vacation with my stupid family.

And here I was and here Dad wasn't.

"The hell with this," I said to Brooke. "I'm going to reschedule and leave for Paris as soon as I can. The sooner I'm out of here, the better." I turned my back to the dining room and started to march upstairs to my room.

I tried to spend as little time at home as possible. Since ninth grade after Mom died, I've been in a boarding school. I came home for the holidays and a week or two in the summer, but I kept my time here limited to the barest minimum. This place was too painful for me, and also this was where my sister lived . . . Grace the Mom killer and the person I despised more than just about anyone.

"Not so fast," Brooke hollered at my retreating back. "We're not canceling the trip."

I pivoted around to face her. "What?" I couldn't hide the surprise in my voice. "You are going to take us out into the wild?"

The closest Brooke ever came to nature was a stroll through our flower gardens.

She shook her head. "Not me. I'm joining your father in Geneva. Your grandfather volunteered to take Paul's place. So, you'll be going with him."

"All right!" Nick shouted, and he started clapping.

We only had one grandparent left—Dad's father, whom we saw exactly twice a year: Easter and Christmas. He never showed any inclination to spend more time with us than this, so going on a vacation with him was slightly bizarre. But he always sent cool birthday presents, particularly for Nick, so my brother loved him.

"Nick and Grace can go with him," I said. "I've got better things to do."

Ignoring the babble of objections from Brooke and Nick, I stomped upstairs to change into my workout gear. The one thing I loved most about our house was the enormous gym we had in the basement. I also liked the pool out back, but so did Grace, so I mostly avoided it.

I quickly changed into yoga pants and a tight-fitting tank before making my way downstairs. On the way, I almost ran down Brooke, who apparently was coming to see me, in the hallway.

"Your grandfather is very excited about this," Brooke said, after planting her lingerie model body in front of me. "Please don't ruin this for everyone. It's only one week. Nick—"

"Yes," I interrupted, "let's talk about Nick. You have him on Zoloft? What the hell, Brooke?"

She let out a long exhale and closed her eyes for a couple moments. "He's had a rough spring, Allie, which you would know if you were ever here. Dr. Wambux—"

"Dr. Want Bucks," I clarified, cutting her off. "That quackster never met a medical condition he couldn't throw pills at. If Nick is having issues again, he needs to see a specialist, not a horse doctor."

"He is seeing a specialist," she responded, a bit testily.

"Right," I said dismissively.

I don't know why Nick's condition made me angry at Brooke. It wasn't like Brooke would want him to have anything less than the best care that money could buy. Still, my mouth twisted into a snarl. If Mom were here, Nick would not be suffering, but I knew this was unjust the moment I thought it.

"Allie, Nick needs help. A lot of help."

"Nick needs a mother."

"That's not fair," she replied sharply. "I'm trying. I'm doing everything I can."

"Okay, okay." My anger deflated. This wasn't Brooke's fault, as much as I'd love to blame her. "Let's talk later. There are ways to help Nick that don't involve drugging him stupid. I—"

"You," she broke in. "Exactly. You can get through to him in a way I can't, in a way no one can. Why not spend the summer here at home instead of running off to Europe for three months?"

Spend my summer here? No way. Not happening. Not unless Dad sold Grace to an out-of-state human trafficker. Besides, this place stopped being my home a long time ago.

"I . . ." my words petered out.

"Think about it," she said softly. "What Nick really needs is someone strong to lean on when . . . when things go south for him. Someone he trusts." She hesitated for a second, bit her lip, and locked eyes with me. "He needs you, Allie."

"I don't belong here anymore," I said softly.

Wait, was I actually being honest with Brooke? Gasp.

"Really?" she replied. "Then where do you belong?"

"Working on it."

She squinted, as if to bring me into focus, but not waiting for a response, I stepped around her and resumed my trek to the downstairs gym. Once there, I climbed onto an elliptical bike, soon found my stride, and cranked up the volume on my iPhone. I wanted to drown out everything around me as much as possible while losing myself in physical exertion and sweat. A half hour into my routine, Grace wandered into the room, wearing khaki shorts and a sleeveless orange blouse . . . a little too preppy for my taste.

I picked up my pace, determined to ignore her, but she planted herself directly in front of my bike and arched an eyebrow up at me. With a scowl, I yanked out my earbuds and let the bike come to a stop.

"You're interrupting my workout," I said curtly.

"What is your problem? Every time you come home, you're more of a bitch than the last time I saw you."

I shrugged. "I guess some people just bring out the worst in me."

Grace rolled her eyes and wearily swiveled her head back and forth. "Allie, Dad gives you everything. So he asked you to go on a one-week trip? You act like he begged you to donate a kidney."

"Everything? What planet do you live on?"

Her eyes narrowed in confusion, as if I said something totally the opposite of what she expected.

"You attend Phillips Exeter," she said. "They buy you anything you want, you study in Paris, you . . . you have it all. I would kill to attend your school."

Yes, Grace would have leaped at the chance to join me at Exeter, but she was dyslexic, and her therapist recommended against taking her out of the special program she was enrolled in. Thank God. The thought of having to interact with her daily was almost enough to trigger cardiac arrest.

After I took a long swig from my water bottle, I met my sister's eyes with unadulterated hostility.

"You're such a waste of flesh," Grace said.

"*I* am? Really? Your hair reeks of marijuana, Grace."

She recoiled as if I slapped her, so, of course, I plowed on.

"Brooke told me about you sneaking out to a hotel last month. Congrats on achieving the trifecta: stoner, loser, slut."

I expected her to charge me with her hands thrust forward to claw my face to shreds or, at a minimum, lob some F-bombs at me, but she just stood there, stunned. Her facial muscles sagged, and the hurt and pain in her eyes was obvious. For a second, I almost apologized, but I didn't. I couldn't.

Strangely, Grace and I were actually close once, but she was always reckless. Still, I stood by her when she got into trouble back in the day. Eventually, though, I couldn't stop resenting all the attention her bad girl antics garnered, while my obedient, loving daughter status was totally ignored. Now, I couldn't stand the sight of her, even though I do envy her for inheriting Mom's wavy, honey-blond hair, while I got Dad's drab and lifeless brown locks.

"I know you don't want to go on this trip, Allie, but do it for Nick. He'll be so disappointed and hurt. You know how he is about being in the woods."

"Since when do you give a crap about Nick . . . or any of us, for that matter?"

"I want to go, too," she said in a quiet voice.

"So go," I replied. "Knock yourself out. Just do it without me."

I waited for a snarky comeback, but she said nothing and wouldn't meet my eyes. In fact, her lower lip was trembling. Was this, like, some designer drug withdrawal symptom?

"I promise not to fight with you," she finally said.

Oh for God's sake. She was making sad puppy-dog eyes at me.

CHAPTER THREE

"This way," I told Nick and Grace, as I quickly walked toward the VIP lounge where we would be waiting for our flight out of LaGuardia. "All of Canada waits breathlessly for us to fly into Toronto."

I couldn't believe I was going ahead with this vacation. A twisted logic existed to doing this back when Dad was coming, too, but now that he bailed, why was I still going? I hated Grace. I couldn't deal with Nick. And I didn't even know my grandfather.

Despite Grace's entreaties, I planned to ditch these losers and go to France, but Dad called me from Luxembourg and pleaded with me not to back out. I finally said yes, but I made it clear he owed me for this, and I definitely planned to cash in my chips very, very soon.

I regretted saying "yes" the second we arrived at the airport and I saw the mass of sweaty humanity clogging the departure area. The going was slow, but once we checked our luggage and made it through security, with only our shoulder bags to slow us down, we raced at a fairly good pace through the concourses to our terminal.

No one put me in charge of getting us on the airplane and making our connecting flights, but if I didn't do it, the chances of us getting to our destination on schedule were remote.

"Where are we going?" Nick asked, as we shouldered our way through the crowds. "There are too many people here."

I gripped his hand in mine and felt his fingers clench tight. His hand trembled. This could signal an imminent meltdown in which fears and anxieties overwhelmed him like a tsunami, leaving him unable to walk—or worse, curled up on the floor in the middle of the Terminal B concourse. Reluctantly, I gave him his Zoloft this morning, agreeing with Brooke it would help him with the plane flight to Canada.

Maybe one capsule wasn't enough. Can you OD on Zoloft?

"We're going to the club lounge to wait for Grandpa," I explained to Nick. "Keep hold of my hand and nothing can harm you."

I had said those same words of reassurance to Nick many times over the years, the first time when he was only five on a day I couldn't forget.

The grounds around our house were enormous, and Nick, Grace, and I spent hours on the north lawn playing a fantasy game about the kingdom of Alithia. In the game, I was always Queen Keelana, wielder of Derthal and keeper of the necklace of Wodin. Grace was Princess Breeta, and Nick was a knight: Sir Captain Captain. He chose the name, which I think was a loose riff on his favorite cereal, but with Nick, who could say.

One of our favorite adventures was the quest to slay the imaginary dragon, Morgon. We always defeated the evil beast. My mind drifted back to the April day when we played the game in the rain . . . the day Nick had his first episode.

"Sir Captain Captain, defend Princess Breeta!" I yelled at my five-year-old brother.

I was ten at the time; Grace was nine. We were probably too old for fantasy games, but it was fun.

"Hurry, Allie!" Grace hollered. "I mean, Keelana! Morgon is about to eat us alive."

Ignoring the gentle drizzle that afternoon, I rushed over to stand between the imaginary dragon and Grace and Nick, jabbing at it with Derthal, the immortal dragon slayer spear. Actually, it was Patty's old wooden yardstick that I borrowed from the kitchen. It was the perfect pretend weapon. With flicks of my wrists, I thrust the spear back and forth, occasionally slashing with it. Nick, meanwhile, had a misshapen stick that he broke off a shrub that served as his knife. He slashed with it with a ferocity that showed that he was really getting into this game.

"Run, Captain Captain! He's going after you!" I yelled over my shoulder.

"Wait," Grace said, "who's going to protect me?"

"Fallayrow, Grace," I answered. "Fallayrow!"

Grace dutifully dived stomach first to the ground and quickly rolled three times away from me, her arms clutched tightly to her chest.

At some point when I was very young, Mom and Dad had talked to me about flames. They said that if I ever caught fire, I was to fall to the ground and roll around. Don't run, they insisted. I adopted their instruction for our games, except that at the time Grace started playing, she garbled "fall and roll" into "fallayrow," so that's how our special, gibberish word for drop and roll came into being.

"He's gone," I announced while breathing hard. "Morgon is gone, but he's coming back."

Grace, who lay on her stomach on the grass, asked, "Wait, he's not dead? I thought you killed him?"

"Not this time. Where's Nick?"

Grace managed to shrug while propped up on her elbows.

"Nick!" I shouted. "Olly olly oxen free!"

Nothing. No Nick. Not even a sound.

"Nick!" Grace shouted. "You can come out now."

Grace and I stood in the middle of a large, mostly square lawn that was groomed to perfection, almost like a giant putting green. Our yard backed up to a strip of woods and tangled brush, which was as effective as a fence in keeping stuff out or in. It was the only place Nick could have fled to.

I waved at Grace to follow, as I strode over to the bushes.

"You think he went in there?" Grace asked. "He's probably upstairs in his room."

"I would have seen him go that way. He's either in here or he sprouted wings and flew off."

Nick didn't sprout wings, and he didn't run into the woods. I found him at the edge of our property where the grass and weeds were high, but a step or two short of where the underbrush started. He lay on his side in a fetal position, thumb in mouth, and shaking as if caught in the middle of a freezing blizzard without a shirt on.

"Nick," I whispered. "Come on. Game's over."

He was unconscious and didn't respond.

"Nick, wake up," I persisted. "It's okay now."

"What's wrong with him?" Grace asked.

"Get Mom," I said. When she didn't move, I added, "Now!"

My hand gripped his, and he responded by squeezing back. Encouraged, I intertwined our fingers and stroked the back of his head with my other hand.

"Hold on to my hand," I said softly. "Come back. You're safe now. Nothing can harm you."

His eyes fluttered open, and his grip tightened until his tiny fingernails bit into my skin.

This was the first moment when we knew something was wrong with Nick, the first time dark clouds formed over him and over our family. A storm was coming, only I didn't understand it at the time.

The memory of that day years ago slowly faded as I marched through the airport, towing a wide-eyed Nick along with my right arm. All these people, the smells, the sounds . . . they threatened to overwhelm his senses and release the demons he battled daily.

"Where is this lounge?" Grace complained. She was wearing fluorescent green yoga pants and a loose-fitting white blouse. "We've walked halfway to Brooklyn already."

"Almost there," I answered. "Let's pick it up."

"Or what?" Grace countered.

Jesus. She had to fight me about everything.

"Or we leave you behind," I answered. "Wouldn't that be sweet."

"Do we have to run, though?" she complained. "We have two hours before the plane even boards."

"I need to make some phone calls," I said. "The sooner there, the sooner we can relax a little."

"Relax," she repeated flatly.

"Don't worry, I'm sure there's a dark corner where you can break out your syringe and shoot up whatever drug you're taking lately."

"God, you're evil."

Possibly.

I glanced down at the sheet of paper in my hand to confirm where the lounge was located. Brooke had choreographed this entire expedition, even though she wasn't coming, and given me a detailed, three-page agenda of our one-week vacation. Every element of the trip was listed, including times, places, reservation numbers, contact info, etcetera, etcetera. I had to give it to her; she was organized. Still, when the Baylors went on a vacation, it was like going into battle; the best war plans, no matter how meticulous and well-thought out, lasted only until the first shot was fired. I didn't know what all would go wrong on this trip, but something— probably many things—certainly would.

"We're lost," Grace muttered, just as I caught sight of our destination.

"Fallayrow, Grace. Fallayrow."

"Stop saying that to me. You may be a little girl trapped in an eighteen-year-old body, but I grew up a long time ago."

"Did you?" I countered.

"I—"

"We're here," I interrupted her.

With a heavy exhale, I pushed through the lounge door, wishing I was anywhere but LaGuardia. I reminded myself that I was doing this not only for Dad, but also to protect Nick. Someone had to, and that someone would never be lost-in-space Grace. Plus, Grace kind of, sort of, asked me to come. I was weirdly curious why, curious the way a person might be who witnessed a car wreck and found themselves inching closer to see the bodies.

Once inside the cramped, functional lounge, Nick recovered his equilibrium enough to wander over and grab food, while Grace melted away into the crowd around the big TV. I had traveled through LaGuardia many times since my earliest memories, and Dad practically lived here. I hated the place. It was small and crowded, and the smell of panic and anxiety seemed to roll off the people thronging its concourses, as travelers scrambled to make their flights or find a taxi. The VIP lounge we were in, which Dad paid a fortune for himself and his family to use, was only a meager oasis from the surrounding chaos.

Slumped in a faux leather couch, I withdrew my cell from my messenger bag and called Olivia, my best friend since grade school. She came to Phillips Exeter with me, and we were as close as sisters. Liv's dad was a wealthy corporate lawyer who hardly batted an eyelash when she asked to go off to boarding school simply because her best friend was going there. I think he was secretly pleased to get rid of her.

"Hey, Liv," I said the second she answered.

"Allie, how did it all work out?"

"Badly. I'm still going on this idiotic trip to the primeval wastelands of northern Canada. And get this, my dad isn't even going."

"Shit," Olivia whispered back. "You're still going to France, though, right?"

"Yes. I have to."

"But what about your dad?"

A deep, ragged exhale slowly drained out of me. Translated into English, it said, "My life is so screwed up right now I want to scream."

"I guess I'll tell him about it after I get back," I said. "I always spend the summer somewhere. So—"

"By yourself, sure," Liv interrupted. "What is he going to say when he finds out you're spending August with Jack?"

"Does it really matter? It'll be history by then. As they say, sometimes it's better to apologize after than ask permission before."

"You are one brazen hussy bitch, A."

I nodded to myself, kind of pleased with that label. "Why, thank you. That's the nicest compliment you've ever given me."

"I want pictures. Lots of pictures. At least eight times a day."

Smiling, I said, "There's no cell service within five hundred miles of this wilderness outpost. Sorry."

I knew she wasn't talking about Canada.

"I don't mean your stupid campfire trip," she shot back. "I want naked selfies of you and Jack in bed with champagne flutes." She paused for a moment. "Well, actually I don't care about you. I want full frontals of Jack, though. I have to live vicariously, okay?"

"I suppose I could manage a few when we come up for air," I teased.

It was all bravado on my part. Yes, I was going to be spending a month with Jack Carter, my boyfriend of the last few months, at a French château, but it wasn't likely to be a lust-and-alcohol infused bacchanalia. First, his parents were going to be there too. Second, Jack was cautious and careful to a fault. He wasn't much for taking spontaneous risks or leaping into the void, unless he checked first to make sure there was a safety net at the bottom. I actually liked that about him. And third, and maybe most important, Jack and I weren't going on this vacation together just to have a good time, although we certainly wanted that. No, we were going to secure his parents' approval; specifically, I was coming in order to get his mother's approval. And I wasn't going to get it if she caught us in bed together texting porn pics to Olivia.

"You are so lucky," Olivia said, sounding wistful. "I wish I were you."

"Maybe."

"What do you mean maybe?"

Yes, what did I mean? I struggled to put my feelings in words. "The trip to France feels forced." I almost said that it felt coerced.

"Are you still hung up over Haiti?" she asked. "It was a tough choice, girlfriend, but it was a choice, and you made it. No regrets."

"No regrets," I echoed.

"Because I can always take your place."

"I'd gladly trade places with you now. This vacation is going to be the most awful seven days of my entire existence."

"Followed by the most amazing time of your life. You're going to be vacationing at a freaking castle in Avignon with the son of the French ambassador. That beats art camp in the Hamptons hands down."

"I don't know," I demurred. "I'm really nervous. This is sort of an audition, you know?"

"Yeah, you two are getting really serious . . . maybe too serious."

"Maybe we are," I agreed. "Maybe we should slow things down."

"You just graduated high school. You're too young to get stuck on one guy, even if his father is on the vice-presidential shortlist."

Things between Jack and me were moving fast . . . too fast. I went from barely knowing the guy to kissing him in an airport in the space of ten days. I never saw it coming. The chemistry between us sparked so quickly.

Jack Carter was in my advanced French class with Mrs. Fèvre, but I said possibly three words to him the entire year until our winter break trip to France. Mrs. Fèvre had chaperoned twelve members of the French club on a ten-day trip to study French architecture in Toulouse, and Jack and I were assigned seats on the plane next to each other. I gave him a curt nod in greeting and expected that would likely be the sum total of our interaction during the flight. I had always pegged him as haughty and aristocratic.

As the plane accelerated down the runway for takeoff, Jack clutched the armrests in obvious fear, and he grimaced the way someone would in a dentist's chair just as the buzzing drill descended into their mouth.

"Have you flown much?" I asked him, trying not to smile at his panic-stricken expression.

"Yes," he said. "Sort of. I hate it. I've even seen a therapist about it."

"Did it help?"

"Not a bit," he said through clenched teeth while chuckling mirthlessly. "He tried reasoning and logic on me. Then breathing exercises and mind games. None of it works. Like all phobias, it's totally irrational. It just is."

I had no advice for dealing with wide-eyed terror. Being on board a plane that crashed into the ocean would be scary, but it wasn't an event I had any control over or could do anything to save myself if it happened. It was one hundred percent fate, and I didn't fear situations that were totally out of my hands.

I decided on distraction.

"You're from Boston, right?"

He nodded but then clarified, "Weston, actually."

"Probably a disgusting Patriots fan," I said in a slightly mocking voice.

"Hey, watch it. Who's your—"

"Jets," I cut in. "I like the pain and embarrassment of always losing. Keeps me humble."

This triggered a genuine laugh from him. "Where are you from? Manhattan?"

"Scarsdale. My trinity is Jets, Yankees, and Knicks. To hell with the Giants, Mets, and Nets. Oh, and the Patriots, too, of course. They're the Antichrist."

He shrugged in resignation, and I noticed his grip relaxed a little. "Ah, yes, cheering for a team that has won the Super Bowl so many times gets weary and boring. But it's the cross we nor'easters must bear."

I grinned and then proceeded to trade sports banter with him about Boston versus New York. When our conversation paused for a couple beats, a ding sounded and one of the flight attendants announced that we were free to move about the cabin. His muscles relaxed like a balloon deflating.

"Don't look now," I said, "but we're at cruising altitude, and you're not even sweating."

"Huh?" he replied, sounding both surprised and amused. "I guess talking sports with the beautiful Alyssa Baylor is the perfect therapy. Who knew?"

"Happy to help."

"Well, now you have to keep it up for the next seven hours so I don't relapse."

I leaned toward him and bumped his shoulder with mine. "I don't have seven hours of sports talk in me, but I can certainly babble on about other stuff for hours on end. Natter-chatter is my superpower."

We blathered on and on, hopscotching from subway systems and cabs to clam "chowdah" and bagels and lox, stopping only occasionally to catch our breaths, as we traded stories about everything.

Time flew. Soon, the intercom came to life again and one of the flight attendants said, "Ladies and gentlemen, we are beginning our descent."

Without either of us saying anything, our hands came together and we interlaced our fingers as the plane dropped toward the ground. I did it because I wanted to help him face down his airplane demons, although my skin tingled with the warmth of his touch. I expected a panicked, crushing grip, but he was gentle. By the time we reached our gate at Charles de Gaulle, I probably knew more about Jack Carter than anyone but his parents. We kept holding hands all the way from the plane door to customs, drawing stares and open mouths from our class companions. Maybe I was an idiot to dive in so fast, but *l'amour c'est être stupide ensemble* – love is being stupid together.

As the memory faded, I switched topics with Liv and asked, "Are you sure you can't come visit me in August?"

"I wish," Liv said, her words trailing off into frustration. "I have to be in Berkeley then. The first semester starts two weeks later."

"Sucks to be you. My first class isn't until the middle of September."

We were both going to be college freshmen this fall, but we would do it two thousand miles apart, and our experiences were going to be even further apart.

"Yeah, and the cherry on top of that suck sundae is that I have to live in the dorms with a roommate," Liv said glumly.

As she relayed this last fact, I spotted my grandfather entering the front door of the lounge. He was tall and rangy, like my dad, and his brown hair showed only minor gray shading at the edges. His primary distinguishing feature was a walrus mustache. He looked like he should be a character on Sesame Street, but he was out of uniform in a blue polo shirt and khaki slacks. He radiated retiree from Florida.

"Got to run," I told Liv. "I'll be on planes and in airports all day. Call you tomorrow."

"Don't forget. I need my daily Allie fix, or I'll go into agonizing withdrawal."

Smiling, I touched the hang-up icon on my screen and rose to greet my grandfather. Where in the blazes Nick and Grace were, I had no idea. Hopefully, Nick wasn't on the floor somewhere muttering "Redrum," and Grace wasn't being arrested for smoking a joint in the restroom.

"My goodness, you're so tall," Grandfather said when I approached. "When did you grow up?" Then he kissed me on the cheek and wrapped me in a hug. It was a little formal and awkward, but I returned the gesture.

"I missed you at Christmas," I said. Usually he visited for a few days over the holiday, but not last year. The only explanation we got from Dad was "he can't make it."

"I had to go in for some minor surgery," he said. "Nothing serious. You looking forward to our back-country adventure?"

"No," I answered honestly.

"Keep an open mind," he replied with a warm smile. "It's not as bad as it seems."

"Weren't those Custer's last words to his men?" I joked.

He laughed and said, "All that is gold does not glitter."

"Where have I heard that before?"

"Tolkien," he replied with a shrug, as if embarrassed. "Where's Grace and Nick?"

As if on cue, Grace and Nick appeared out of nowhere, each sporting broad grins at the sight of their grandfather. Grace wasn't in handcuffs, so that was a good sign.

"Sorry to break up the reunion," I said a few minutes later, "but it's time to head for the gate. Our plane is boarding in five minutes." I held up Brooke's pages as proof.

"You're wearing the watch," Grace observed, dipping her head subtly at my wrist.

She referred to the Cartier watch Dad got me as a graduation present. He bought it in a small jewelry store in Atlanta while scouting film locations. He said that the girl who sold it to him was so cheeky that he had to have her in one of his films. We'll see how that goes.

The watch itself was magnificent, crafted from pink gold with a ring of diamonds around the rectangular face. I hadn't taken it off in the weeks since I received it, except for baths and showers. The design was simple, elegant, and it reeked of opulence and extravagance. I liked the statement it made about me: rich bitch.

"So?" I countered.

"What if you lose it?"

"I won't," I snapped. "Come on, let's get out of here."

So, the moment had come to leave the giant, unwashed armpit that was LaGuardia and fly to Toronto. None of us had any idea how long it would truly be before we saw New York again.

CHAPTER FOUR

When Air Canada flight 1834 finally lifted off, after a twenty-five-minute delay, I leaned my head back, slipped on my noise-canceling headphones, and closed my eyes. The music from my playlist thrummed in my ears, and sleep began to settle over me, although taking a nap was probably a waste of time since it was only an hour-and-a-half flight. We were seated in first class with my grandfather, Grace, Nick, and myself occupying all four seats in the first row. I had an aisle seat next to my grandfather, and Nick and Grace sat across the aisle from us.

Lost in my music, I tuned out the rest of the world and let my thoughts drift along, dwelling on buying new shoes and getting my nails done next week. A tap on my shoulder caused me to jerk my head back and tug my earphones down.

"What are you listening to?" Grandfather asked, smiling pleasantly beneath his bushy mustache.

"What?" I sounded a little annoyed.

"I said what are you listening to?"

Did he really want to know?

"Five Finger Death Punch," I replied.

He silently mouthed "oh."

"You know who I liked to listen to when I was eighteen?"

I shook my head. The question was rhetorical, of course; how would I know? In my head, I quickly did the math. I knew he was seventy-one, so he would have been eighteen in 1967, give or take. Then I took a guess.

"The Beatles?" I ventured.

"Nah. They were okay. I was always partial to the Stones, though. But the group I really liked was the Rascals."

"Who?"

"I thought you might say that. Can I give a listen?"

I shrugged and handed him my Bluetooth headphones. He slid them over his ears as I tapped the play icon. His eyes widened and he blinked several times before handing the phones back to me after twenty seconds.

"Cool, huh?" I teased.

"Bitchin'."

I grinned and went back to my music, only to fall asleep ten minutes later. I dozed for less than thirty minutes when turbulence jolted me awake, and I blinked several times in confusion. Then I leaned forward, slid my headphones down to my neck, and massaged my temples with two fingers. Headaches always attacked me when I flew, and today was no exception. The pain seemed to worsen if I ate anything, so I told the flight attendant I didn't want any refreshments, particularly the chocolate chip cookies she offered. Refined sugar was only slightly less poisonous than drinking Liquid-Plumr.

Later, the flight attendant—Jenna—approached me grasping a glass tumbler of booze in one hand. Was this a joke? But, even though her eyes were on me and she stopped next to my seat, I was wrong. The drink wasn't for me. She handed the glass to my grandfather.

What is he doing?

My grandfather didn't drink. When he visited for Christmas, he strictly avoided the wine, spiked eggnogs, and big snifters of expensive cognac that were hallmarks of Dad's holiday merrymaking after Mom died. So, what the hell? I gawked at the glass clutched in his hand.

"You're staring," Grandfather observed.

"What are you doing?" I asked.

"I'm having three fingers of miruvor."

Looked like whiskey to me, but whatev. He must have noticed the confusion on my face.

"Cordial of Imladris," he clarified.

I swept a hand across my hair in a way-over-my-head gesture.

"Today we call it bourbon," he added.

"Today?"

"Didn't you ever read *Lord of the Rings*?" he asked in a chiding tone.

"Saw the movie. Don't remember whiskey. Lots of ale, though."

He shook his head slowly as if disappointed.

"You're not going to book shame me, are you?" I asked.

"This is one case where reading is better than watching."

"Okay. Putting it on my bucket list . . . right up there after item number nine hundred seventy-four."

He smiled. I didn't. The drink in his hand—whatever he wanted to call it—distracted me. When did he become a booze hound again . . . or *un ivrogne*, as the French would say?

He nodded at my unvoiced question.

"Yeah, I know. I haven't had a drink since way before you were born for . . . for reasons that don't matter anymore."

"Oh," I replied lamely and let it go. This was a weird conversation.

I guess it wasn't my issue, really. My dad might have a different reaction, but he wasn't here. Mom had once hinted that a rift opened between my dad and my grandfather over the hard stuff. She never talked about any of the details, but I picked up enough to understand that my grandfather had been a raging alcoholic. So, seeing him knock back a slug of Jack Daniels, swish it around his mouth, and then swallow was slightly unsettling.

"You want a sip?" he asked.

My face scrunched up in revulsion and I shook my head. Bad memories lingered too fresh in my mind. Liv and I smuggled a bottle of vodka into her bedroom during a sleepover at her house. After mixing the stuff with pink lemonade, we drank way too much with predictable results—we both spent the next morning puking our guts out in her bathroom.

I wasn't ready for another drink yet. Maybe by this fall at a freshman party, I'd have my sea legs under me again, but not now. I slid my headphones on and slipped back into my music.

A few minutes later, Jenna gestured at me to take my headphones off. Why did I even bother? Soft dings reverberated through the cabin, and the captain's voice came over the intercom telling us we would be landing in ten minutes at Toronto Pearson International Airport. Stage one of my descent into hell was nearly over. I dutifully brought my seat back to its upright position, stowed my phones in my bag stuffed under the seat in front of me, and fastened my seat belt.

After a flawless landing and temporary confusion when we deplaned, we hustled over to our connecting flight to Winnipeg, only to discover we had a two-and-one-half-hour layover. Brooke's detailed notes omitted this fact. Thanks for that, Stepmom. Might have to put Nick's snakeskin down the sleeve of her favorite coat when we got back.

As if to sprinkle salt in an open wound, our next plane was much smaller and didn't have a first-class section, which not only meant more cramped seating and no meal, but the surly flight attendant lacked Jenna's smile and eagerness to please.

Things went considerably downhill on the third and final leg of our all-day journey, which took us from Winnipeg to Kenora, Ontario, by way of an ancient turboprop plane run by Bear Paw Airlines.

Yeah, what a name; it kind of says it all.

The tiny plane afforded us about the same level of accommodations as the baggage stored in the hold, but thank God the flight was only forty minutes. By the time we landed, over eight hours had passed since we left LaGuardia, and I was tired, hungry, sweaty, and dirty. If Jack saw me now, he'd probably make the finger cross used to ward off vampires.

I glanced at my phone as I deplaned with Nick's hand in mine. He was as tired as me, and exhaustion and Nick could be a bad combination.

It was ten minutes after six. Kenora was our destination today, but it lay two hundred and fifty kilometers to the south of the Lasley Wilderness Lodge, where our, quote, vacation, end quote, would officially begin tomorrow.

My eyes roved over the one-room terminal at Kenora Airport. Small. Essentially, a room with a high ceiling and lots of glass. Our house was probably six times as big as the entire building, but who was keeping score.

"Why did Brooke put us on all these planes?" a slump-shouldered Grace asked.

"Yeah, why didn't we use the jet?" Nick added.

"Exactly," Grace agreed. "Dad wasn't using it. He flew to London on the studio's plane."

Often, for a big family outing like this, we would fly on the private jet Dad sometimes used. He doesn't usually put us through stuff like sitting in coach, layovers, and airport terminals. Grace had a point. Why did we fly commercial?

"Probably Brooke wanting to torture us," I suggested. "She can be petty sometimes."

"Not your stepmother," Grandad said. "I insisted on no private jets."

"Why?" I immediately replied.

"It seemed like a good way to start easing folks into this," he answered. "We're going to be roughing it for a week. Flying like normal people seemed like a nice way to get you all in the mood."

"That so doesn't make sense," Grace said half under her breath.

Grandfather shrugged. "It's what your father and I did when we made this trip thirty years ago."

"Because you had no choice," I said, as I ambled over to a person in a uniform to ask where the hell our baggage was. "Dad was years away from becoming rich and famous."

"True enough," Grandfather agreed. "He was like you, Allie. Just about to head off to college and begin chasing his dreams. So very long ago. Yet, some mornings I wake up and it seems like only last week."

A far-off look of nostalgia came over his face, which meant it was time for me to separate, lest my grandfather start babbling about the good ole days. I didn't care about my father's family history; I cared about my mom's, only there was no one alive to tell it to me.

By the time we retrieved our luggage and trooped out the exit, all of us were dead on our feet. According to Brooke's master list, private cars were supposed to be waiting for us to whisk us away to a local hotel, but they never showed. I was going to kill Brooke for this. Of course, I tried to call the morons, but the phone number Brooke gave us was disconnected.

"This blows," I told the others. "We'll have to call a couple of cabs."

"I'll handle this," Grandfather said. "I'll go back inside and talk to the nice lady in the terminal. I'm sure she can get us pointed in the right direction."

A half hour passed before the first of three cabs pulled to a stop in front of our heaping mound of luggage. Other than telling them the hotel address where to take us to, few words passed between us and the cab drivers, although one did mutter something about how many suitcases we brought. He had a point. I had three and my carry-on. Grace had three, a computer case, and a large carry-on. Nick had two and a half, plus a duffel bag with his video game controller and accessories. Grandfather only had one bag.

"Tell me this isn't where we're staying," Grace said, when our taxi fleet came to a stop in front of a sickly beige, two-story building.

It looked like it doubled as a penitentiary.

I wasn't expecting luxury, and I was so tired luxury would be wasted on me anyway, but come on, Brooke, couldn't you do better than this?

Grace, on the other hand, began to sulk when Grandfather and I checked us in and the front desk clerk explained there was no room service, no in-room mini-bars, and no pay-to-view movies. What we did get were three rooms, each with an old TV, a plastic ice bucket, disposable cups wrapped in cellophane, and a cheap clock radio.

"If you think this is primitive, wait until you see where we're sleeping tomorrow night," I told Grace when we reached our rooms. "It'll make this feel like the Plaza."

"Yeah, but that's way out in the woods. We'll be camping, and it's supposed to be rough."

"Whereas we're still in a city tonight," I said, "and sleeping rough—"

"It's called being homeless," she interrupted.

Brooke had selected the rooms and organized the sleeping arrangements. I wasn't happy with it. She had me staying with Nick in one room and gave Grandfather and Grace their own rooms. My room and Grace's had a connecting door. Brooke told me she had to pay a premium for the hotel to guarantee adjoining rooms, which ended up being a complete waste of money since Grace immediately locked the door between our rooms.

When I turned off the lights and climbed into one of the double beds, all I wanted to do was close my eyes, but Nick sighed heavily the way he did when he was about to ask me something. I rubbed one eye with the heel of my left hand in frustration. Can't we just not talk and say we did?

"I'm going to have nightmares," Nick whispered.

"I'll bet."

"Bad."

"You'll have to do whatever it is you do to deal with it," I said, not sounding too encouraging.

"But . . ."

Always a but. He sounded the same as he did when he was six, when he had wake-up-screaming nightmares at least once a week. I was eleven when it started. I didn't want to remember, but I did.

I awoke one night to find Mom leaning over me with her fingers clutching my arm. "Allie," my mother said that night, while shaking my shoulder insistently.

"What's wrong?" I asked. It had to be something major. My first thought was that our house was on fire.

"I need your help with Nick," she said.

Wordlessly I climbed out of bed in my *Frozen* movie pajamas and followed her down the hall toward Nick's room. As we drew close, I heard him moaning. Once Mom pushed through his bedroom door, I saw Nick on his bed writhing on top of his blankets in the dim illumination of his nightlight. He was muttering unintelligible words.

"I can't wake him," Mom said in a very quiet voice. "I think he's stuck inside a bad dream."

Stuck in a dream? To my eleven-year-old brain, this sounded frightening enough to stop my breathing and make my heart race. And, what was I supposed to do about it? I tried to appear baffled and confused, but I knew.

"You helped wake him last summer, remember?"

I nodded and kneeled beside his bed, half frightened to death myself. Still, I would rather die than disappoint my mother, so cautiously I extended my hand to place it on top of Nick's mop of dark brown hair. My fingers stroked his head.

"It's safe now," I said to him. "Come home."

"Morgon," he replied breathlessly.

"Is gone. He can't hurt you."

"Morgon," he repeated.

"Captain Captain. Queen Keelana needs you."

I pulled the names up from the depths of memory. We hadn't played in Alithia since Nick's incident nearly nine months ago. Too afraid. Too guilty.

Nick's seizures weren't new by now, but always Mom drew his trembling body into her arms, and he came out of it. Not tonight.

I had an idea. Without a word, I sprang up and ran to my room.

"Allie!" Mom yelled after me.

"Be right back," I replied without looking back.

Moments later I returned and kneeled beside Nick, who was still out of it. My right hand grasped a string of purple, yellow, and green Mardi Gras beads Dad gave me when I was Nick's age.

"I am placing the necklace of Wodin around you," I whispered in Nick's ear. "You have sanctuary."

His body shook as if hit by a sudden blast of frigid air.

My body shook as if hit by that same blast of frigid air.

The memories from that night years ago faded, but not the routine that began afterward. I left all of it behind when I ran off to boarding school, but Morgon always returned.

"Help me with the blankets, Nick."

CHAPTER FIVE

The rattling noise of the cheap air-conditioning unit coming to life woke me again. The AC turned off and on all night, grinding away each time as if it was shedding nuts and bolts. This time I didn't fall back asleep.

"Wake up," I told Nick, my throat hoarse from sleep.

I groaned from the sore, pinched nerve in my neck. I fell asleep with my head twisted in an awkward position; plus, my right arm tinkled with numbness from having the circulation cut off for God knew how long.

"Nick, it's time," I said and gave his shoulder a gentle shove. "It's Saturday morning. Rise and shine."

Nick and I slept on the floor between the two beds in the room with a bed sheet stretched over the top of us, making for a tent-like enclosure. The sheet overhead was anchored in place on the mattresses by a Gideon's bible, an iron, a small, folded luggage rack, and the budget, one-cup coffee maker. We stripped the blankets off the bed for makeshift sleeping bags. The mishmash was a tolerable re-creation of the sanctuary tent I created in my bedroom years ago where a younger Nick could flee to when the demons came. Many a night I slept in that tent holding his hand while he fell back asleep.

"Just a little longer," Nick groaned.

"I'm going to take a shower. You need to be up and ready when I get out."

Later, Nick wandered to the open bathroom door while I delicately stroked on mascara while wearing the cheap motel robe I found in the closet. As always when I concentrated, my tongue stuck out the side of my mouth.

"Don't put it on so thick," Nick said. "Just a light—"

"Excuse me," I interrupted, shooting a death ray glare at him.

"I mean, you should—"

"Wait," I cut him off again, holding up one hand in a stop where you are gesture, "are you, like, mansplaining makeup to me? Because if you are, don't. Just. Don't."

"Don't. Right."

Twenty minutes later, as we prepared to leave our dive hotel room, I placed a twenty-dollar tip on the bureau for the housekeeper, who would have to clean up the trashed room Nick and I were leaving behind. The poor woman's mouth would surely drop open in a dismayed expression when she saw what we did to the beds.

"Shit, we're pigs," I murmured and left a second twenty.

Moments after Nick and I arrived in the lobby and grabbed two stale bagels from the free breakfast area, Grandfather and Grace waved us over to where our luggage was stacked in mounds in the middle of the lobby waiting to be loaded onto our yet-to-arrive transportation. A stranger glancing at all our suitcases and trunks might think we were about to embark on a three-month African safari; the only items missing for that were guns and crates of ammo.

"Any sign of our cars?" I asked Grandfather.

He held up his android phone. "I called them. They're on the way."

I nodded and collapsed on the lobby sofa. What I really needed was a grande cup of dark roast.

Reading my mind, Grace said, "There's a pot of gooey coffee burning over there."

Unlike the airport, our rides showed up more or less on time. They must have received some intelligence about us, since one of the vehicles was a pickup truck that was more than adequate for our baggage. After a short conversation with one driver, Grandfather signaled for us to follow him out the lobby door.

"Hallelujah," Grace muttered. "Time to blow this popsicle stand."

I climbed into the front seat of a rusted, dented SUV to ride shotgun alongside a girl who might have been Grace's age, or even a year younger. She was tall, broad-shouldered, and tan-skinned with black hair. She looked . . . what was the term in Canada? First Nation?

Grandfather, Nick, and Grace slid into the spacious back seat. Each of us gazed expectantly at the girl.

"Hey, everyone, my name's Nokes," the girl said, glancing over at me and then in the rearview mirror at the rest of the gang.

"Nokes Lasley. Settle in. The lodge is a two-hundred-fifty-kilometer-ride north, so we got some driving to do."

Nokes? What the? What kind of name is Nokes? It had to be short for something else. No-can-do? Nokey-dokey? Gnocchi alla Sorentina? I fought off an impertinent giggle.

"I'm Jim Baylor," Grandfather said, "and these are my granddaughters, Grace and Allie, and my grandson, Nick."

Each of us simultaneously murmured some version of hello. I didn't feel very talkative, too preoccupied with my sore neck and pissed off at the prospect of living like the Swiss Family Robinson for a week. By the time I remembered to call Liv and tugged my phone out of my back pocket, we had no cell service on the long, lonely road to wherever we were heading.

"You're going to have the best vacation of your life," Nokes assured us out of the blue, after miles of driving in silence.

"Do we get a refund if it sucks?" Grace asked with a scowl.

Instead of being offended, she smiled and said, "It won't suck. My grandfather owns the lodge, and he's been running the place for forty years. It wouldn't have lasted as long if we were peddling awful experiences."

This conversation was getting a teeny bit awkward. Grandfather seemed to sense it, so he stepped in to take over.

"You know," he said. "My son and I came to your lodge thirty years ago. The only person whose name I remember from back then was a fellow named Gary. He flew us out to our cabin and told us all about the history of the area where we were staying. I never forgot his stories."

"Seriously?" Nokes said, sounding very excited. "That's crazy. Gary was my great-uncle. He and my grandfather started the lodge way before I was born. Back then, it was just the two of them."

"So, is Gary still flying bush planes?" my grandfather asked. My eyes snapped open. Apparently, the uncomfortable silence drove him to small talk.

Nokes swallowed a couple times in obvious discomfort and then cleared her throat. She didn't want to answer the question, but she was going to anyway. "No. Uncle Gary passed about twenty years back," Nokes said. "He was on a supply run when his plane went down. My great-aunt Cheryl was with him. She died too."

Even though I didn't know these people, my insides twisted at the idea of them dying in a plane crash. What upset me in particular about plane crashes was the thought of passengers knowing for a couple of minutes while the plane was on its way down that it was going to smash into the ground and they were going to die a horrific death from blunt force trauma and fire. My entire body shivered until I jerked my brain away from these thoughts.

Think about . . . French pastries, I told myself. *Paris-Brest. Canelé.*

Delicate, sweet, and yummy. Tongue cocaine.

"I'm sorry," Grandfather said to Nokes. "Gary was a perfect guide and host to us. I didn't mean to bring up a painful subject."

The taste of the imaginary patisserie items turned bitter. I was momentarily tempted to tell Nokes I lost someone close when I was young, as if this would matter to her at all, but doing so would violate my rule against ever discussing Mom with anyone, even

Dad. If I spoke of her, I was afraid it would be like scratching a scab off a slow-healing wound and causing it to bleed all over again. I couldn't do that to myself, so I clamped my mouth shut.

"It's okay," Nokes said. "It happened before I was even born. Took a month to find him. He . . ." She stopped to exhale heavily and run her tongue over her lips. "He survived the crash, but according to the autopsy, he had a broken arm and a couple busted ribs. Apparently, they got tired of waiting for a rescue, and after five days, they tried to hike out. Searchers eventually found the two of them a month later in a small cave twenty kilometers from the crash site."

"Oh God." The words slipped out of me involuntarily.

"Yeah, it shook people up pretty bad at the time," Nokes agreed. "The worse part of it was that if they had stayed with the plane they likely would have survived."

"They probably thought they could make it to a road," Nick suggested.

I had forgotten about Nick. The last thing he needed to hear about was a tragic plane crash just before we were about to board the same kind of plane. My concern seemed unfounded, though; when I glanced back at him, he appeared entirely unaffected by the story.

"Road?" Nokes repeated, her voice sounding a little bitter. "There wasn't a road for a hundred kilometers. He knew that. Trying to walk out was suicide. He knew that too."

Okay, let's move on. I glanced back at my grandfather, who shrugged at me with a pained expression on his face. We locked eyes for a moment and silently agreed to change the subject.

"So, are you going to be running the lodge one day?" Grandfather asked.

"Nah," Nokes replied. "I just work here for the summer. My cousin, Trevor, is the heir apparent. He's one of the bush pilots. You'll meet him later."

"Sounds like a cool job," Grace remarked.

Nokes shrugged. "The money's decent. It pays for my hockey equipment and league fees."

I nodded, but said nothing. I never played sports at Exeter. Watched a lot and followed all the New York teams, but any activity requiring muscular strength or hand-eye coordination was beyond me.

I turned my head to gaze out the window. Sadly, the scenery didn't engage. The land was heavily forested with evergreens and some hardwoods, and when it wasn't, the ground was mostly flat and rocky. After a few miles, the view became too repetitive to warrant any attention, as if the same two-mile stretch of trees and boulders was cloned over and over again.

After nearly three hours of driving with the soft hum of the engine as the only sound for the last hour, the vehicle slowed. I squinted to make out the reason for our deceleration.

"Well, that wasn't here the last time," Grandfather said.

He pointed out the window, and I leaned forward to stare out the windshield to see what had caught his attention. As we paused to make a turn, I saw what he was pointing to. Off to our left, a large wooden sign spanned a driveway and proclaimed in big, yellow letters: *The Lasley Wilderness Lodge*.

We were here.

My mind shifted to the class I took last semester on Dante's Inferno.

We were crossing the river Acheron and Hades awaited us on the other side.

CHAPTER SIX

"Sorry for the delay," a young guy said upon entering the foyer of the main lodge building where we all sat waiting.

He was a couple of years older than me, decked out in jeans and a red flannel shirt. His black hair was buzz-cut short. In one hand, he held a clipboard, and he had a pen stowed behind one ear. Instinctively, I compared him to Jack: a little shorter, more muscular, squashed-in nose, and a smirk that made me bristle with annoyance.

"No problem," Grandfather said. "Is everything okay with our reservation?"

No problem? We spent the last two hours stuck in the lobby of the main lodge bored silly and forced to listen to piped-in country music. I'd say that was a *big* problem.

The architecture of this lodge place was mildly distracting, I'll concede that. The building was made of enormous, blond-colored logs, which gave the place the appearance of an old trading post but for the absence of horses tied up to a hitching post out front. The reception area, where we passed the time spread out on chairs and couches, had walls crowded with stuffed animal heads—at least a dozen deer, a big moose, and some sort of sheep. A huge, stone fireplace sat in one corner with a genuine bear rug in front of it . . . or so said the "do not touch" sign.

Surrounded by dead animal heads and pelts was ultra-creepy. They kept staring at me accusingly, as if I was the human who killed them and orphaned their kids.

I was on the verge of suggesting we bag this vacation and vamoose, when that "sorry" guy showed up.

Damn.

"My name's Trevor," the guy said. "Thanks for your patience. There's been a big mess-up with your reservation, but I think we got it all straightened out."

"What mess-up?" I asked, rising from the couch I was slumped on.

"The original reservation was canceled," Trevor said. "Then it was reinstated a few hours later. The cancellation made it into our system all right, but not the reinstatement. So, we've had to scramble a bit to accommodate you."

"Scramble?" Grandfather repeated, as much to himself as Trevor. His walrus mustache twitched a little.

"Yep," Trevor said. "The cabin we originally had reserved for you was given away to a party from our waiting list."

"So much for the vacation," I said, barely able to contain my urge to yell, "Woot yeah!"

"Nah, we're good," Trevor replied. "We have a cabin way to the north I'm going to put you guys in. It's on Lake Makwa, which is Ojibwe for 'bear,' or some shit like that. We just finished building a cabin there. It wasn't supposed to be completed until the fall, but we got word this morning that they're done."

"Lake Bear?" I said.

"Yeah, it used to be a hunting camp, but it was abandoned back in the sixties. We bought it from a first nations band a couple years ago." He chuckled and shook his head. "They thought the place was cursed, so we picked it up for a song."

"Aren't we so dang lucky," I said, but he missed my sarcasm.

"Exactly. Perfect timing. We haven't even had a chance to log the place into our inventory. Everything is brand-new: appliances, solar panels, furniture, the whole enchilada. You're all set."

His comment "you're all set" was bitter to hear. For an instant, hope flared that this mess-up meant we could head back to the airport and I could return to my normal life. For Nick's sake, whose expression went from tense to relaxed, I forced myself to maintain an outward appearance of serene acceptance.

"However," Trevor went on, "our schedule is absolutely jammed today, so we need to get moving. Your bags are already being loaded. Make whatever last-minute pitstops you need to make and follow me down to the docks."

This Trevor guy windmilled his arm for us to follow, which we did like obedient sheep being herded to our demise. Once outside, I glanced around the lodge complex, as Nick slipped his hand into mine and squeezed. The main building sat inside a cluster of smaller ones on the edge of a large lake with water almost black in color, its surface roiled by whitecaps from small waves. I raised my free hand to shield my eyes as I studied the sky to the north. A strong gust of wind blew my hair around, while dark clouds hovered ominously on the horizon. A storm was coming, and we were about to fly a small plane into the teeth of it.

Just perfect.

Grace trailed along behind Nick and me, apparently oblivious to everything around her . . . as usual. Her presence here seemed gratingly out of place. Wearing two-inch wedges, a garish layer of makeup on her face, and sporting designer sunglasses, Grace looked like she had recently teleported from the red-light district of some urban wasteland.

Clueless. Not a surprise.

One of Frederick's duties included chauffeuring Grace to and from school every day; and when she was not in school, she'd either be in our mansion, being doted on by maids and servants, or at the mansion of one of her rich friends. She couldn't peel a potato without assistance, let alone build a fire. Poor Grace had no idea what a week in a remote cabin was going to be like.

Trevor led us onto a floating dock, where two people were tossing our gear into a plane. I stared at the aircraft and gulped. A shiver ran down my spine.

Are you kidding me?

"Is that what we're flying in?" I asked.

"That's it," Trevor said, beaming proudly at me. Then he pointed at it. "This here is a de Havilland Otter, one of the best planes in the world."

"Oh, sweet vanilla fudge," I muttered.

We had begun this vacation by sitting in first class on a Boeing 787 Dreamliner, and from there everything slid downhill, ending with us crammed in narrow seats on a regional crop duster. But we hadn't hit bottom yet. Not by a long shot. That happened when I gazed out at the old plane in front of us, which looked like it was on loan from an aviation museum. It had a large, clunky tail; wings stretched across the top of the cab; and a big, fat propeller rested on the end of its snout. The thing was painted glossy yellow, but even from a distance I noticed numerous dents, scrapes, and imperfections. This was disturbing. I liked my planes shiny and free of fender-bender scars.

"Oh my god," Grace said in a breathy voice when she realized this was our transportation to the cabin.

"Hope you like turbulence," I whispered to her.

I watched two of Trevor's aides-de-camp finish gorilla-throwing our bags into the plane along with numerous blue bins of supplies. Brooke's notes said we paid extra to have the lodge acquire all of our food rather than doing it ourselves. I only hoped that they managed to get at least half of the stuff on my part of the grocery list.

One of the guys loading our stuff stood abruptly and shook his head. Then he tossed a few brief words to Trevor before stomping away . . . and he left half our junk in a disorganized heap on the dock. The way his upper teeth ground into his lower lip left no doubt he was dropping a couple F-bombs with Trevor. Apparently, he didn't like our baggage very much.

Sorry.

"All right, everyone," Trevor said, "time to get on board and get in the air."

"What about the rest of our stuff?" I asked him. I kept my voice low, as if he and I were having a confidential aside.

"We can't fit it all," he answered. "It'll put us over on weight. We'll bring in all your food and half your gear this round. I'll come back tomorrow morning with the rest of your stuff. You'll be charged for that, though."

"We—"

"The weight restrictions were pretty clearly flagged in your confirmation receipt," he interrupted, sounding a little peeved. "Normally, I'd let you guys paw through your junk, see what can be left behind, and then try to squeeze under the weight limit, but we don't have time. And besides, you're too far over the limit to bother."

Ah, the confirmation receipt I never saw, the one Brooke made no mention of in her write-up. So, weight limits? What weight limits?

My immediate urge was to hit back with a growl that all our stuff was absolutely critical and necessary and his weight limits were stupid, but then I remembered the smoothie maker I crammed into my larger suitcase. I clamped my mouth shut and swallowed the lump of indignation I was about to spew at him.

Trevor and his remaining assistant helped each of us step from the dock up into the plane, taking our arms and steadying us as we climbed a short, aluminum ladder. The interior was functional and lacking in both aesthetic appeal and comfort. There were six seats and a narrow aisle down the middle. The good news was that everybody had a window seat.

"This is a bigger plane than what I remember," Grandfather said, as he settled down into his seat.

"Seriously?" I replied. "Anything smaller than this is one of those cans you pack the little fishies into."

He winked at me and grinned. I couldn't help smiling back at him, but I shook my head in a "we're so screwed" gesture at the same time.

We taxied away from the dock, picking up speed as the plane glided over the surface of the lake. I clenched my teeth anxiously, half expecting the front of the skis to catch in the water and cause the plane to pitch forward nose-first into the lake. Of course, if that were to happen, sealed up inside this leaky tin can as we were, all of us would drown horribly before we even had a chance to undo our seat belts.

My fears were misplaced. Instead of crashing, the plane lifted off effortlessly from the water and climbed into the sky.

The noise from the plane engine was near deafening, but we each had bulky headphones, so I put mine on. The loud roar instantly shifted to a dull thrum, sparing my eardrums further torture. The headphones, alas, did nothing for the shimmying and shaking. I hadn't eaten since breakfast, so my stomach was mercifully empty; otherwise, its contents would have been shaken into a froth of undigested food and likely I would have hurled.

We flew low, and the view of the forests and numerous lakes below us was arresting, but I was unable to relax and enjoy the sight. At times, it seemed like we were barely skimming over the tops of the trees beneath us. This was nerve-racking, since I felt like there was zero margin for error. The slightest misstep and we'd crash into the top of a giant Douglas fir or face-plant into the side of a granite escarpment.

But I had to give Trevor some credit. Noise and vibration aside, the flight was smooth and uneventful . . . all three and a half hours of it. The only moment of terror came when we dropped out of the sky to land on the surface of a large lake below.

Our destination.

This was the body of water Trevor named Lake Makwa. Once again, my throat constricted in raw fear over the prospect of crashing nose-first into the water, resulting in a cabin full of dead, mangled bodies still strapped into their seats. It didn't happen. In fact, the landing was actually smoother than a jumbo jet landing on a runway. Go figure.

As we taxied across the lake toward a distant shore, a slight smile crept over my face at the sight of the deep blue sky overhead and the rugged majesty of the surrounding, dense forest that came down right to the lake's edge. During our flight, Trevor said that in the lands around the lake there were places no human had ever visited before. Pure wilderness no different than what it was thousands of years ago when the last ice age ended. Cool but scary too.

Then the cabin came into view in the distance. Full realization of what we were in for hit home like a stomach punch.

Shit. Kill me now.

With a heavy sigh, I reminded myself that this was only seven days. A week. One-fifty-second of a year. The time would pass in a blink of an eye. Before I could say *"crème glacèe,"* I'd be home again and packing for France.

If God existed, then somewhere out in the dark, empty universe she was laughing her lungs out at me.

CHAPTER SEVEN

I was the first one off the float plane, helped down and onto a very new-looking dock by Trevor, who grasped and pulled my biceps as if they were the rung of a ladder he was climbing.

"Ouch!" I said and jerked away.

He didn't apologize. Once everyone had deplaned, I glanced around at the others, trying to see if they, too, still felt their bodies shaking from the flight. My legs wobbled with phantom vibrations, but they quickly recovered.

So, here I was.

Lake Makwa.

One hundred and fifty miles from the nearest human, so Trevor said. A few light-years from a Wi-Fi hotspot and a couple galaxies from home.

I wasn't nervous or frightened about being in the middle of nowhere; I was merely put out, annoyed, and impatient. I agreed to come on this trip, but now that the moment of truth had arrived, I wanted out. I wanted to get back on the plane with Trevor and leave Nick, Grace, and my grandfather to do this tour of duty in purgatory without me. But as self-centered as I felt, I couldn't leave Nick. I wouldn't be able to live with myself if I did that to him. Again.

"Help me get the plane unloaded," Trevor said in a raised voice to all of us. "We're burning daylight here, folks. Come on, Allie-gator."

Wait, did he just mangle my name? I'm Allie. Not Allie-gator. What a dick.

Grace smirked, making sure I heard her amused chuckle.

"I'm sorry," I said, rounding on Trevor. "I missed the part where you explained why I give a crap about your daylight."

"Have you ever tried a night landing on a dark lake?" he replied. "It's called crash and die. So I needed to be back in the air ten minutes ago. Capisce?"

He had an icy condescending tone that pissed me off, and he glared at me like I was an airheaded ten-year-old. No way I was taking *that* lying down.

"My name is Miss Baylor to you," I shot back. "Call me Alligator again and I'll kick you in the balls. Capisce?"

"Whatever," he muttered.

I rolled my eyes and walked away.

We spent an hour unloading food and gear and lugging it up a slight hill to the cabin where we were staying. I expected primitive, but the place surprised me. It wasn't the hovel I braced myself for. The house was square in shape, dirt brown in color, and sported a chimney pipe thingy and a number of windows. Also, solar panels covered the roof. That's right, solar panels.

Solar panels meant electricity. Electricity meant modern conveniences. Modern conveniences meant using my smoothie maker.

My tiny spark of elation died quickly. Sure, we had electricity, but turned out it was only for lights and the water pump that gave us our shower and flush toilet. There were no electrical outlets. I wanted to grip the front doorjamb in both hands and bang my head against it a few times and scream, "Why, cruel universe, why?"

Still, our home for the next seven days exceeded my admittedly low expectations. Yes, it was small, but we wouldn't have to sleep on a dirt floor, huddled around a firepit like a tribe of Neolithic hunter-gathers. All in all, the place looked like a humble bungalow you might find in any town . . . well, not Scarsdale.

"Okey doke," Trevor said, once all our stuff was piled in what passed for the living area of the cabin. "Grand tour." He made a sweeping gesture of his arm toward the kitchen corner.

"Propane fridge and stove, and electric lights throughout," he said. "Hot and cold water. New shower in the bathroom. Flush toilet. But the outhouse is just over the rise in case of emergency. You'll see the trail outside."

The rest of the tour only took a few minutes. Not much to see really. Half the floor space consisted of one big open room with the kitchen area in one corner, a plain wooden table and six chairs in the middle of the room, and a pleather couch and a couple overstuffed chairs by the wall opposite the stove and refrigerator.

The other half of the floor space contained three small bedrooms with two twin beds in each, along with a small closet of a bathroom. The cabin had no pantry; instead, apparently, we were supposed to store our food on floor-to-ceiling bookshelves by the refrigerator.

"As I'm sure you noticed," Trevor said, "you have two boats with motors tied up to the dock. Do you need a quick lesson in how to operate them?"

I could tell he didn't want to waste the time on us.

"No, I know how," Grandfather answered. "Where is all the fishing gear and gas? I believe you were supplying them?"

"You may have seen the shed down by the water," Trevor said. "There's gas in there. Also, the work crew was supposed to leave some tools behind—shovel, ax, that sort of thing."

"Fishing poles, tackle?" Grandfather repeated.

"In the plane. I'll move it all to the shed before I leave."

"Then I think we're set," Grandfather said with a nod of appreciation. "We're not in Rivendell, but we should be comfortable enough."

"What?" Trevor said, scrunching his eyebrows together in confusion.

"Classical reference," I murmured to him.

"Right," Trevor replied, still not understanding. "Well, time for me to go."

Then he smiled for the first time since we got here, doubtlessly as happy to get rid of us as I was to get rid of him.

"I'll be back tomorrow with the rest of your stuff," he went on. "You also paid for two check-in flights. Tomorrow will be the first. I'll swing by Wednesday afternoon for the second. In the meantime, use the sat phone if you have any problems. Our number is in the contacts."

Grandfather nodded and patted the bulky phone clipped to his belt. I gazed at the device in sudden appreciation. Hot damn with chocolate sauce. I could call Liv on that thing. Maybe I wasn't as cut off from the outside world as I thought. I'd have to talk to my grandfather later about it.

Meanwhile, Nick and I followed Trevor out of the cabin, but at a distance. We halted at a point twenty yards from the lakeshore and watched Trevor and Grandfather unload the fishing poles and a large tackle box. Soon, Trevor readied the plane for departure, untying it from the dock and climbing inside with deft ease. Within minutes, the plane taxied away from the dock and, with much buzzing, headed out toward the middle of the dark-blue lake.

As Trevor made a wide turn to give himself the length of the lake to take off from, Nick said, "Look at the birds."

Shielding my eyes with one hand, I squinted in the direction he was now pointing. Sure enough, a dozen large black birds wheeled about in the sky above Trevor's plane as it roared with acceleration.

"What are they doing?" he went on.

"Ravens," I said. "Maybe they're attracted to the shiny yellow."

"Morgon," he whispered. "Morgon sent them."

Oh, not Morgon again. Nick loved the woods and loved walking trails, and over the years, we had spent many hours on the weekends visiting parks for his sake. That was, before I left for Phillips Exeter. This vacation was supposed to be nirvana for Nick, an escape from all of his demons . . . particularly Morgon. I knelt on the tussocky ground and drew his small, wiry body into mine for a hug.

"Morgon is gone," I said gently. "He fled. The battle of the gazebo, remember?"

"Here. He came here."

"He didn't," I insisted, but then added, "Even if he did, we'll defeat him again. We always do, you know."

Nick let me tug him back to the house, but both of us kept glancing back over our shoulders at the lake. Those darn birds followed Trevor's plane as it sped up down the lake, breaking off only when his floats left the surface of the water and the craft banked sharply upward toward the clear blue sky.

Weird. I remembered from a class I took on mythology that in some cultures the raven was considered a powerful trickster, while in others it was a harbinger of death. Neither boded well for Trevor, but these were only stories and fairy tales.

Back in the house, Nick and I unloaded food bins, placing the dry stuff on shelves and the rest in the refrigerator. We had a lot of pretty strange junk, some of which I could associate with one of us and some not.

Strawberry syrup.

That would be Nick. Even though we had no ice cream, he liked to drizzle it on anything sweet: Oreos, Captain Crunch cereal, graham crackers . . . you get the picture.

A dozen cucumbers.

Those were for null space Grace. Not sure if they were for facials or salads.

And tofu. That would be me.

Next, I paused to examine a trapezoid-shaped can with a picture of some kind of mystery meat on the label. Corned beef? In a can? My God.

"That's mine," Grandfather said. Then he added, "Nostalgia."

"At least it's not Spam," I replied with a shrug, hiding my revulsion.

"Oh, that's in there too," he clarified. "More nostalgia."

"Are you really going to eat it?" I asked.

"Sure. It's not elvish waybread, but it's not orc flesh either."

"Do you always quote *Lord of the Rings*?" I asked sarcastically.

"Pretty much."

The expression of disgust on my face slid away at the sound of someone crying out in anger and panic.

"Where's my suitcases?" Grace hollered.

Grandfather and Nick chimed in that they were missing stuff too. Me? All of my luggage was present and accounted for.

"They couldn't fit it all in the plane," I quickly explained. "Trevor said he'd bring up the rest of our stuff tomorrow morning. So take it down a couple notches, Grace. I'm sure you can survive twenty-four hours without your thong collection."

"Of course, you got all *your* junk," Grace observed sarcastically. "No surprise there."

From the anger sparkling in Grace's eyes and her aggressive hands-on-hips posture, I could tell she was spoiling for a fight. I wasn't in the mood, so I did what I almost never did when it came to my sister. I walked away.

"Come on, Nick," I said. "Let's go check out the lake."

We wandered out onto the dock and stared across the water at the far off shore, as the water lapped against the wooden pilings. The sun was sinking fast, casting long shadows over the lake's surface from the large trees surrounding it.

"We'll go fishing tomorrow," I told him.

"In the boat?"

"Of course."

My voice sounded nonchalant, but I was leery of launching out into the middle of the lake inside one of the two flimsy-looking rowboats that came with the cabin. I could swim fine, but I never particularly liked being out on the water. Dad long ago stopped asking me to go on the yacht outings when studio head, Luke Adams, would invite our family to join his off Newport, Rhode Island.

"Is Grandpa coming with us?" he asked.

"Yeah. He's the only one who knows how to operate the motor," I explained. "Why do you ask?"

"You know the movie *Alien*?"

"You shouldn't be watching that kind of crap," I scolded. "It'll only keep you up at night."

Normally, I was preaching to the choir on this point. Nick had no desire to take in monster movies. He shied away from scary shows and stories without any prompting from Brooke or me, knowing full well that evil beasts might upset him for days.

"I had a dream, and one of those things was coming out of his chest," Nick answered. "He was standing on the edge of a cliff."

"Grandfather?" I asked skeptically.

He nodded.

"It's a dream. You said it yourself. A really ugly, terrifying dream. Let it go, Nick. I know it's hard, but try to forget about it, okay?"

"Oh, oh," he said, staring past me bug-eyed.

I pivoted to see what had transfixed him. Grace. She stomped toward the dock, toward me, with a determined, angry face not unlike Almira Gulch from *The Wizard of Oz* coming to get Toto. Our grandfather followed a few yards back, his legs moving in a rickety, stiff gait.

"Wait," Grandfather said to Grace. His voice had a stern tone to it.

Grace ignored him. She stepped onto the dock and advanced to within three feet of me before stopping. Her narrow, glaring eyes radiated "ugly confrontation on the way." No walking away this time. What happened to her promise not to fight with me on this trip?

"The suitcase with my travel bag is missing," she said accusingly. "I *need* it."

"Sorry," I said, not sounding a bit sorry. "You'll have to wait until tomorrow to get your dope."

"You did it," she said. "You had them leave my stuff behind."

I responded in a respectful, genteel fashion by biting my lower lip and shoving my middle finger in her face.

"Go to hell, Grace," I added. "You know what your problem is? Mom—"

"You!" she interrupted through gritted teeth. "You're my problem. You're always my problem."

"Good. I hope it hurts."

"Girls," Grandfather said. "Enough. Come on, Grace. Take a walk with me and Nick."

"Bitch," Grace spat.

"Killer," I lobbed back.

"Me?" she answered, sounding genuinely surprised. "You're the one—"

"Shut up!" I said, cutting her off.

So far, this exchange was within historic boundaries for us. We had fought like this before over the years, and so far this fight was clocking in at the high end of the ugly scale. Still, to this point, our only weapons were words. Usually our battles ended when one of us gave a parting shot and stormed off. Not this time. A coiled, twisted band of pent-up anger and resentment inside me snapped.

My hand swung forward with all the force I could muster. I slapped Grace across the cheek so hard my hand stung and Grace stumbled backward, reeling from the blow.

Oh God. What had I done?

"Allie!" Grandfather barked.

Grace recovered and took several steps forward, holding one of her hands to the side of her face, while her mouth hung open in complete shock. My anger instantly drained away, and I closed the distance between us intending to apologize profusely.

"Grace, I'm—"

The word "sorry" never made it out of my mouth. Grace hauled off and punched me in my left eye with her closed fist.

Blackness and pain exploded in my head beyond anything I had ever experienced. Unlike Grace, I couldn't recover my balance. Instead, I staggered backward, and my heel caught on a dock cleat.

And that was all she wrote.

I fell backward, grasping desperately at the air. My fall seemed to happen in slow motion as I waited for impact.

"Grace!" Grandfather yelled, even louder than before.

Then my head hit the edge of the dock. Another layer of pain blanketed me, but this time, my eyesight blurred and my brain began to shut down. I stopped moving my arms as I slid into the lake. I sank beneath the surface like a bag of rocks. With my last shred of consciousness, I told myself not to breathe, but my lungs refused to listen. I couldn't stop myself.

My last thought before a curtain of darkness descended was that Grace had just killed me.

CHAPTER EIGHT

"Her eye opened," a voice said. My half-dead brain recognized the person. Nick.

"And she's got snot dripping out of her nose," he added.

My eyelids struggled to lift. I woke.

My first sensation was a raw, swollen soreness that ran from the back of my mouth, down my throat, and into my lungs. Next, I became aware of a dank rotten taste inside of my mouth, and my stomach spasmed to throw up. Painful cramps in my abdomen squelched the effort to empty my digestive tract inside out. Lastly, my left eyelid would only open halfway, and efforts to do more hurt. Grace had punched my lights out . . . at least one of them anyway.

"Gross," Nick observed. "She's leaking green stuff again."

"Back off and give her some space, son," my grandfather said. "She doesn't need your color commentary."

Gradually, nerves in my body relayed news about my situation to my brain. I was lying on my side on a wooden floor with a blanket draped over me. My head rested on a pillow. My clothes were soaked. And Nick was right. I needed a box of tissues to mop away the muck that clung to my upper lip. I rolled onto my back. Immediately, my lungs convulsed, and I started coughing. The convulsions became deeper and more wracking, as my body tried to hack out some unknown invader.

"Easy," Grandfather said, swiping my nose with a paper towel. "You swallowed a ton of water, girl."

"What . . ." I tried to ask. I couldn't finish the question because my vocal cords were sore and inflamed. Also, my mind couldn't figure out which of the thousand questions swirling around inside me it wanted to ask first.

"You've been out for over an hour," Grandfather said. "We almost lost you."

"We *did* lose the sat phone," Nick added. "It's at the bottom of the lake. Grandpa lost it pulling you out of the water."

"Never mind that," Grandfather scolded. "Sat phones can always be replaced."

After lying on the hard floor of the cabin for another hour or so—my sense of time was vague—Nick helped me struggle to my feet and shuffle off to the bathroom for a shower and change of clothes. My hair and the rest of my body was coated in lake water that was like a tea brewed from rotting vegetation. Unfortunately, my lungs had no easy way to flush away the water other than to cough it out. While I showered, I became aware of a gauze bandage taped to my forehead right at the hairline. This awareness seemed to waken the wound, and suddenly my head began to throb with a dull pain.

Exhausted, sore, and able to breathe only shallowly, lest I unleash a bout of uncontrolled coughing, I let Nick direct me to the bed someone had assigned to me. I collapsed on it and rolled onto my side. Of course, Nick and I were sharing the same bedroom; I expected as much.

Sleep clawed at my consciousness, but before I drifted off, I noticed Nick sitting on the edge of his bed across from mine holding a flashlight that was turned on, but pointing at the floor.

"What the fu . . ." I muttered, my voice fading off into silence.

"I'm supposed to keep watch over you," he said. "Make sure you don't choke on your own vomit, Gramps said."

"Lovely," I croaked. I meant to say more, but for the second time that day a tsunami of darkness flooded over me and I sank into inky blackness.

I awoke early the next morning in a cold room, every muscle in my body, except possibly the ones that operated my toes, was stiff as starch and sore as sin. The gray light of dawn filtered through the windows without drapes as I shuffled to the bathroom. My lungs were heavy and congested, my bladder was at DEFCON 2, and my eye ached. After dealing with the bladder situation, I studied my face in the square of reflective glass that hung above the sink.

Not pretty.

Gingerly my fingers felt the bandage on my forehead, which hid a lump the size of a hard-boiled egg. Painful. Wacked in the head with a baseball bat painful. When I raised my arm, I noticed a jangle sound from my wrist. I still had my Cartier watch, and unlike me, it survived the lake baptism just fine.

The worst outcome of my fight with Grace was my eye. With it half-swollen shut, I didn't recognize the left side of my face. Deep-purple bruising around the eye extended to the cheekbone below. How long was this going to last? I was supposed to meet Jack in Paris in ten days but not if I looked like this. I'd never make it through customs . . . France had a strict policy against letting pizza-face zombies into the country.

The noise of a clattering pan accompanied by the creak of cupboard doors opening snapped me out of my thoughts. Someone was up and probably needed to use the bathroom I was hogging. If it was Grace, I wasn't sure what I'd say or do.

Not Grace.

I found Grandfather in the kitchen area fumbling around to make a pot of coffee. He had located all the necessary elements except the paper filters. Fortunately, I remembered shelving them yesterday, so I marched over, snatched the box from behind the peanut butter, and handed it to him.

"Thanks," he said. "I need a cup before I'm functional and lucid."

"What? No miruvor?" I chided.

He shook his haggard, just woke up face and said, "Not this early."

Then he got his coffee brewing and sat down at the table while I put a teapot on the stove for myself. Unlike me, he was already showered, dressed, and pressed. He wore a Hawaiian shirt with lots of blue and gold, and his bushy mustache was trimmed and combed.

"I'm going to need more than caffeine," I said.

With a dry hacking cough, I sat down on a chair across from him. I had come to a decision in the half hour or so since I awoke. Spending the rest of the week here with Grace was ludicrous.

When Trevor the dick showed up in his plane, I was getting on it and leaving. Nothing could talk me out of it. My only concern was Nick.

"You want to leave," Grandfather said matter-of-factly. I noticed he had a foil Pop-Tarts envelope in his hands.

"Sure do."

He nodded, tore open the foil pouch, and extracted two chocolate-iced Pop-Tarts. He broke off a corner and put it in his mouth as he rose from his chair to pour himself a mug of coffee.

"You know, the sugar in those things will kill you," I observed. I could be a bit of a food Nazi sometimes.

He shrugged. "It will have to get in line. Plenty of other things are already queued up to take me down."

I wasn't sure what he meant. I let it pass.

"You *should* go," he went on. "All the lake water in your lungs is liable to cause an infection. Pneumonia maybe. You need to see a doctor."

"I need to kill my sister."

"Understandable," he conceded, tossing another chunk of Pop-Tart in his mouth. "Grace did help pull you out of the water, though. Nick and I couldn't have done it without her."

A derisive snort escaped my nostrils. "She was only trying to avoid a murder charge. Some vacation, huh?"

"Very reminiscent," he said. "Your dad and I didn't punch each other, but we came close."

I stared at him. From all the stories Dad had told us about their trip thirty years ago, I imagined Carl and Russell from the movie *Up*.

"I thought your trip was this big bonding adventure."

"Not at first," he said, leaning back in his wooden chair and taking another sip of coffee. He sighed and exhaled. "We fought for the first two days. We were awful. I—"

"Unless he punched you and shoved you into the lake," I interrupted, "you guys aren't in the same league."

"We did get into a shoving match, though," he noted. "We both ended up on the floor, and one of us knocked out a table leg."

"Sounds like a couple of five-year-olds," I commented.

"Near enough."

"You keep going at it?" I asked.

He shook his head and smiled. "No. We burst out laughing at how idiotic we were acting. And then . . ."

His voice faded out.

"Then what?"

"We started talking," he mused. "We sat on that damn floor for two hours talking, sometimes yelling. We didn't solve anything, but we let out a lot of pent-up manure that had piled up inside both of us for years."

"And you lived happily ever after. Blah, blah, blah."

"Well, you know that's not true," he replied with a raised eyebrow. "I was still the same apathetic, lousy father I was before and he was still the same disrespectful, punk kid."

"But?" I prompted.

"But we developed a bit of an understanding of why we were the jerks we were. And I stopped pushing his buttons, and he stopped pushing mine. Mostly anyway."

He took another sip of his coffee, placed the mug on the table, and stared at me. His gaze felt uncomfortable, so I glanced away to study my suitcases, which still lay in a jumble in the middle of the room.

"Anyway, once we got past all that shit," he went on, "we were able to go fishing, enjoy ourselves, and talk about things like baseball, stuff we hadn't talked about in years."

"Never going to happen with Grace and me," I observed with a shake of my head. "Too much water under the bridge . . . and in my lungs."

"Don't say never," he replied, his tone serious. "It's easy to slam the door on your sister and walk away. Don't do it. Leave the door open a crack. Someday—maybe not in my lifetime—you're going to need each other."

"That'll be the day. I need Grace the way I need the bubonic plague, and I don't see that ever changing."

Time to go outside and wait for the plane. I gulped down the rest of my tea and rose.

With Grandfather's help, I wrestled my luggage out of the cabin and down to the dock, where I stacked everything neatly, and then sat dangling my feet over the edge, after Grandfather returned to the cabin to check on Nick. I hoped to board Trevor's plane and get out of here without having to see Grace. Once I got home, I would arrange my life so I never crossed paths with her again . . . at least, not for a very long time.

Given how far north we were, I reasoned Trevor would start out his day by visiting us first before doing anything else. I guessed he'd show up about 11:30, give or take. As I waited on the dock, the air fast became hot and muggy as the morning aged, but I was ready for it. I wore a pair of fluorescent orange shorts that served as my uniform last semester in my badminton class, which one of the girls said looked sharp and sexy on me. So, of course, I wore them every chance I got afterward. For a top, I had on my Yankees jersey—white with pinstripes. It was baggy but airy and comfortable.

After a few hours, a glance at my phone revealed that it was noon. Where in the crap was this tool? He said he'd be here in the morning with the rest of our stuff—including Grace's missing suitcases that meant so much to her that she tried to kill me. If this guy were part of our staff back at home, I'd have Brooke fire his ass. But with a heavy sigh, I forced myself to calm down. After all, morning had only just ended. I would hold off on going nuclear-war ballistic for sixty more minutes.

A half hour into my countdown, I spotted Nick exiting the cabin with a covered plate in one hand. A groan bled out of me. If Nick thought I needed cheering up, he'd make me something to eat. Usually, it had peanut butter and was inedible.

"What you got there?" I asked, as he drew near.

"Lunch."

"Thank you so much," I gushed while accepting the paper plate with a sandwich on it, covered with plastic wrap. I couldn't tell what lay between the slices of white bread.

"It's your favorite."

"Really?" I remarked with a raised eyebrow.

"Lettuce." He paused for approval.

"I love lettuce," I said.

"Tomato slices."

"I love tomatoes too."

Then he added the kicker . . . and there was always a kicker.

"Plus, lots of Nutella." He smiled with a ta-da expression. "It sounds weird, but trust me, you got to try it."

"Wow," I said, while trying to keep my stomach from making *urp* noises. "You know what? I'm going to save it and eat it on the plane."

He kicked off his flip-flops and sat beside me, but his legs were too short to reach the water.

"Do you have to leave?" he asked quietly.

"Look at my eye. What color is it?"

"Purple," he replied, sounding a little confused by my question.

"Canada doesn't allow purple-eyed nonresidents to stay in the country . . . It's an immigration thing."

"Shut up, Allie. I'm not six years old, and I'm not stupid."

"Sorry."

Nick left me after that to return to the cabin, clearly unhappy with me leaving. From my vantage point, I noticed Grandfather on the porch sitting in a knobby wooden chair. Where Grace was, I had no idea. The cabin had no air-conditioning, so it must be warming up like an oven in there.

At one o'clock, my stomach cried out from hunger, but all I had was Nick's sandwich, which had begun to deteriorate in the sun. Not unless the alternative was instant death would I eat Nick's creation. If I wanted something decent, my only option was to return to the cabin, except to do that was to admit defeat.

Instead, I rose to my feet and stood on the edge of the dock.

"Where are you!" I yelled out across the lake. "Well, screw you, asshole!"

There. That felt nice.

My yelling did not make the float plane appear. Its only effect, beyond the therapeutic benefits from screaming my lungs out, was to scare a bunch of ducks at the far end of the lake.

This was un-freaking-believable. Where was this guy? Half our luggage sat somewhere at his stupid lodge. Probably the jerks just threw our stuff on the grass and left it there overnight.

"He must have got delayed," I muttered to myself. "He'll be here sometime this afternoon. He has to."

I tried to grab on to those words to calm me down. Five hours ago I had hoped to be out of here in time to catch a flight out of the Kenora Airport, but at this point that hope had evaporated. I would have to spend the night in some derelict motel before starting back for New York tomorrow. Now that I had made up my mind to leave Lake Woe-be-me, I couldn't stand waiting any longer.

Finally, at three o'clock, I had enough. I needed to pee, I needed water, and I needed something other than Nutella to eat. In that order. After more yelled curses, I stomped up the small incline to the cabin, walking at as fast a pace as I could manage, leaving my suitcases on the dock. I had this irrational anxiety that, while I was in the bathroom, Trevor would fly in, toss our junk on the dock, and fly off before I had time to even pull my shorts up.

"Where is he?" Nick asked as I barged through the cabin door.

"Jerking off somewhere," I muttered.

A few minutes later, I sat outside on the porch in a chair next to my grandfather with a plate of food on my lap. My late lunch consisted of grapes, apple slices, and some celery sticks. Grandfather nodded to me and took a long drag from a silver flask. More miruvor. I rolled my eyes.

"I don't think he's coming," Nick remarked, having come out to sit on the porch steps.

I couldn't think that, so I changed the subject. "Where's Medusa? Feeding her snakes?"

Nick blinked at me several times and started to ask "what."

"Your Neanderthal sister," I clarified.

"In her room," he answered with a shrug. "I think she's waiting for you to leave."

I went back to my lunch, remembering the last time I was as angry at someone as I was at Grace. The day had gone from one of the worst of my life to one of the best in an eye blink. Could that happen again? Not a chance.

It was the last day of our French club trip to Toulouse, a trip during which I focused almost all my attention on Jack. We weren't able to spend too much time alone. Mrs. Fèvre organized group activities that took up most of each day, but we were able to steal some time together. Fèvre knew something was blossoming between us, though, which the old spinster didn't approve of. While she and I had never been particularly warm and fuzzy before—she wasn't warm and fuzzy with anyone—she became brusque and imperious with me after Jack entered the picture.

The situation with Fèvre went from worse to worser the night before we were supposed to fly home. Fèvre stopped four of us, including Jack, from sneaking out of our hotel after midnight on a quest to find a local night spot. She and I argued rather heatedly in the hotel lobby, exchanging harsh words in French.

"*Fille blanche choyée,*" she hurled at me in a raised voice, calling me a pampered white girl.

"*Chienne,*" I shot back, naming her a total bitch.

We said more, but I only remember my two hotel roommates yanking me away from her by the shoulders and leading me back to our room. I was still angry the next day at the airport, where Fèvre and I didn't speak but traded icy glares. While we waited for our flight back to JFK to board, Jack approached with a box of macarons he bought at a Ladurée store in the terminal nearby.

"You're still pissed," he observed, plopping down in a seat next to me.

"I am."

I had my arms crossed over my chest and my lower lip stuck out in a sulky way that radiated supreme anger.

"Here. Blue macaroons help." He handed me the box of confections. "That and cocaine . . . so I'm told."

"Fèvre and I don't like each other very much," I said, accepting the box with a rueful smile. "You don't want to get caught in the crossfire."

"I'm counting on you to get me through the flight back," he said.

"I'm running out of things to talk about," I answered with a laugh, which wasn't actually true at all. If pushed, I could easily blather on about movies, candy, clothes, Manhattan, pizza, etcetera, etcetera, until the next ice age arrived.

"Then I suppose you could kiss me all the way to New York."

My lips parted as I started to reply with some smartass remark, but before I could speak, his lips were on mine . . . right there in Terminal 2E in front of one hundred and fifty thousand people. Maybe not quite that many. The kiss was gentle and quick and completely, shockingly unexpected. I blinked several times, but otherwise, every muscle in my body was no longer functioning. He broke it off and tipped his head back a couple inches. After inhaling a deep breath to armor up on oxygen, I leaned forward and immediately restarted the kiss, this time tuning out the world around us and letting the electricity between us spark on for a full minute. We were both breathing a little rapidly when we stopped.

"I'm not sure I could survive seven hours of that," he said with a gasp.

"No, me neither."

My stroll down memory lane was cut short by my grandfather, who cleared his throat and said, "I hate to say it, Allie, but it's too late for Trevor to fly in, drop his load, and make it back before dark. I don't think he's coming today."

"We could call him," Nick suggested, and then he added, "Except the sat phone sleeps with the fishes."

I rose to go down and begin bringing my junk back inside the cabin. "Son of a bitch!" I yelled.

CHAPTER NINE

Around six in the morning on Monday, I stumbled out of bed, let loose with a couple of hacking coughs, and headed for the kitchen to make tea. I was the only one up.

The second full day of our glorious vacation had begun, and I had high hopes Trevor would show up nice and early in the morning with the same brusque manner he left with on Saturday afternoon. He would toss us an apology and make some excuse for yesterday's no-show, and I'd probably glare at him while he was doing it. But truthfully, seeing him glide out of the skies to land on the lake would be a huge relief.

Dressed in baggy sweats and a T-shirt, armed with a cup of tea and a slice of the biscotti I brought, I pivoted away from the stove and took one step toward the door. I wanted to sit outside, drink my tea, and do some serious wallowing in self-pity at how effed up my life was this week. Then a bedroom door opened, and Grace stepped out, her normally gorgeous blonde hair disheveled and stringy.

I froze.

She froze.

"You slapped me," she said dryly.

"You *punched* me."

"Yeah, I did."

"Yeah, I did," I echoed.

And that was it. She marched off to the bathroom, and I went outside.

I spent a good portion of the morning drinking tea. I also took a short walk, venturing to the edge of the woods that surrounded the small clearing in which our cabin sat. Other than a few bugs and birds, the forest was silent.

As I scanned the tree line, trying to see into the gloom and shadows under the canopy, my gaze froze on an odd sight. Several small trees, each a little bigger than a sapling, lay sprawled about on the dirt. They had been snapped off their trunks a few feet above the ground and tossed about like kindling. Branches were ripped off and bark was shredded. Something very big had really torn up the ground and destroyed the trees in the area. A moose? I read that they used their massive antlers to tear up the brush sometimes. Whatever it was, judging by the damage, it must have been seriously pissed off. Shivering, I headed back to sit and wait on the porch and steer clear of the trampled area.

I did whatever I could think of to kill time. Every few minutes, my eyes drifted skyward, hoping each time I would spot a plane emerging from the clouds to the south. No plane came. By noon, all hope left me, even though a three-hour window, give or take, remained. He wasn't coming. The *asshat* wasn't coming!

Well, misery loves company, and I had plenty of it. As disappointed as I was about not leaving today, Grandfather and Nick might be worse. They had lost suitcases they needed.

I could only guess at the frustration Grace had to be feeling. All three of her suitcases were left behind; if this rankled her yesterday, it drove her insanely crazy today, judging from the sound I heard earlier of a chair being thrown against a wall. Knowing she suffered more than if she lost a leg comforted me amid my crushing disappointment. Somebody had it worse than I did, and what better someone than my psycho sister.

Four o'clock arrived, but no bells sounded to signal the official death knell of any plane arriving today. Four was the latest we could possibly expect him to show up.

To commemorate the occasion, I relocated to an Adirondack chair beside a fire ring that was downslope from the cabin, where I vegetated and gazed blankly at the horizon with my sunglasses on. I sat still enough, long enough, that a stranger passing by might mistake me for a slovenly attired mannequin. Except, there were no strangers, unless you counted the wildlife.

What is Jack going to say when I tell him this story?

I agreed to meet him in Paris in mere days. Then, four glorious weeks with him and his parents would follow, nestled in luxury inside Château d'Amour Fou outside Limoges. The giant castle had it all: an Olympic-sized pool, a spa, a vineyard, twenty-seven bedrooms . . . *et ainsi de suite.*

Jack and I had planned bike rides into the city, picnics in the scenic hills around the château, and parties. We would also be attending the formal dinner his father was hosting for the minister of culture, Edmond Chabaud. This excited me. In the midst of my agony, I smiled.

"I'm missing my duffel bag," Nick said, coming over to sit in a chair next to me. "I have no underwear or undershirts. And, my Nintendo Switch is in there."

"What? Nick, we have no electrical outlets, you know. It can't be recharged."

He shrugged. "Still."

Tempted as I was to toss out a few more words of chastisement, I swallowed them. After all, didn't I have a useless plug-in smoothie maker in my suitcase?

"Maybe Wednesday," I said. "He's supposed to check in on us twice—yesterday and Wednesday. I mean, we paid for it."

"What if he doesn't show?"

It was my turn to shrug. "I guess you won't be changing your underwear. Or, worst case, you go commando for a week."

"In jeans?" he asked incredulously.

"Why not?"

"Because you need a protective cloth barrier between the zipper mechanism and your junk." He let out an annoyed sigh. "You wouldn't know."

Good point. I was about to suggest an ad lib loincloth from a dish towel and duct tape when Grandfather came over to join us, taking the third of six chairs.

"Why don't we go fishing?" Grandfather asked. "Take a whirl around the lake and catch enough for a fish fry tonight."

"All right," Nick quickly answered. "Allie?"

Exhaling heavily, I rolled my eyes. Maybe if I said nothing and froze as still as a granite column, this cup would pass from me. No such luck.

"Allie?" Nick repeated.

"Fine," I said, shaking my head. "But I have three rules. One, someone has to cast my line for me. Two, I don't bait hooks. And three, I never touch the fish. Agreed?"

"Just like your late grandmother," Grandfather said. "Agreed."

Soon, the three of us were gathered on the dock, and Grandfather chose one of the motor boats tethered to one side of the dock. The thing was disturbingly small and fragile looking. Made of bright aluminum with a flat bottom, the boat had an outboard motor attached to the back. The two bench seats inside were plenty big enough for us to sit with ample space, but the cold metal slats looked far from comfortable. Before helping each of us into the craft, Grandfather handed us orange life jackets that tied together with white nylon straps. Once we were all on board and seated, the motor roared to life after a couple yanks by Grandfather on the pull cord thingy . . . or whatever you called it. Within moments we picked up speed and shot out toward the middle of the lake.

"This is a big lake," Nick observed, almost yelling to be heard over the motor.

My vocal cords were still raw too holler back, so I merely nodded.

From the map Trevor had left us, I knew that Lake Makwa was shaped like a giant cashew nut. The cabin sat on the inside of the concave part of the cashew shape about midway along the lake's length. We were headed toward the western end. Grandfather cut the motor, letting us glide silently through the water. We came to a stop close to shore at the opening of a small cove. A reedy quagmire ringed the water near the shoreline fifty yards away; it made me shiver with visions of water snakes slithering among the swamp vegetation.

"Fish like weeds," Grandfather said. "Let's see if they're biting."

I chose to sit out the first few casts, content to wait on the sidelines and watch Nick and Grandfather go at it. Nick caught the first fish.

"Got one!" he yelled, and the excitement in his voice brought a smile to my face.

Grandfather coached him to keep his rod tip down and pull back slowly before cranking the reel. Once Nick got the creature on board and unhooked it, he held it up triumphantly. I didn't know what kind of fish it was, except that it was a member of the green slimy thing family.

"That is one nice walleye," Grandfather said, patting Nick on the back. "Good eating."

Ugh. Eating first meant cleaning. Note to self: when we returned to the dock, evacuate the area.

In the end, I acquiesced in holding a pole after Nick did a perfect cast for me, sending my funky-looking lure flying until it hit the water at the edge of the weeds with a plop. Following Grandfather's instruction, I reeled in my line. By the time I finished reeling in three casts, Grandfather caught a walleye and Nick got another one. On my fourth cast, a yank on the line almost jerked me over the side and into the soup.

Nick, my cheerleader, shouted encouragement at me to keep reeling.

"Big one," Grandfather said while scooting over to help me. With a grunt of exertion, he hefted the netted fish out of the water and into the boat.

"That is one hell of a northern," he said. "Christ, it must be three feet long."

Nick tugged his phone out of his pocket and said, "Hold it up, Allie. I want to get a picture."

"I said no touchies."

His mouth dropped open, and he gave me sad baby lamb eyes.

"Fine," I said in a huff.

With Grandfather's help, we held up the mucous-slick fish for Nick. Grandfather called the fish a northern, but that seemed a little vague for an official name. I decided to call it a dino-snapper, since it looked like an ugly prehistoric remnant from the Triassic period with its toothy mouth and snaky body.

"I want to throw it back," I announced.

Grandfather nodded, and Nick frowned but didn't object. Grandfather and I leaned over the edge of the boat and let the slickery, snot-slimy monster glide out of our hands into the lake. As I straightened, rubbing my hands on my shorts to get the phlegm off, a crashing noise exploded from onshore, directly in front of us. More limb snapping and bush-shaking sounds followed. All of us held our breaths, waiting to see what might emerge from the tangle of trees and bushes. We didn't have to wait long.

"What is it?" Nick asked no one specifically.

"T-Rex?" I ventured.

I was joking, of course, and opened my mouth to laugh when a hairy black blob the size of an Amazon delivery van crashed through the brush at the water's edge. It had a stubby, honey-colored snout and nub-shaped ears. Fifty yards of water lay between us; it wasn't nearly enough.

The beast that ambled out of the forest was the most massively humongous mammal I had ever seen in all my years of watching the National Geographic channel. We weren't quite into elephant territory, but a hippo or rhino had nothing on this colossus.

"My god," Grandfather gasped.

"Mine too," I agreed.

The beast saw or smelled us because it immediately froze and stared in our direction. Then it twitched its nose, apparently testing the air in order to get a clue as to what we were.

"Bear?" I whispered-questioned.

"It's got to be twice the size of a polar bear," Grandfather said, sounding truly awed.

Exactly how big this monster really was we found out an instant later when it rose to stand on two feet, gazing across the water at us.

"It's ten feet tall," I said.

"More like fourteen," Grandfather corrected.

After more sniffing, bearzilla bellowed at us, caught its breath, and bellowed some more. The roar had a paralyzing effect, nearly turning my muscles into useless jelly. My hands yanked up instinctively to stop my ears, and my blood morphed into a cocktail of fear, amazement, and shock. A primordial urge to run clawed at my body.

Throat dry, I asked, "Can bears swim?"

"Like an otter," Grandfather replied.

"Let's get out of here," I suggested. "It looks pissed."

Grandfather and I stared at the growling bear transfixed, forgetting all about Nick . . . until we heard *clunk-bang*. I jerked my head sideways to discover Nick on the bottom of the boat beginning to shake. Quickly kneeling beside him, I lifted his head onto my lap as his eyes rolled up and backward.

"Nick!" I pleaded.

He said one word before the shakes started again. "Morgon."

"What's happening?" Grandfather asked. His voice reeked of panic.

"He's having a seizure," I said. "We need to get him back to the cabin. Now!"

With a couple tugs, Grandfather yanked the motor to life, and in seconds, we were roaring across the lake surface. I glanced up to check on the bear monster, but the shoreline was empty, just tall weeds, bushes and trees where the thing had stood moments before. Was it all an illusion?

The spray of water from our wake quickly soaked my shirt and drenched my hair, but I barely noticed. For about one minute, this seizure was like so many Nick had experienced before over the years, seizures that led Mom to take him to doctor after doctor in search of a way to put the cracked pieces of Humpty Dumpty back together again.

Then blood began to stream out of his nose, and his face darkened to a plum-purple color.

"Hurry!" I screamed. "I'm losing him!"

CHAPTER TEN

"What's wrong?" Grace practically yelled as Grandfather carried a twitching Nick into the cabin.

"Seizure," I answered. "Bad one."

"Put him on the bed. Turn him on his side." Grace shot the instructions at Grandfather like bullets from a gun.

I went for the largest of my suitcases, the one with my makeup, toiletry bag, smoothie maker, and other non-clothing stuff. Rather than rummage through it, I simply turned the suitcase upside down and let the contents spill out on the floor.

"Allie, what are you doing?" Grace shouted, glancing over her shoulder. She was helping Grandfather position Nick on the bed.

"Rescue meds," I responded.

I quickly located my pink pill bag, which not only had stuff like Tylenol, Midol, and allergy pills but also Nick's emergency seizure meds. Nick never went anywhere without them. They were what we used when bad stuff hit the spinning blade device. The goal was simple: prevent a meltdown that required a trip to the emergency room. They could not be more critical today, since the nearest hospital was a few light-years on the other side of Alpha Centauri.

Of course, so much junk filled my bag I couldn't immediately locate Nick's drugs. I dumped it out on the floor just like my suitcase.

There.

The meds were lying on the wooden floor next to a square white package that held a condom.

Oops. How did that get there? No time.

"Hurry," Grace urged.

My hand clasped the foil-backed package, and then I raced to Nick's side. My fingers fumbled with the blister pack. I was so nervous and upset I couldn't stop shaking. This was an emergency. Why were my stupid fingers not working?

"Here, let me," Grace said, taking the med pack from my bumbling grasp.

She scratched at the back of the package with her long, purple-enameled nails and swiftly peeled away the foil backing. Her fingers were calm and controlled. After prying out one inhaler, she handed the package back to me. Each foil pack held two disposable inhalers and one dose required the use of both. Grace shook her head to get her hair out of her face, leaned over to shove the nozzle into one of Nick's nostrils, and then squeezed down on the plunger. I handed her the second inhaler, and she repeated the process.

"Well, we haven't had to do that in a while," Grace said.

"Thanks," I replied, and I meant it. I tottered on the edge of panic, but Grace was as cool as the cucumber slices she liked to put on her eyes.

"It was for Nick," she said, straightening. "Let's hope it works."

It *did* work.

The seizure faded over the next hour until Nick became a normal sleeping boy. He rarely had episodes this bad, but when it happened, someone stayed with him until he woke and was up and about like his old self. Grace volunteered to take the first shift by his bedside while I helped Grandfather make dinner. Although my eye was still swollen, purple, and tender, my roaring flames of anger at Grace had subsided into glowing embers. When things went south, she answered the bell and helped with Nick. I wouldn't say that I couldn't have done it without her, but it would have been tougher.

I found Grandfather in the kitchen area rinsing a bunch of fish fillets in the sink in preparation for what he called his famous fish fry. I joined him at the counter and started chopping vegetables for one of my easiest to make and favorite dishes: spicy minestrone soup.

The incident with Nick had mostly driven the bear from my mind. Mostly.

"What was that thing?" I asked. I didn't need to be any more specific.

Grandfather shook his head. "I'm not sure. I've never heard of bears getting that big."

"At least we've got a huge lake between him and us. He'd have to walk ten or twenty miles around the water to find us, right?"

"How's Nick?" Grandfather asked, changing the subject.

I exhaled slowly. "He'll be fine."

"Paul told me he had epilepsy, but I didn't realize how severe the seizures are."

"They're not," I said, sounding a tiny bit defensive. "Usually they're mild and they happen very seldom."

He mouthed "oh" and went back to his fish.

I didn't like the word epilepsy, so I avoided using it. Yes, according to the technical medical definition—whatever that was, come to think of it—Nick had epilepsy, but the term bothered me. Calling Nick an epileptic meant putting a label on him, a label that came with the subtitle disabled, defective, and handicapped. Okay, Nick was different. I got that. But couldn't we just leave it at that?

"What triggers the seizures?" he asked after several minutes of silence.

"Lots of things really," I replied. "But in this case, stress. He has panic attacks sometimes, and they can lead to seizures."

"The bear?"

I nodded and repeated, "The bear. And can you blame him? *I* almost had a seizure."

"I didn't understand," he said softly. "Your stepmother said being out in the woods would be therapeutic for him. She said he would excel out here."

"He will. This was a one-off."

What I didn't tell my grandfather was that the type of stress that sent Nick over the edge came from a fantasy game I invented when Nick was five. For him, the fantasy world of Alithia blended with the real world of Scarsdale around him. Grace and I stopped playing the game when we realized what it was doing to him, but whereas we could shut down Alithia and get on with real life, he couldn't.

Part of the reason I left for boarding school was that my being around was what helped keep the game alive for him. At first, it seemed to work, but this past year, things had gotten much worse, even though I was two hundred forty miles away.

Anyway, my soup came out great. Too bad I had little appetite to eat any of it. Grandfather insisted on having a bowl, more out of politeness than true desire I'm sure.

"This is the best soup I've had in a long time," he said.

I think he was engaging in a little praise therapy to make me feel better. I mean, fried fish and minestrone? What a combination.

Neither Grandfather nor I said much while we ate. A pall hung over the room as we waited to see when Nick would resurrect and how he'd feel. Hard to enjoy a meal when Grace was on the front lines. With a sigh, I dropped my spoon into my half-filled bowl with a clank.

"I'm going to spell Grace," I said and left the table.

As soon as I entered the bedroom, Grace rose and started to head out. She was simply going to leave without a word to me. I blocked the doorway, and we locked eyes. As much bad blood as there was between us, we had to get past yesterday if only for Nick's sake.

"You almost killed me," I told her. "I'm not going to forget that. But I'm going to put it aside for now, since I threw the first punch. So, truce?"

"I don't need a truce," she shot back. "And yeah, you did throw the first punch. But don't worry, it wasn't gender-based, so your rep is safe."

She pushed past me without another word. I flinched slightly at the jibe. She was referring to the kerfuffle I started at school last year that almost got me expelled. My mind wandered back to that day.

Ava was more than an acquaintance but less than a full-time friend, when I came upon her and Franklin, her boyfriend, arguing in a parking lot outside Phillips Hall. The sun had set, streetlights were on, and we had returned from the Thanksgiving break only two days before. The sound of Ava's and Franklin's raised voices reverberated through the crisp, autumn air and attracted my attention, as each hurled expletive-filled phrases at one another. Slightly shocked, my first impulse was to turn around and walk away from this embarrassing lovers' squabble, but *it* happened too fast.

Unaware of me standing twenty yards away, Franklin stopped in the middle of a curse-filled rant and grabbed Ava by the throat with both hands. He shook her violently a couple times and then shoved her backward, and she tumbled onto her back on the asphalt. Ava promptly began sobbing. Franklin and I stood gaping at her, both of us utterly shocked at the explosion of violence. I ran to Ava's side. Franklin stared at the two of us for several seconds before simply walking away with his fingers twisted into his hair.

"Please don't," Ava begged me later.

"I have to," I replied, "This is about more than just you."

I wanted to report Franklin to the school. Having seen what he could do when angered, I was afraid of him and wanted him punished. So, over Ava's protests, I filed an official complaint against her boyfriend.

Amazingly, nothing happened. A bureaucratic blackhole of indifference sucked in my complaint. In fairness, this was largely due to Ava, who pleaded with people to let the matter go. I refused. In the end, Franklin got a semester of probation. That was, he received a slap on the wrist.

I was pissed. I made sure every breathing mammal on campus knew what went down. I circulated a petition. I organized rallies against male violence against women. I made people listen, and I gathered an army of angry students behind me. Then, after a week of protests, I and seventeen of my fellow students stormed the dean's office and engaged in an impromptu sit-in. A local news station came by to film the event and interview me. The story made it back to Dad, who was not pleased.

In the end, they almost expelled me and probably would have if not for Dad cutting a backroom deal. No one else was disciplined seriously. Both Ava and Franklin withdrew from school after the Christmas break and never returned.

Looking back, when all the effects of my crusade were netted out, I wasn't sure much of anything positive came out of it. What *did* come out of it was that I had a rep. What that rep was exactly depended on who you talked to. The thing about reps was that you didn't even know you had one until everyone knew you had one. It was like waking up in the morning and discovering a tattoo on your arm you didn't precisely remember getting. "Margaritaville."

As for Franklin, he would have found delicious irony in watching me go at it with Grace down on the dock. Our little fight was far worse than his and Ava's, at least physically.

Later, I was half asleep with a sore neck from sitting awkwardly on the chair when Grace came to relieve me. It was one o'clock in the morning, and Nick still hadn't woken up. No concerns, though. He needed sleep.

"Thanks," I said. "I'll set the alarm for three hours."

"Don't bother. I'll come and get you if he wakes. Until then, you might as well get some sleep too."

"Thanks."

She extended her hand toward me and said, "If you're still up for a truce . . ."

I shook her hand. "Truce."

Exhausted as I was, I spent the next couple hours rolling around on the lumpy, uncomfortable mattress in Grace's room, rethinking whether I should leave this place early as planned . . . that was, whenever Trevor deigned to show up again. Running away from Grace wasn't going to solve anything. I wasn't sure *anything* was going to solve anything, but escaping to Paris would certainly make the Grace issue worse. Also, while bears now owned the top spot on everyone's things-to-avoid list, who could say what might sent Nick over the edge again. And if that happened, I needed to be here for him.

Strange, but I sensed Grace was also battling her own monster. My sister would never have blamed me for her stupid suitcases to the point of starting a fight if she wasn't staring at something bad in the rearview mirror.

"Fallayrow, Grace," I murmured to myself. "Fallayrow."

Then sleep finally dragged me under.

CHAPTER ELEVEN

Monday morning arrived cool and crisp, and when I sat up in bed, I discovered mosquitoes had dive-bombed my exposed flesh during the night, leaving a trail of welts. Disgusting. After a few seconds of thought, I decided we were far too north for Zika, but who knew what other unknown killer viruses lurked up here near the arctic circle.

True to her word, Grace had taken the entire night shift and let me snooze. I found her asleep on the wooden floor with a pillow and a sheet while Nick still dozed, and I decided to let her rest for a while longer. Even though his door was shut, I heard Grandfather's snoring.

It was six o'clock in the morning, approximately forty-one hours since we first arrived at the cabin.

With my fingers wrapped around a warm mug of tea, I sat outside in one of the Adirondack chairs near the fire ring, watching the fog on the lake and the occasional splash of fish jumping. At least, I hoped they were fish.

When I finished the tea, I went inside to make breakfast for everyone. I was no cook, but Mom had taught me how to make French toast and a few other idiot-proof dishes. I mean, who couldn't fry bacon and put bread in the toaster? Beyond that, my repertoire was limited, but I was proud of my skills in dorm room cuisine at school. We weren't allowed to cook in our rooms, but, come on, who obeyed that rule? Yes, sir, I could make my friends a dang fine grilled cheese sandwich on an iron turned upside down . . . if I did say so myself.

As soon as I started setting out breakfast on the table, Nick and Grace emerged from the bedroom, each rubbing their eyes and stretching.

"Just in time," I told them. "I—"

"Can't talk," Grace interrupted around a yawn. "Code blue. Have to pee before all of my internal organs shut down."

Grandfather stumbled out of his room, no doubt awakened by the others. His eyes were bloodshot, and he looked hungover. His usually well-coiffed hair and mustache were disheveled.

"I made French toast," I announced, once Grace was back, "but come to find out we didn't bring any syrup."

"I saw a thing of Karo syrup in the far cabinet," Grandfather said, pointing over my shoulder. "That'll work."

"Excuse me?" I said.

"Corn syrup," he replied. "It's great. I like it better than maple."

Since I was having oatmeal, it wasn't my issue. Still, one side of my mouth slipped down in a half yuck-face expression. Corn syrup on pancakes? Jesus wept.

A few minutes into breakfast, Nick asked, "What happened yesterday? I don't remember much."

"An episode," Grace said dryly just before pushing a forkful of food into her mouth.

I nodded in agreement and repeated, "Episode."

The term "episode" was a euphemism, but I liked it better than seizure, even though it made his epilepsy sound like a TV show.

"Shit," he muttered.

"That about sums it up," I agreed.

"You think Trevor will show up today?" Nick asked.

What he was really asking was whether I might fly home with him.

"Maybe," I answered casually. "But I won't be leaving with him if he does."

Nick's features brightened instantly. "Really?"

"I can't let Grace have *all* the fun."

Grace rolled her eyes while shaking her head. "Please, help yourself to my serving of fun, and take my whoopee sauce too."

Nick didn't seem the slightest bit phased by yesterday's events. Whether he remembered the bear or not, I couldn't tell. I wasn't going to bring it up.

"So, what do we do today?" Nick asked.

The question hung in the air as he rose, carried his dishes to the sink, and dumped them. So, who did he think was going to wash them thar dishes? Me? Sorry, housewife was not part of my job description.

"Maybe we go fishing again," Grandfather suggested.

"Awesome," Nick agreed. His face lit up at the prospect.

Didn't he remember yesterday?

"I'll be ready in a few minutes," he added.

As soon as he darted from the room, Grandfather said, "We'll stay in the middle of the lake away from the shore. It might be best if one of you came along." He paused to inhale deeply before adding, "Just in case."

Yes. A good idea. I jumped on it lightning fast before Grace could do more than blink a few times. I jabbed my oatmeal-coated spoon at her.

"Grace should go," I said. "I went yesterday. It's her turn."

She exhaled dramatically. "Fine."

When Grandfather left to change, Grace and I remained seated. She finished eating, but made no move to leave, instead staring at the middle of the table. This could only mean she had something to say, and I was fairly sure I didn't want to hear it.

"What?" I finally asked.

"I need my suitcases, Allie."

I sighed deeply and massaged my forehead with my thumb and forefinger. No migraine yet, but one could be on the way.

"I'm not responsible for your damn suitcases," I replied. "I had nothing to do with any of it."

She nodded. "I know. It's just . . ."

"Just what?"

She exhaled a breath, letting her cheeks puff outward. "Never mind. Dickless better show up today. That's all."

Her chair scraped backward, and she rose to leave. At this point, it seemed a near certainty Trevor would show up today with our missing luggage. Standing us up yesterday was bad, but doing it again today would be insanely evil. He had to know we needed our stuff. Could he have forgotten us? I seriously doubted it. I mean, how do you forget four people who are paying your idiot business thousands and thousands of dollars?

If I may approach the bench, Your Honor, and introduce into evidence the way Trevor stared at Grace's chest when she cluelessly bent over on the dock. Ladies and gentlemen of the jury, I ask you, is this a man who would forget our existence?

After the others left on their fishing trip, I spent the morning pacing the cabin and then reading. Every few minutes, I would pause and listen for the thrum of an incoming plane that never came. To cope with the stress and anxiety, I decided to eat. I sat at the table with a jar of creamy peanut butter and a package of pita bread, and I used a spoon to slather the spread on thick and heavy. To add a little zing, I sprinkled fresh blueberries on top. The combination worked. I ate until I came right up to the edge of getting sick, and then I stopped. Stress eating sucked. Ugh.

The buzz of a motor sent me racing outside, but the noise came from the motorboat. Grandfather and crew returned from a three-hour fishing trip with tired but contented expressions, except for Grace, who appeared wrung out. She lifted her eyebrows at me as she approached, silently asking me if I had any news of the plane . . . as if it might have landed and left again without her hearing or seeing it.

I shook my head.

Her mouth moved as if making the sound for an F-bomb, but she didn't utter the actual word.

Out of earshot of Nick and Grandfather, she confessed, "This whole trip sucks. Why would anyone totally cut themselves off from the outside world and think it was fun?"

"Well, we have a sat phone," I said, before adding sarcastically, "Oh, wait, our phone is buried in the mud under twenty feet of water. I forgot. My bad."

"Don't blame me for that!" she said way too loudly. "You shouldn't have hit me."

"You started the whole thing!" I blasted back.

Why were we fighting? I had no new killer arguments or zinger comebacks to hurl at her. She had nothing new either. So, why waste our time treading over the same ground?

"Go to hell, Allie."

"News flash, Grace. We're already there."

Grandfather led Nick toward the cabin, promising him bologna sandwiches, tomato soup, and Oreos. At the mention of bologna, I stuck two fingers in my mouth in an "I'm going to gag and throw up" gesture. Nick laughed.

While the rest of gang was eating, I wanted to find a way to kill three hours doing something other than waiting around the cabin for Trevor to show up.

Nature walk!

I would amble along the well-maintained trails, commune with the squirrels and other harmless animals, and try to ignore the swarm of flies and bugs that buzzed around me whenever I was outside.

My biggest, nearly pathological worry about hiking? Ticks. As if sucking my blood wasn't revolting enough, these little monsters were disgusting disease vectors . . . Lyme disease, Rocky Mountain spotted fever, rabbit fever, and so on and so forth. For me, the strongest question mark about the existence of a benevolent God was ticks. If God really loved us, then what the heck was going on with sprinkling ticks all over the world?

The first speed bump on my nature walk? There were no trails.

"So, what happened to the yellow brick road?" I asked out loud to a mostly silent, brooding forest that crowded in around me.

I did find a narrow, trampled line that might have been an animal trail. Whatever it was, it dead-ended after a quarter mile, forcing me to go off trail. By dead end, I meant fallen trees and brush piles blocked it, requiring me time and again to scramble over scratchy limbs and bark. After an hour of hand-to-hand combat with dead tree limbs, I quit and collapsed on a log near the lake's edge to sit. Exhausted and thirsty, I decided I would turn back after a short rest. I unslung the small rucksack I carried on my back, packed with a Nalgene water bottle, two bags of nuts, and my bricked iPhone that still took pictures.

"I'm so thirsty," I said, as I unscrewed the lid from my quart bottle and started to guzzle. The water leaked out of my mouth and trailed down my throat, drenching the front of the bright yellow tank top I wore. Since it was already soaked with sweat, I didn't mind and welcomed the cool liquid.

"All right, time to head back," I explained to the lake in front of me, as water lapped gently at my feet. "But first things first."

The generous swigs of water I took had certainly rehydrated me, but now I had to go. Even though there couldn't possibly be another human within miles of me, still I sought out a sheltering screen of bushes to squat behind. I wandered at least a hundred yards into the forest before finding an acceptable spot, but no sooner had I finished when a nauseating stench slammed into my nostrils, almost driving me to my knees.

"What is that smell?"

The forest didn't respond. Forcing myself to breathe through my mouth, I staggered back toward the lake . . . or so I thought. My sense of direction was off. After stumbling around for hundreds of yards, I didn't find the lake.

I found something else.

My feet skidded to a halt at the edge of a small clearing, in the center of which was a mound of brown fur, blood, meat and guts, and a black cloud of buzzing flies. What appeared to be a hoofed leg stuck out at a forty-five-degree angle from the slaughter pile. I wretched uncontrollably several times, triggered both by the sight of the eviscerated animal and by the odor. Yes, I found the source of the stink, and, of course, instead of walking away from it, I had floundered straight into it.

"Oh my God."

The ground around the carcass was torn up with bushes ripped out of the ground and small trees snapped in two. Also, I saw lots of tracks. Huge, clawed feet had left perfect impressions in the soft dirt. Although I don't have any Daniel Boone DNA in me, I had little trouble guessing a ginormous bear made the prints.

Studying the head of the slaughtered animal, I also guessed the bear had taken down a full-grown freaking moose.

So, was this Nick's bear from yesterday?

Probably. What else could have butchered a thousand pound moose like this?

I backed away from the massacre site, but the carnage so flustered me that I careened through the trees with no idea of what direction I was going, let alone the direction in which the stupid lake lay. Finally, a tiny shred of rationality returned, and I paused beside a tree, my chest heaving from exertion that could only come from scared, mindless lurching around in a wilderness area.

"I'm lost," I confessed. "Must get back to the cabin. If I'm still here when darkness comes, then kill me now."

Once my heartbeat slowed, I remembered one of the few shreds of backcountry lore I knew: If you got lost, pick a spot and stay put. I didn't remember if there was an exception to the stay-put rule if a flesh-eating zombie bear was in the woods around you. Plus, it seemed that the premise of hanging out in one spot was trusting in competent rescuers to find you. My grandfather and Grace?

"Remain calm," I coached myself. "Don't panic."

Slowly, step by step, I backtracked. After an hour, I found myself back at the carcass. I resisted the urge to run. The bear would come back to finish its meal. You didn't leave a half-eaten Big Mac and fries sitting out on the kitchen table; you were coming back for them. And when Papa Bear did return, I sure didn't want to be here.

So, I continued retracing my steps, a little surprised at how chaotic and zigzagging my trail was. The process dragged on for what seemed like hours, and I smacked myself around mentally for how stupid I was to get lost. To be honest, I didn't remember ever being truly and thoroughly lost like this before. Sure, who hadn't misplaced their mother at the mall when they were five, but this transcended "little kid" lost. Unless I got myself oriented and back in familiar territory soon, I would be spending the night out here.

Spending the night meant freezing or . . . worse.

Freezing or worse both meant dying.

I dodged the bullet.

Eventually, after losing and finding my trail time and again, I spotted the lake through the thick brush and let out a deep exhale of relief. All I had to do was follow the water's edge back to the cabin.

I walked for over an hour as the sun plummeted below the horizon, the air chilled, and the light beneath the tree canopy dimmed. This was taking too long, and suddenly the idea hit me that maybe I was walking around the lake in the wrong direction. Instead of getting closer to the cabin, maybe I was actually getting farther away. The thought horrified me, but I had committed myself to going this way.

Stick with it.

Then I froze.

Off to my left, I heard a crashing sound a hundred yards out of sight in the now inky blackness of the forest.

What was *that?*

The woods went silent. The cheeping of insects died out. I stopped breathing.

Something was out there in the dark, something big.

Cursing under my breath, I stumbled forward, clawing my way through brush and limbs, giving up any effort to be quiet. I couldn't hear anything over my own panicked blundering through the underbrush, but I had to assume that whatever was out there was after me.

Just as I was about to seriously consider splashing out into the ice cold lake and swimming parallel to the shore, the lights of the cabin came into view. The sight was like a shot of adrenalin directly into my pulmonary artery, and I charged forward with redoubled speed.

Once I broke out of the brush into the clearing around the cabin and lurched toward the porch, I heard loud, mournful cries erupt like a chorus from across the lake. I laughed with relief. Those were wolves. Had to be. Lots of them, but just normal, ordinary mean and nasty wolves. Not the giant monster from yesterday.

Still, I didn't stop to listen further. I rushed up the cabin steps, flung open the door, and dashed inside.

CHAPTER TWELVE

According to Brooke, and as Trevor himself agreed, our contract with the Lasley Wilderness Lodge stipulated a plane would come to check in on us. We paid for that damn flight. Yet, like the days before, Wednesday came and went with no sign of a plane. This callous disregard of us hit me like a punch to the gut. I felt like I got mugged.

Now it was Thursday morning. My emotions the last two days had swung wildly up and down, pinballing from extreme anger and curse-filled tirades to uneasy dread mixed with fear. What was going on? Why were these people doing this to us?

If only we still had the sat phone, we could solve this problem in thirty seconds. I would call Dad, he would have the US government mobilize the 101st Airborne Division, and in twenty-four hours the army would invade Canada and rescue us. Piece of cake.

Of course, we didn't have a sat phone any longer. We didn't have a shortwave radio either. We didn't even have a flare gun.

Wrung out from stress, I prepared myself to embrace another day of boredom. We were all tense, so no one wanted to sit around the campfire and sing ninety-nine bottles of beer on the wall . . . or whatever the heck people sang around campfires. No one wanted to go fishing. No one wanted s'mores. And no one wanted to put together the one-thousand-piece jigsaw puzzle of tropical fish swimming around pink coral.

My dad spent thousands of dollars on this vacation and look at us! We were having about as much fun as the British POWs building the bridge over the river Kwai. I knew this movie since it was one of Dad's favorites. He said he learned more from watching that film than from all the classes he took at UCLA.

The one sunny side up egg in all this was that no sign of the bearasaurus had manifested since my frenzied dash through the forest. I assume he had bigger fish to fry—or moose to maul—than a few scrawny humans.

Dieu Merci.

With these thoughts swirling around in my head, I went outside, intending to sit on the porch with my mug of tea and dream about Paris. It was early in the morning. No one else was awake . . . or so I thought. No sooner had I sat down when I spotted a lone figure sitting cross-legged on the ground near the lake.

Grace.

Oddly, she had her back to the water and sat facing the trees. After a couple sips, during which time Grace never moved a muscle, I decided to check on whether she OD'd on some new opiate that caused you to become comatose in a sitting position.

I approached her tentatively, not wanting to invade her space in case she was meditating or whatever. She blinked as I came closer, tears on both cheeks. So, not comatose and not meditating.

"You okay?" I asked hesitantly.

"Do I *look* okay?" she answered. "I'm wearing your underwear and baggy shorts, an undershirt from my grandfather, and a bathrobe. This is so degrading."

"We'll get even with the bastards."

"I don't want to get even," she replied. "I want my suitcases."

"You can borrow anything of mine you want," I offered, getting a bit alarmed at Grace's imminent meltdown.

"I don't want your stuff," she said with an impatient groan. "I just want to know. Is that so much to ask?"

"Know what?" I asked, not sure if I really wanted an explanation.

"Remember the hike in the Hudson Highlands?" She asked.

How could I forget? That day was in the running for the worst day of my family's life in which somebody didn't die.

"Last week, I would have said that sitting on those rocks was the scariest day of my life."

Then she squeezed her eyes shut and another rivulet of tears streamed out of both eyes.

What was going on with my sister? Did I want to know? If Grace was this upset, it was bad. Best to keep my distance, lest she drag me down with her. She was like a soldier who said, "Here, hold on to my hand grenade while I run off and find the pin for it."

The Hudson Highlands. I haven't been back in years. Not since that day. I remembered it rained on the early morning drive there, and my earliest memory of the actual hike was twenty minutes past the trailhead on our way to Breakneck Ridge. I didn't know it at the time, but such a prophetic name.

"Grace, keep up," I yelled over my shoulder at my laggard sister.

Dad said the trail had some very rugged and difficult spots, but we hadn't reached them yet. If Grace couldn't keep up on the easy part of the trail, what about the hard part? I was thirteen at the time, Grace twelve, and Nick eight. I worried least about Nick, who loved the woods and had the climbing agility of a spider monkey. I worried most about myself. I hated hiking, camping, and Mother Nature in general. Still do. Mom persuaded me to come by promising to go shopping with me the next day at Sericris—best clothes shop ever . . . at least in Scarsdale at the time.

A half hour later, after the trail became jagged and steep as Dad warned, I glanced over my shoulder to see how far behind Grace was. I expected maybe twenty yards or so. That was how far Mom and I were behind Dad and Nick. Seeing no sign of her, though, I paused and tugged on the back of Mom's shirt. She was preoccupied with the panoramic vista of the Hudson River that had opened up in front of us, so I had to tug a second time more insistently.

"What?" Mom responded.

"Grace."

"All right," Mom agreed. "We'll wait here for her to catch up."

She never caught up. Instead, a shrill scream pierced the air. The previously loud birds went instantly silent.

I knew that shriek. My sister.

In seconds, I scrambled back down the trail, my heart pounding in my chest. The thump of boots behind me signaled Mom was following.

"Grace!" I yelled, grabbing tree limbs to steady myself as I rushed toward the place where I heard her scream.

"Grace!" Mom echoed.

Mom and I covered thirty yards when we heard Grace yell, "Help!"

I made for the sound of her voice. Then my breath caught and my chest tightened when I realized the sound came from over the edge of a cliff.

"Hold on!" Mom yelled.

"Mom!" Grace hollered back.

I peered over the lip of the escarpment, moving cautiously on the rain-slicked rocks, and found myself staring down into empty space that stretched for what seemed like a mile before terminating below on a floor of trees and boulders. A wave of vertigo slammed into me. Then horror walloped me in the face, and my vision blurred. No one could survive that kind of a fall, except Captain Marvel and a few other superheroes. Grace was no superhero.

My eyes searched the ground below for some sign of her, for a mangled corpse I didn't want to see.

Nothing.

But wait. She cried out for help. She must not have fallen all the way to the bottom.

Duh.

A meek, frightened voice said, "Mom?"

The sound came from directly below me. And sure enough, I saw the top of a blonde head fifty yards below the edge.

Grace?

Yes. There she was.

My sister stood on a rock protrusion no bigger than a dinner plate and clung to the side of the cliff with obvious desperation.

As Mom later quipped, "Like Groucho Marx said, if she hugged it any closer, she would have been in back of it."

The drama played out for hours. Other hikers gathered around to watch the spectacle. Calls to 911 were made. Park rangers came. EMTs came. In short order, a throng gathered around the place where Grace went over the edge. Rescue ideas were floated, the most common of which was to lower a rope to Grace, but trusting her to let loose of her handholds and cling to a rope while people reeled it in was a dubious proposition.

Then the rain came back and dumped buckets on us. So, Grace went from scared and exhausted to scared, exhausted, and freezing her ass off.

Finally, a helicopter was brought in with a rescue basket. A brave guy dressed in an orange jumpsuit managed to coax Grace off her ledge and into his arms. Once he wrestled her into the basket, they hauled her in, and off they went.

Hours later, we picked up Grace from a nearby hospital. The story was all over the news for days. Famous movie director's daughter stupidly wanders off the trail and almost dies. Major embarrassment. A month later, Dad got a bill from county search and rescue for twenty-six thousand five hundred dollars. He paid it.

My eyes closed, and the memory of the hike years ago petered out. The memory of that day pained me but far less than it did Grace.

"What's going on, Grace?" I asked softly.

"Do you know why I left the trail that day?"

I shook my head.

"I saw something shiny. It was your emerald bracelet."

My eyebrows furrowed at this, and my mouth scrunched into a silent "O." I remembered losing the bracelet I had gotten for my thirteenth birthday—Dad regularly showered me with jewelry—but I didn't know where for sure. Grace never mentioned finding it that day nor did she return it to me afterward.

"I climbed down a couple feet to get it," she went on. "Then I slipped and slid down the cliff face until I landed on the ledge, where I spent the next four hours standing all alone."

"Uh," I began uncertainly, "I don't remember anything about you finding my bracelet."

"That's because I never said anything." She sighed and added, "I lost the bracelet during the rescue, so what was the point of it all in the end."

"I thought—"

"You *thought*," she interrupted, "that I was being an idiot. Everyone did."

"Sorry."

She shook her head. "The point is, I never wanted to be stuck like that again—helpless, powerless, trapped."

"Is that what this is about?"

"I'm more scared now than I was then."

"Grace—"

She interrupted me again. "I have a pregnancy test in my suitcase, Allie. I need that damn suitcase. I need to know. Okay?"

CHAPTER THIRTEEN

"What's going on?" Nick asked, his brows furrowed in suspicion.

Grace and I sat outside in chairs by the fire ring talking. It was dusk. We talked all afternoon. A couple times Grace broke down and cried. The last time—gasp!—I put my arms around her and said "shhh" for ten minutes.

In *The Wizard of Oz* terms, "Oh, what a world, what a world."

"I'm consulting with Grace," I told Nick. "Can you give us some privacy?"

"Yeah," Grace agreed. "Isn't there like a squirrel around here you can catch and torture?"

"Real funny, jerko," Nick shot back. "I wouldn't do that."

"It was a joke," I intervened. "A really dumb joke. Why don't you work on the puzzle with Grandfather?"

Nick sighed and shook his head. "He's passed out in his room. He drank like fifty-seven glasses of whiskey this afternoon."

"Any left?" Grace asked, not entirely sarcastically.

"That's what I call falling off the wagon," I added. "He's been sober all these years and now . . . kaboom!"

"He's dying," Nick said in a matter-of-fact voice.

"What?" Grace and I cried out at the same time.

Nick shrugged and explained, "It's what I see when I look at him."

After several seconds of silence, Grace said, "Okay, roger that, paranormal dude."

Nick, the coat of many colors: boy, brother, epileptic, delusional fantasist, and now death seer.

Grace and I fell silent, waiting for Nick to leave, but he didn't. Instead, he remained next to me as if waiting for us to tell him something important. His eyes flitted from me to Grace and back again.

"What?" I finally said.

"It's our last night here," he said, sounding like a whiny five-year-old. "We have to have at least one campfire before we leave. Come on!"

Grace leaned her head back and gazed up at the sky in a silent plea to our heavenly father to work some little brother mojo on Nick to make him leave us alone. The oddness of this caught my attention. Since Mom died, the three of us lived in silos, having only the barest minimum of interaction. And here we were interacting *too* much.

"Fine," Grace agreed. "But Allie and I get to sit here and do absolutely nothing. You're in charge of the fire. You and Grandfather . . . if he should regain consciousness, that is."

This satisfied Nick, who bolted inside to get supplies. We had plenty of firewood stacked along one side of the cabin, but who could say how many monster-sized black widow spiders lurked in the dark crevasses of that wood pile. Wait, were there black widows this far north? Who knew. If not, surely some other human-hating creation of a compassionate god skulked within.

"So far, you're only late," I said to Grace, once Nick was out of earshot. "You haven't officially *missed* your period yet."

"What's the difference?"

"The difference is late equals hope. Missed equals you're dead and I should start planning the baby shower."

"I'll get an abortion when we get back."

I blinked. "Just like that? You make it sound like a change of clothes. There's always adoption."

Grace started to zip out a comeback, but Nick interrupted us, dragging a bleary-eyed Grandfather by the hand. Grandfather stumbled a bit at the fast pace Nick set but recovered enough to keep up.

"We have to start the fire," Nick said to Grandfather. "Come on."

"We'll talk later," I told Grace.

"But what am I going to do?" she replied. "I want to know right here and now. I can't wait any longer; it's killing me. Am I or am I not? Isn't there some home-based test I can take?"

"You mean like shampoo or vinegar?" I recited the urban myth tests I had heard of.

"Exactly. Or Pine-Sol or bleach."

Hadn't heard of those. "Grace, none of that stuff works. It's all snake oil and voodoo."

"What if I took all of the tests at once? I mean, if I tested positive on all, or negative on all, that's probably reliable. No?"

I closed my eyes and muttered, "Oh my God," under my breath. "I can't believe we're having this discussion in the twenty-first century. Grace, peeing in shampoo is like tossing a girl into a pond to see if she's a witch. *Maybe* legit in the seventeenth century, but we've moved on since then."

"I just want to know," she said, repeating her new mantra.

"We're going home tomorrow. We'll take a real, scientific test then. Okay?"

"You said 'we.'"

I shrugged. "Yeah. So?"

"So when did you and I become a we?"

I let out an exasperated sigh. "Just go with it . . . and try not to get rolled by the waves."

She was right, though. When did we become a we? This was Thursday. On Monday, three days ago, we slapped and punched each other and I almost drowned. Where was my anger? Where was the hate I used to give? I didn't know. Maybe all the bad feelings and resentments were hiding in the shadows of my brain, waiting to leap out of the darkness when I got mad again.

Maybe.

Or maybe they were simply gone.

I really didn't know. Why? Well, strangely, I think I knew the composition of a pine cone better than I knew my own self.

What I did know, what I had to admit to myself, was that I cared about Grace. I didn't want her to suffer. She was my sister, a sister who once looked up to and idolized me. And I once had been so protective of her. Suddenly I felt that way again.

"What do you say we upgrade our truce to an alliance?" Grace said. "You know, like NATO."

"NATO sounds cool," I replied with a couple nods. "So, who are we allied against?"

"The dark side of the force," she answered with a chuckle.

"I feel like we're mixing metaphors here, my young padawan."

"Guys," Nick interrupted, "get your marshmallow sticks."

Grace and I slumped back in our chairs, ready to experience our last night in Paradise City. Both of us wore tired expressions; we had exchanged more words in the last few hours than in the four years before. Like marathon runners at the end of the race, we were exhausted . . .verbally at least.

By now, Nick and Grandfather had a robust fire going, and all four of us sat in a rough semicircle around the burning ring of fire that was banked on all sides by smooth stones. We glanced at each other in silence, long poky sticks in hand, waiting to see who would break first and start roasting marshmallows. Grandfather swayed a little like he was having trouble staying awake, so it wasn't going to be him.

"When are we getting picked up tomorrow?" Nick asked.

"After lunch," I answered. "Any last-minute things you want to do, Nick?"

"Swimming," he said with a smile. "Although my swimming suit is in my lost suitcase."

"Ditto," Grace said. "So, why don't we move onto playing with matches and starting a forest fire?"

"Who needs swimming suits. How about skinny-dipping?"

I almost had to pick my jaw up off the ground. Temporarily

speechless, I blinked rapidly, as if I was sending out a message in eyelid Morse code. Nick and Grace also sat with their mouths hanging open.

"Don't look so surprised," Grandfather said. "Skinny-dipping was pretty common on the ranch where I grew up. We didn't have swimming pools. You wanted to swim, you swam in ponds. And when the mercury hit one hundred, as it often did in Nebraska summers, you didn't always worry about bathing suits."

"Did you . . . with . . . with Grandmother?" Nick burbled.

Grandfather shook his head with a hint of a smile. "No, I didn't meet her until college. Sadly, my skinny-dipping days were over by then."

"Then who?" Nick continued.

"Anybody really," Grandfather answered. "There was always a gang of us. My brother and sister. Cousins. Friends. It was usually like a big party."

I glanced over at Nick. He looked scared at the prospect, while Grace was gorping like a fish. Grandfather, on the other hand, was nonplussed. I stared at him, noticing for the first time how gaunt he looked with his rail-thin frame, baggy jeans, and loose-fitting golfing shirt. The white streaks in his hair reflected the flames, giving his head a washed-out orange appearance. I tried to visualize him as a fourteen-year-old boy splashing naked in a farm pond in Nebraska surrounded by a bunch of guys and girls. Couldn't do it. My imagination went sideways on me.

My brain pulled up an image of myself when I was fourteen, staring at my chest in the mirror as I took a selfie of my boobs. My cheeks heated at the memory of me taking that damn picture and then, after a deep breath, tapping the texting send button. In the time it took to lick my lips, my nude breasts pic dinged its arrival on Janna's phone. I remember shaking my head as if I was emerging from a trance and asking myself, "Why did you do that, you idiot?" My immediate answer at the time was because Janna had sent me a selfie of her breasts only minutes before. But that was a pretty lame explanation, and I knew it at the time.

Janna almost instantaneously flipped my pic to her circle of friends, and from there, it more or less circled the globe . . . or the entire school, anyway. I wasn't surprised or mad. I knew she would do it. I knew it, and I sent her my boobs anyway. Why? Did I simply succumb to a moment of wild exhibitionism? Sort of. Was I acting out some weird sex fantasy? Uh . . . no. Attention? Maybe. Or was I being a bad girl from the safety of my own room? Meh. Then what? Validation? Yeah, that was mostly it, I thought. I wanted to show the world, show myself really, that I had arrived. I wasn't that little girl with braces and a flat chest anymore. I had a real body now, so choke on it, world.

I never texted a nude selfie of myself again. The next week at school—in the classrooms, in the hallways—whenever a guy looked at me, I felt like he had x-ray eyes and was staring not at me but gazing through my clothes at my chest. I had enough guy self-confidence issues without body adequacy worries on top of them.

"If nobody is going swimming," Grandfather said, "then we should spend tomorrow eating as much as possible. There's a ton of food left. It's use it or lose it."

"I want s'mores," Nick said.

"I want my clothes," Grace muttered.

"I want civilization," I added.

Grandfather suddenly leaned forward in his chair and began coughing violently while pounding his chest with a fist. Then he cleared his throat a couple times, apparently in an attempt to hack out a lung.

"Swallowed a bug," he said.

It didn't look like he swallowed a bug. Yes, a cloud of tiny flies and mosquitoes constantly enveloped you everywhere you went outside, but his face was pale, and his hands trembled.

"You okay?" I whispered to him.

"Yes and no." He took a deep breath and, as if to catch himself, said, "Actually, I'm fine."

"Maybe take a break from the headache juice," I suggested. I bit my lower lip as soon as the words left my mouth. His drinking was none of my business. Nobody had appointed me a member of the alcohol police.

He chuckled. "That's not the problem."

Of course, I wanted to ask what the problem was, but he didn't seem inclined to talk about it. So, I let it go.

"I'll get the food," Grandfather said, rising from his seat. "Then we can play a game, how about?"

"Goods and bads!" Nick shouted.

"Please crucify me upside down," Grace said with a groan.

I hadn't played goods and bads since my one year in the girl scouts, back when my favorite TV show was *Hannah Montana* and before Mom put all my Barbie dolls in storage. While I was ready to suck it up and play for Nick's sake, it wasn't meant to be tonight.

As soon as Grandfather rose to go inside, a chaotic mishmash of yips, barks, and howls erupted across the lake. Wolves again. A lot of wolves. Their mournful baying sent shivers down my spine, but their cries were also strangely entrancing. The pack sang its haunting, wild chorus for several minutes before dying out for a few moments. Then it started up again.

Nick began to shiver. Was he about to have another episode?

"Come on," I said to Grace. "Let's get him inside."

Tomorrow was D-for-departure day, and it couldn't arrive soon enough.

CHAPTER FOURTEEN

Friday, our go home day, arrived with gray skies.

It rained all day.

Water fell in torrents from the moment I woke at 5:45 a.m. until now . . . 11:05 p.m. The downpour showed no sign of easing up, having soaked the ground around the cabin until it became a field of mud and grass. We spent the entire day inside the cramped confines of our shack, waiting and waiting and waiting.

Everyone was asleep now but me. I couldn't make my mind close down and let go of the questions that kept running in a loop in my head. Why? When? My eyes locked on the sliver of moon barely visible through the overcast sky.

Our vacation, our rental period, officially ended this afternoon, but no plane came to pick us up. My packed suitcases still sat on the porch waiting for someone to carry them down to the dock.

When we sat down to eat dinner earlier—me, a salad with tofu; them, hamburgers—Nick asked, "Do you think they forgot about us?"

"It's the rain," Grace said. "They're probably not allowed to fly in a monsoon."

"Planes fly in the rain," I disagreed.

"Yeah, but not when it's this heavy," Grace countered. "It's a rain shear thing."

"*Wind* shear," I corrected. "And there is no wind."

"No," she insisted. "When the rain falls this hard, it pushes down on the plane's wings and drives it into the ground. That's gotta be what's going on."

Too tired to argue, I said, "Whatever."

After dinner, Grandfather taught us to play pinochle, but enthusiasm was lacking, so we only played a few hands. All of us felt abandoned and disrespected by the Lasley Wilderness Lodge, the province of Ontario, the nation of Canada, and the entire universe. Was this all because I was a tiny bit of a bitch to Trevor? No one could be that petty, could they?

Nick went to bed a couple hours ago, perfectly content apparently to live out his life in this place. He didn't remember much about his meltdown.

Grace and Grandfather, on the other hand, went to bed convinced the plane would show tomorrow, that bad weather today kept the plane grounded . . . or watered . . . or whatever you called a float plane unable to fly.

Why did we keep saying tomorrow? The plane was supposed to show up Sunday, then Monday, then Wednesday, and finally today. Each time we speculated and made excuses for the bastards, reassuring ourselves the stupid plane would come *tomorrow*. It didn't before, why would it now?

A cold spike of dread shivered down my spine. What if we were lost here forever? What if the plane never came back? What then, Allie?

The answer to those questions was obvious.

We died.

Yes, we had shelter and plenty of water, a lake full of it if push came to shove, but what about food? Maybe we had a week of groceries remaining, give or take. Then what? Would we all sit around until we became emaciated, walking skeletons and eventually fell over dead? Or, would we go all Donner Party? A vision of Nick gnawing on somebody's arm intruded in my brain, and I clamped my eyes shut, forcing my mind to think about . . . doughnuts. Glazed doughnuts with pink frosting and multicolored sprinkles. This worked. The parade of horribles about to take over my mind vanished, leaving me to stare out at the night and suck in several heavy breaths.

Can't panic. Have to stay rational.

Fact: Brooke and my father would be at LaGuardia to pick us up in thirteen hours. They might send Frederick, but the basic fact remained we were expected, awaited, wanted. And when we didn't show, it would cause nothing less than a tear in the fabric of the space-time continuum itself.

Fact: When we turned up missing, all hell would break loose. Dad would go into full-out, ninja kick-ass mode. The press would be all over the story. Famous film magnate's family was missing in the Canadian wilderness. Alien abduction had not been ruled out.

Fact: The search effort for us would be epic. It would be on the scale of the Empire invading the tiny planet of Tatooine in search of Luke Skywalker.

So, if all of this was true, why was I engaged in hand-to-hand combat with fear and terror?

Because I was not a rational creature. Not completely, anyway. I jumped to conclusions that weren't warranted. I let my imagination run wild sometimes. I ran when I should walk, and I walked when I should run. I let emotions get the best of me. Hadn't I learned this lesson last winter? Yes, I had learned a lesson, but exactly what lesson was that?

My mind wandered back to January and my Thursday afternoon encounter with Riona, who was a year behind me. Riona came from Alabama and had the accent to prove it. She was incapable of discretion; secrets, private confidences, they all cascaded out of her like the water of a fast-moving, bubbling brook. Behind her back, we referred to her as the mouth from the south.

"Allie," Riona gushed that day as she plopped down in a chair next to me. "Saw your boyfriend last night."

I glanced up from my iPad I was preparing to use to take notes and raised an eyebrow at her. Riona and I, along with four others, sat around a circular table waiting for our advanced Latin class in Ovid to start. Mr. Tableri, our teacher, was occupied with rummaging through his leather briefcase for his battered copy of the *Metamorphoses*. My copy was electronic.

"Dinner at Brouillard's last night with my parents," Riona went on. "Jack was there with his parents too."

"I know. They came up from DC for a visit. He told me about it."

"He had a date," Riona said in a hushed voice that was nevertheless loud enough for everyone to hear. "Not local. A blonde model."

That, I didn't know. Jack only told me that he was meeting his parents for dinner.

"It's going to be awful," he confided to me beforehand. "My dad will tell me how much of a failure I am, and my mother will tell him to stop browbeating me. But once they inhale a couple martinis, they'll loosen up, forget about me, and talk too loud to each other about embarrassing stuff they did this week."

I started to respond, but he silenced me with a full-on kiss that dragged on for several moments. We broke it off, and each of us glanced around the room, slightly red-cheeked and flustered, since we were standing in the Academy Center with crowds of students flowing around us.

"I'd take you along," he continued, "but I couldn't subject you to my parents in good conscience."

"That's okay," I replied. "I've got an essay to finish tonight anyway. Call me after."

"Later then," he said and kissed me quickly on my forehead.

Jack didn't call after his dinner, and in fact, I hadn't seen or talked to him at all prior to my encounter with vomit mouth Riona in Latin two days later. When class was over, I headed for my dorm room, distracted and queasy about Jack. Did he lie to me? If so, why? I skipped my next class, something I very rarely did, lay on my bed, stared up at the ceiling, and moped. In retrospect, I was a pathetic, jealous monstrosity.

Jack found me the next morning in the dining hall, as I used my spoon to rearrange chunks of cantaloupe and honeydew melon in my bowl. My drowsy mind tried to remember if I had an assignment due in my nine o'clock class—Global Topics in Women,

Gender, and Society. If so, I wouldn't be turning it in that morning. Surely, it was due next week, I remembered thinking.

"Hey you," Jack said as he approached my table. He wore a cheery smile.

"Hey back."

"I thought we were going to study together last night?"

"We were?" I asked cluelessly. "I must have missed your text . . . or call . . . or whatever."

He sighed heavily and sat down across from me. After drumming his fingers on the table for several seconds of awkward silence while I made a show of spearing a melon square and jabbing it in my mouth, he said, "I've been busy with my parents. They finally left this morning."

And busy with Miss Blondie, I thought.

"I also had to babysit my stepsister."

"Stepsister?"

He nodded. I exhaled wearily, grabbed my tray, and rose to leave. Apparently, Jack forgot he had already told me all about his stepsister. Arden. As in Dale Arden of *Flash Gordon*. Who would name their kid Arden? Anyway, I knew for a fact that Arden was twelve. More to the point, she was *not* the *Vogue* cover girl Riona described.

"Wait," Jack said.

"Listen," I began, whirling about to face him, but he cut me off.

"It wasn't Arden," he said in a rush. "I was just trying to avoid a *War and Peace* length explanation."

"Just . . . don't lie."

"Her name is Cailee." He gazed down at his shoes, as if he was confessing to a crime. "My parents volunteered me to take her to Hanover. She's up from DC to visit Dartmouth. I've known her since we were in kindergarten, and our parents have been trying to hook us up since forever. We play along, but there's nothing between us. She has a boyfriend."

"There," I said. "That wasn't so hard."

He made it up to me that week, taking me out to dinner and even buying me an expensive bouquet of red roses and orchids in a white china vase. Nothing happened between him and this Cailee, he swore, and I believed him. Actually, I was more annoyed at myself than him. I acted like some raging jealous girlfriend. I was determined never to be that girl. No boy was worth corrupting my soul . . . not Jack, not anyone.

Yet, Riona had said Jack and Cailee were holding hands at the dinner table. The mouth from the south was many things, but liar wasn't on the list. So, who was Jack stringing along, her or me? I pondered that question after I told Jack goodbye that morning and headed to class.

It rained all that day.

PART II

"Lose yourself wholly; and the more you lose,
the more you will find"

—Catherine of Siena

CHAPTER FIFTEEN

"What else?" I asked Nick, who stood on his toes rummaging through the top shelves of our primitive pantry.

"A second jar of peanut butter, Ritz crackers, and two cans of baked beans," he summarized.

I sighed and slumped back in my chair. "Okay, that's our food inventory."

"How long will it last?" he asked.

"However long it needs to," I answered.

The better question was how long did it need to last? And the answer to that was who the heck knew. An entire week had passed since the day when the Lasley Wilderness Lodge was supposed to pick us up and take us back to civilization. Two hours ago, we officially hit our two-week anniversary here.

Our hopes a plane would come and get us lay in ruins on the cabin floor. After a week of waiting, praying, wishing for a savior to glide down from the sky, all of us were despondent and drowning in misery. One fact seemed crystal clear—something very bad happened out in the real world, something so bad that the outside world had deserted us.

Where was everyone?

Why had no one come to get us?

I had no answers, not even a good guess.

In thinking about our abandonment, I remembered a film I saw years ago about a pair of divers who were left behind in the middle of the ocean when their dive boat accidently forgot about them. Was that what was going on here? Except, how could people forget us? It made no sense. *Nothing* did. But here we were, abandoned and left behind. I was about to take a swan dive into the deep end of the pity pool when Grace stomped in from outside, slamming the door behind her.

She was sweating so hard through the oversized white under-shirt that I said, "Uh, skinny-dipping means swimming without clothes."

"Ha, ha," she replied. "I just spent three fricking hours spelling out 'SOS' with large stones. Nick and I also gathered wood earlier for a signal fire in case we hear a plane approaching."

"Excellent."

"You?"

I shrugged, slightly annoyed at her "why did you lay around on your butt all day" tone. "I think I figured out a way to use foil, toothpicks, and forks to hack into a communications satellite and route a call for help through the international space station."

"Really?"

"Grace," I chided, "don't be so freaking gullible."

"You're a real tool."

Nick, who now sat next to me, started to laugh. Grace pointed a finger at him and added, "And your little dog too!"

Once Grace returned from cleaning up, she took a chair across the table from me, holding a cool tumbler of water between the insides of her wrists. She seemed in a good mood for a person staring starvation in the face.

"So, what do we got?" she asked, pointing at my list.

"Not a lot," I replied. "We're down to the dregs of the stuff we brought. We still have an unopened jar of peanut butter and one of grape jelly. Sounds great, but we have no bread."

"And?"

"We have flour tortillas for the Tex-Mex we never made but no meat, unless you count fish. We also have a couple dozen canned foods, including tuna fish. We're out of milk, soda, and coffee."

"No coffee?"

I shook my head. "However, we do have a thing of Pillsbury biscuits in the refrigerator and two thingumabobs of Jiffy Pop popcorn."

"What else?" Grace asked.

"Half a bag of family-sized Doritos. Some dry goods: flour, instant mash potatoes, oatmeal, spaghetti noodles, and a few other stray cats and dogs."

"What are *you* going to eat?" she asked

I inhaled deeply and sighed. "We have no produce, except a half a head of wilted lettuce. No tofu, no rice, one baggie of trail mix." I scraped my teeth across my lower lip. "I'll harvest what greens I can outside and try to make do."

"What about dessert?" Nick chimed in.

"One bag of Jet-Puffed marshmallows and six packs of hot chocolate."

"Our food won't last a week," Grace said glumly. "What are we going to do when we run out, Allie?"

"The only thing we can do," I replied, just as glumly. "We have an entire lake of fish. When we run out of everything else, that's what we'll have to eat for breakfast, lunch, and dinner."

Grace groaned in obvious distress.

"Nick will catch us a passel of fish every day," I added and mussed his hair.

Nick beamed. "Oh yeah. I got this."

"On the non-food side of the ledger," I went on, "we're down to three rolls of toilet paper, two travel-size shampoos—"

"Two!" Grace interrupted.

"Two," I repeated. "And one spare bar of soap. But, cue the applause, we have an industrial-sized bottle of dish soap that came with the place."

"My cup runneth over," Grace muttered.

Hours later, when the sun set, Nick, Grace, and I sat outside around a massive fire Nick built. In addition to fishing, I learned Nick was a budding arsonist who loved to burn stuff. Grandfather didn't join us. He spent most of the day in bed or throwing up in the bathroom, so he was in no shape to roast marshmallows to-night. While we were skewering our little white pillows, the muf-fled sound of a person heaving violently drifted out from inside the cabin.

"He's going to kill himself if he keeps drinking," I muttered to Grace.

"It's not drinking," she said. "He ran out over a week ago."

"Then what?"

She shrugged. "Who knows? I guess he's even more sick of this place than we are."

"And how are *you* feeling?" I asked her.

She shrugged again. "I'm officially three and a half weeks late but otherwise fine. No morning sickness or anything."

Changing subjects, I announced to my siblings, "Guys, let's analyze this. Here we are stuck in this place. Our transportation is a week overdue. I can't figure out any scenario for how we got marooned here. People should have come for us days and days ago. So, it has to be—"

"Something completely unexpected," Grace cut in. "For some reason, people can't get to us. Why?"

"Zombie apocalypse," Nick said in almost a whisper. "Got to be it. Right now, the entire world is overrun by people-eating monsters. Civilization has totally broken down. Mom and Dad are probably stranded in Europe somewhere surrounded by the walking dead."

Grace snorted, and for the first time in a while, her dour exterior gave way to an amused smile.

"Zombies. Right," Grace said dismissively. Then she decided to play along. "I'm going with alien invasion. Like *War of the Worlds*. While we've been out here communing with Mother Nature, creatures from the planet LV-426 have devastated the major cities of Earth and are harvesting humans to feed their famine-stricken world."

"Pandemic," I said, joining the game. "Everyone's dead or dying from a new disease." Then I decided to add a science fiction element. "A virus hitchhiked a ride to Earth on a rogue meteor. All the airports and major roads are clogged with dead bodies."

"This is beginning to sound really creepy," Grace said.

"What about the rapture?" Nick asked.

"Sorry?" Grace said, a confused expression on her face.

Nick started to explain, "You know—"

I interrupted him, "Where all the good people are whisked away to heaven to spend eternity at a five-star resort, while all of us bad people are left behind to fight amongst ourselves in the Bronx."

"Typical," Grace murmured. "Everyone's going to Antonio's house on Friday night for the big party, but I get left off the invite list."

"No dice, Nick," I said. "If it was the rapture, you'd be gone."

He smiled at me.

"I'm rethinking my guess," I said. "Maybe this is purgatory. Like the TV show *Lost*, except we're all stuck here by a lake instead of on an island."

"So, we're all dead?" Grace said skeptically. "And I thought zombies and aliens were creepy."

"Did they ever get off?" Nick asked. "The island, I mean."

"Sort of," I said, sounding a little uncertain. "It was a little fuzzy at the end."

We paused our speculations to eat the burnt marshmallows on our sticks. I only nibbled at mine, but Nick slid all three of his off his skewer and into his mouth in one motion. My spine shivered at the massive sugar hit Nick was injecting into his system.

"It doesn't matter," I went on. "We'll never know what happened until we get back to civilization. The fact is, we're stuck here for now."

"I know what it is," Grace said, nodding as if the truth was finally dawning on her. "It's one of those deals where the power grid gets fried." She snapped her fingers a couple of times while she tried to remember the name.

"EMP," I supplied. "Electromagnetic pulse. It would brick anything with an electrical circuit. Not a bad guess."

"Or," she paused, apparently wanting to amp up the suspense levels, "time travel. We passed through a wormhole and we've landed a thousand years in the past. No one's coming to get us because the airplane won't be invented for centuries."

"Uh, that would be purgatory," I commented. "It's already on the list."

"I'll bet a plane shows up tomorrow." The suggestion came from Grandfather, who walked toward us, apparently having regained his sea legs. "In a week, we'll all be laughing at this. Allie will be negotiating with Hollywood types about a movie or reality show, and we'll all be celebrities."

I couldn't tell whether he honestly believed this or he was only saying it to cheer up Nick.

"Nice," I replied. "But I'm not doing any TV shows unless Nick is my co-star."

I leaned over and fist bumped with Nick, who grinned up at me as if we were already deep in talks with producers.

CHAPTER SIXTEEN

Day seventeen of our wilderness incarceration began with me experimenting in the early morning hours with tea brewed from pine needles. The idea came from Marina, who roomed next to me at Exeter. We had all kinds of odd ducks in the dorm. Marina was one of them. She called herself a Gaian, but what that had to do with pine needle tea, I never knew. What I did know was that Marina promoted the tea as if it was an immortality elixir.

We'd see about that.

I took a tentative sip of the greenish water. An astringent, slightly bitter taste. I expected some hint of turpentine but found none. The drink wasn't as smooth as other herbal teas I favored, but it wasn't bad. Since we had no other tea and no coffee, pine needles would have to do.

Halfway into another sip, the lights went out. The cabin interior went from dull yellow to dim gray. The sudden change startled me, and I set down my tea while my brain processed what happened.

No lights meant no power. No power meant . . . no running water.

With dread creeping up my backbone like crawling spiders, I flipped up the faucet handle in the kitchen sink. A spurt of water sputtered out for a second, quickly petered out to a slow trickle, and then became a sporadic dribble.

"Oh Lord," I murmured.

To confirm what I already knew, I tested the shower. It was a goner. So was the toilet. Thankfully, the refrigerator and stove ran off propane, but how long would that last?

Okay, so we would have to haul water from the lake. And we'd have to boil it. No way was I drinking unsterilized brown water. Also, we'd have to start using the outhouse.

"Ugh," I muttered at the thought.

Recalling a discussion in one of my history classes, I remembered Mr. Reynolds explaining that the modern flush toilet in the US dated only to the late 1800s. So, outhouses were the norm for most of human existence. If Emily Dickinson, one of my literary idols, could sit on a wooden plank with a hole in the middle, then I could too. Grace? Well, she was going to freak.

As I turned to leave the bathroom, my eyes caught sight of a pill bottle sitting by the side of the sink. Who left their prescription in the bathroom? The only one who had prescription meds was Nick, and I was careful to keep his meds zipped up in the side pocket of one of my suitcases. Had I left a bottle out?

I grabbed the orange plastic container and raised it closer to my eyes to read the label: James E. Baylor. So, it belonged to Grandfather. Not a surprise. Old people were always taking prescription meds. Then I read the name of the drug: Oxycontin. The big kahuna of pain meds . . . or one of them, at least. Why was he taking Oxy?

The question had to wait. A strangled cry erupted from the room where Nick slept. Slipping the pill bottle into the pocket of my shorts, I raced to Nick's bed, where he lay writhing in apparent pain. I grasped him by the shoulders to keep him still, but I did little good. His muscles were so tense I worried that tendons were going to snap like piano wires.

"Nick, wake up!"

Was he having another episode?

"Nick, come back."

"I'm not a coward," he said through clenched teeth.

My heart squeezed at these words. I knew what he meant, and I hated myself for it. I kept trying to bring him out of this fit, but my mind drifted back to our last game fighting Morgon in late September many years ago. I had buried this day in the back corner of my mind, but now it blossomed in my memory as if it had happened yesterday.

"It's getting dark," Grace had whispered to me that day, as we crouched behind a line of hedge roses.

"Where's Sir Captain Captain?" I asked. My right hand gripped Derthal, my magical spear.

"Behind the oak tree," she replied. Without raising her hand, she wiggled her index finger in the direction of a massive tree some twenty yards away.

"Good. I'll attract Morgon's attention and lead him between you and Captain. Then, you guys jump out and ambush him."

She nodded. Grace—Princess Breeta—held a bow, which she had crafted out of twine and a slender branch, and used sharpened chopsticks for arrows. She possessed the only functional weapon, the lethality of which she demonstrated the day before by killing a slug and a daddy longlegs with it.

"Wait until I run past," I told her. "Then come out shooting. We'll push him toward the gazebo and finish him off there."

"Got it."

As Queen Keelana, I wasn't supposed to be risking my life. My loyal subjects and protectors—Grace and Nick—were supposed to defend me from Morgon. But, standing around in our gazebo, tapping my shoe on the floor, was really boring. I was a fighting queen, a ruler who charged first into battle. Besides, I made up the game, so I got to say how we played it.

I crawled out from behind the roses on my hands and knees. The meticulously manicured lawn felt soft on my knees. The landscapers had watered it earlier, so my jeans quickly became damp and stained. My immediate objective was the giant hydrangea bush by our patio.

I made it.

Deep breaths. Count to three.

Straightening, I glanced over at the roses where Princess Breeta hid and then over to the oak tree. With the shriek of a banshee, I took off running across our lawn, angling my route so as to pass between Sir Captain Captain and Princess Breeta and draw Morgon after me.

"Get ready!" I yelled.

Up until now, Morgon was a make-believe monster I created as part of our fantasy. I didn't have a clear vision of what Morgon looked like; I described him to Nick as a flying dragon-like creature, except no fire breathing. His skin was black and scaly like a lizard. Beyond that, I hadn't bothered to imagine any other details.

As I drew near the ambush point, jogging along at a fairly good clip, I glanced back over my shoulder for no reason really. I expected to see our slate patio with teak furniture and behind it the doors to our house, but my eyes didn't focus on these things. Instead, a creature the size of a tractor-trailer lumbered after me on two legs as big around as massive tree trunks. Black scaly skin. Its head was as large as a king-sized bed, but in place of bed sheets and blankets, the leathery skull had a mouth of foot-long fangs and orange eyes.

My breath caught. What the?

Morgon roared at me. His breath smelled like hot, rotting fish.

My make-believe monster seemed to have gone from fantasy to reality. And he was going to rip my body in half, slurp down my insides, and burp out my bones. My shrieks became genuine cries of terror.

"Run!" I yelled at Grace as I ran by.

"What?" she shouted back.

From the annoyed expression on her face over my seeming change in plans, I guessed she didn't see Morgon. At least, not the way I did.

My pace accelerated into a sprint or as much of one as a ten-year-old could muster, and I headed toward the gazebo. It would offer some protection but not much.

I made it to the gazebo but, from the ear-shattering bellows behind me, just barely. Although I wanted to cower in a corner, I forced my body to pivot, and I confronted Morgon. He stood at the gazebo steps, his big fat head lowered as if to squeeze it inside. My hand whipped forward to swing my weapon at him. I expected to see the old yardstick in my grasp, but it wasn't there. I held an actual silver spear that was as tall as me and sharp pointed with blades running down the shaft. Well, if I had to suffer an attack by an ugly illusionary monster, at least I had a nice illusionary spear to fight with.

I swung, slashed, and stabbed with Derthal, inflicting cuts and gashes on Morgon's snout and face. Green blood spilled from the wounds.

"Ya, ya, ya!" Princess Breeta yelled from somewhere off to my right.

Morgon swiped a clawed paw in her direction.

"Fallayrow, Grace!"

She dipped a shoulder and executed a perfect roll. She came out of it with bow ready.

Chopstick arrows arced in my direction. These slivers of wood could barely kill a grasshopper at close range, but when they struck Morgon's flanks and ribs, they hit with the force of great projectiles. More green blood spurted from Morgon's hide where the arrows hit. We were winning.

Then I lifted my spear to take a swing at Morgon when a sharp pain exploded in my right temple. My mind spun in circles, my feet staggered backward a couple steps, and then my body fell over backward into an abyss of blackness. I remembered the sensation of falling into a void before everything blinked out. The next thing I experienced was a voice.

"Geez, wake up already."

My eyelids fluttered open. My brain was totally disoriented. Very slowly, memories oozed back into me, filling up the emptiness the way a trickle of water gradually collects in a glass. My senses became aware of pressure on the side of my head. A hand pressed against me. Instinctively, I jerked away from it.

"What happened?" I asked in a hoarse breath.

"I think I knocked you out."

I recognized the voice. Grace.

"Sorry," she continued with a shrug. "A couple of my arrows hit you in the head. Just missed your eye."

I became aware of sticky wetness on my cheek. After dabbing at it with a couple fingers, which I held up before my face, I saw blood. Lots of it. It covered the side of my face. I almost fainted again at the sight of it.

"You shot me."

"That's what I said," Grace replied. "You look really gross. I may have to throw up in my mouth."

Feeling groggy and dizzy, I managed to sit up. "What happened to Morgon?"

Grace shrugged again. "I guess he's gone?"

She lifted both eyebrows and looked to me for confirmation.

"Didn't you see him? Didn't you hear him?"

"See who?" she answered. "Hear what?"

"Morgon."

She paused to study my face for several seconds.

"Sort of," she offered tentatively, as if fishing for the right response.

"He was here," I insisted before giving into a groan from the pain in my throbbing temple.

From the confused expression that rippled across her face, Grace clearly was puzzled by the statement. She hadn't seen what I'd seen;

she hadn't heard what I heard. I could tell. And what exactly *had* I seen and heard? A hallucination? A phantom apparition? Was I schizo?

"Never mind," I said. "I need a Band-Aid."

"Let's go inside," Grace suggested. Then she helped me to my feet.

"Where's Nick?"

We found Nick sitting at the base of the oak tree with his arms around his knees and his head bent forward. He was crying. I guessed he saw Morgon the same way I did. I should have felt compassion for Nick, but I didn't. Instead, his cringing behavior pissed me off. Why? What did I expect from a five-year-old?

"Where were you?" I said to a blubbering Nick. "You were supposed to defend me, you miserable coward. I almost died."

"Allie—" Grace began.

I cut her off. "We're not playing this game again . . . ever."

Nick's cries turned into sobs. I felt a stab of remorse like you'd feel if you kicked a defenseless puppy dog, and regret slashed at my insides. Still, I wanted to lash out even more but swallowed the words. With a dozen emotions warring inside me, I had to get out of there, so I stomped toward the house with the palm of one hand pressed against my wound.

We never played our game again. I never saw Morgon again. But I understood Nick in a way no one else did or could. I had seen what Nick saw every time we played our game. The monster was terrifying beyond anything else I ever experienced. No wonder Nick was the way he was.

At times later, when I lay in bed waiting for the onslaught of sleep, my thoughts would wander back to that day and what I saw

. . . or thought I saw. What *did* I see? Eventually, my memory of the day faded, and I put aside the whole event, convinced I suffered from a temporary bout of delusional psychosis. I left the whole matter in the past and moved on.

Nick didn't.

I stared down at my brother, who shook with a seizure

"You were never a coward," I whispered to Nick, shoving aside the uninvited and painful flashback.

Slipping my hands under his shoulders I raised him off the bed and pulled him into an awkward hug. He squeezed back, returning the embrace. His muscles went slack the way violin strings relaxed when loosened.

"Can I make you some breakfast?" I asked softly. "It'll have to be peanut butter and Ritz crackers."

I felt him nod against my chest, and I gently released him. When I left the bedroom, Nick sat on the bed rubbing his eyes with the palms of his hands.

"Can I have some of that too?" Grandfather said.

He sat at the table in the kitchen area with a glass of water. What any of us would have given for caffeine.

Grandfather wore the same blue flannel pajamas he had every night since we arrived. How he could stand it I didn't know. The summer temps outside soared into the low eighties the last few days and the cabin had no AC, of course, so it became pretty stifling inside during the day. We kept the windows open, but with the humidity, the air was immobile like a block of pudding.

"Sure," I said. "By the way, the power's out, so we have no running water and no toilet."

"So I found out," Grandfather said. "It's been a few decades since I had to use a real outhouse. This one even has a catalog for reading . . . and for other things."

"Can you and Nick get some fish today?" I asked, changing the subject. "We're about out of everything."

"Yep. Was already planning to. What about you?"

I sighed and sat down at the table across from him. "I'll gather some dandelions and other greens for a salad. I have a tiny bit of dressing left."

He was about to say something in response when I pulled the pill bottle out of my pocket and plopped it down in the center of the table. Both of us stared at it for several seconds before he leaned back and let his shoulders slump. He looked tired and beat up.

"Well, I guess it's time to come clean."

CHAPTER SEVENTEEN

"Are those what I think they are?" I asked, pointing at the paw impressions in the damp soil. They were each the size of a cookie sheet.

Grandfather leaned over to study the prints that lay along the lake's edge, less than seventy-five feet from our outhouse. We had wandered out from the cabin to talk privately about his pills, only to come to an abrupt stop at the sight of the trampled earth. I stared in growing alarm at the chunks of clawed up ground that marked a large animal's passing. This thing had come right up to the cleared land around the cabin and patrolled the perimeter, careful, it appeared, to stay just far enough back for the brush to screen its movements.

"They look like bear tracks. Either that or one of the fighting Uruk-Hai," he mused.

"The what?"

"The Uruk-Hai are a breed of super orcs."

I rolled my eyes. "Not the *Lord of the Rings* again, old man."

He shrugged apologetically, "Sorry." The amusement in his voice a moment before evaporated. "It's just that I've seen bear tracks before, Allie. These are way bigger than those of any bear I've ever heard of."

"Really?"

He mopped his forehead with the back of his hand. "I've been thinking, thinking a lot, about that creature we saw on the other side of the lake."

"Creature? Uh, you're scaring me."

"You ever been to the La Brea Tar Pits in LA?"

I shook my head. I had heard of it, of course. "Bunch of animals fell into the muck and fossilized, right?"

"More or less. They have an exhibit showing a reconstruction of one of the victims. A giant, prehistoric bear. If I remember correctly, it was easily two or three times the size of the biggest bear we got today."

I stared in horror at him.

"That thing we saw the other day," he went on, "it sure looked like the picture in that exhibit—tall, stubby nosed, long arms, all of it."

My mind drifted back to the brief comments Trevor made about this place. "Remember what he said?"

"He? He who?"

I rolled my eyes. "Trevor. You know, Mr. Douchebag."

"Oh, right."

I sucked in a deep breath before continuing. "He said they bought this place from a first nations band who thought the land was cursed. Lake Makwa means Lake Bear."

His mouth tightened in a grimace. "Maybe we shouldn't say anything to the others about—"

I cut him off, "About us camping in Jurassic Park with a giant, prehistoric bear monster? Agreed."

"In the meantime, no one goes out at night, no one goes out alone, and no one goes into the forest."

"Okay," I murmured.

I suddenly felt very exposed and vulnerable. We had no weapons to defend ourselves with, other than some kitchen knives and, possibly, blunt projectiles such as my smoothie maker. I hated guns, but in that moment I would have gladly joined the NRA if it meant we could have an AK 47 and a dozen high-capacity magazines.

We made our way down to the dock, where we stood beside each other gazing out at the distant shore on the other side of the lake. Neither of us wanted to talk about the bear anymore, but we hadn't come out here to discuss that anyway.

"Meanwhile back at the ranch," I finally said. "You said you didn't want to talk inside."

When he didn't respond, I added, "The pills?"

He dragged a hand through what was left of his thinning hair and cleared his throat a couple times. Nervous much? Whatever the pills were about, he didn't want to discuss the subject. Too bad. He had to.

"I have a cancer," he finally said. "The meds are for when the pain gets too strong to take."

"How—"

"Bad?" he interrupted. "Pretty bad. My doctor has a couple of last-ditch things he wants to try when we get back, but he told me not to get my hopes up."

"*If* we get back," I clarified.

"If."

"Why come on this trip?" I asked. "You're in no condition for this."

My voice sounded angry but not at him. What angered me was my father canceling out on us and then cajoling my poor, possibly dying grandfather to take his place. Dad could certainly be a dick sometimes; boy, did I know that. But getting my grandfather to sub for him on this vacation, my *cancer-stricken* grandfather, was low. Really low.

"It wasn't your father's idea," he said, apparently reading my mind. "It was mine."

I opened my mouth to ask a question I had yet to formulate, but he beat me to it.

"Actually, I pleaded with him to let me take his place. I wanted to try and fix things with you and Grace and Nick."

"You had nothing to fix as far as I'm concerned."

He jammed his hands into his pockets and turned to gaze out across the lake. The dark water rippled with the slight breeze that was blowing.

"I'm seventy-one years old, granddaughter. I've had a full life mostly. I haven't done everything I wanted to do, but who ever does? My life hasn't been as fulfilling as some, but it's been better than most. My joys outweigh my regrets."

"But?"

"So, you'd think that when the time comes, I could make my peace with life and accept dying, but it scares the beans out of me."

"That sounds pretty normal . . . but what do I know."

He shrugged indifferently. "The fact is, after I'm dead, no one is going to remember anything about me beyond a name, maybe a face, and some brief lines in a local paper obituary. It's not that I want marble monuments erected in my name, but I would like at least one person to remember me when I'm gone for who I really was."

"I'm glad you came on this trip," I whispered.

"Well, that's a start."

I should have shut up at that point, but I couldn't. I had to ask.

"Is the cancer why you started drinking again?"

He turned to face me, a grim expression on his face.

Then he said, "I was sober for thirty years because the stuff was killing me. Now that I'm dying anyway, what's the point? At least, that's what I told myself a couple months back. I didn't plan to bring anything with me on this trip, but once I let that monkey climb back on my shoulder, there was no getting it off again."

"Except you ran out a week ago," I noted.

"That I did."

We didn't have much else to say after that, so we walked in silence back to the cabin, both of us lost in thought. I slipped my hand into his and squeezed. He squeezed back.

So, now what? I thought.

My sick grandfather added new pressure and stress I didn't need. If he was dying of cancer, then we really had to get out of here. Now.

Grimacing, I remembered I still had to make my breakfast of Ritz crackers and peanut butter. To add some variety, I put both peanut butter and jelly on half of the crackers. Grandfather watched me for a few minutes before popping the lid off his bottle and taking one of the pills. Glancing over at him, I noticed how haggard he appeared, a fact I hadn't picked up on before. His skin was pasty, and his facial muscles sagged as if they no longer had the strength to hold his features in place. Grace and Nick wandered in just as I was finishing up a plate of my suck breakfast.

"We can't sit around and do nothing," Grace said, after jamming a cracker in her mouth and chewing. "We're completely lost, and nobody is coming for us."

"We're not doing nothing," Grandfather countered in a patient tone.

"Somebody explain how sitting on our ass is doing something," Grace persisted.

"The signal fire," I responded.

I pointed vaguely in the direction of the dock. A few feet down the lakeshore from it was a blackened pyre of logs. For the last three days, I had started a giant bonfire in the morning and tossed branches and chunks of wood on it to keep it lit during the day. Currently, my fire blazed away, belching dark-gray smoke into the air.

"That fire is what's going to save us," I went on.

"Bullshit," Grace countered.

"The line of smoke from that fire can be seen from the air for miles and miles," I said. "If a pilot sees it, they'll come to investigate."

"Whatever," Grace said and stuffed a cracker PB and J sandwich in her mouth.

Actually, I agreed with Grace that we were doing mostly nothing, but it wasn't as if we had a lot of options at our disposal. We didn't. The fact was, we weren't lost. I knew exactly where we were; in fact, I could consult the one map we had and recite our precise longitude and latitude. The problem was that no one else apparently knew where we were, and we had no way to contact them.

"What do we do then, Grace?" I said. "What's your plan, huh? You don't get to crap all over my idea and not come up with one of your own."

"We walk out of here, of course," she said. "We pack what we have, and we take off right now."

"Are you serious?" I replied. I sounded incredulous, and I was. "The nearest road is a hundred and fifty miles away. That's like walking from Scarsdale to Schenectady."

I didn't say anything about a giant bear prowling the woods.

"So what?" she countered. "If we walked fifteen miles a day, we'd reach your stupid road in ten days. Ten days! I won't speak for anyone else, but if I have to go ten days without food to get the flip out of here, then that's what I'll do."

"Fifteen miles! Dude, have you actually stepped into the forest around us? Well, I have. It's a jungle. We'd be lucky to make two miles a day slogging through the underbrush. Instead of ten days, try two and a half months. And that's assuming we don't get lost or injured or attacked by a . . ." I paused, suddenly aware of Nick's penetrating stare.

"By some wild animal," I finished. Best not to mention prehistoric monsters.

"I'd rather die trying," Grace said sullenly, "than sit around and die doing nothing."

"Somebody will come. How could they not? We just have to be patient, okay?"

"We're out of food, Allie," Grace said. "We don't have the luxury of waiting for weeks, months, or whatever."

What she meant, or *one* of the things she meant, was she didn't want to have a baby out here in the wilderness. She didn't want to have a baby *period.* I couldn't blame her for feeling trapped. And like any animal caught in a trap, sitting around and patiently waiting for someone to come along and rescue you wasn't an appealing strategy.

"I understand what you're saying," I told Grace.

Grandfather and Nick both sat quietly, having witnessed our debate in silence. The fact was, neither of them could survive a two months' long trek through the forest. Grace and I couldn't make it, so how could they possibly survive? Although both of us were physically fit, if I was being generous, neither of us had any survival skills. I couldn't start a fire without matches. I had no idea how to find water, make a camp, or build a shelter. Plus, we didn't have enough food to bring along on an overland hike. What would we do? Hunt? In Buddy Holly terms: That'll be the day.

Yes, the obstacles to hiking out were legion . . . without even getting to the issue of evading hungry bears.

"Not all of us can walk a hundred and fifty miles, Grace," I added.

"I know. So maybe some of us stay here. Not all of us need to try and hike out."

Our impromptu strategy meeting broke up after Grace's comment. Grandfather and Nick wanted to go out on the lake and catch enough fish for dinner. Grace actually volunteered to go with them, although she knew less about fishing than I did about astrophysics.

A few minutes after the others left, I went outside to pace about, careful not to stray into the forest. The bear tracks we saw this morning scared me. I didn't know if bears hunted in the afternoons, but I wasn't taking any chances.

My mind went over and over my debate with Grace. Maybe someone *should* try to hike out of here, as impossible as the venture seemed. It might be a suicide mission, but with a generous amount of luck, maybe a person could stumble onto something or someone who could help. I kicked this thought around for over an hour as I walked the circumference of the cleared land around the cabin many times.

Finally, I nodded to myself. Grace was right; we should at least *try* to get help. The bear frightened the hell out of me, but in the back of my mind I was thinking that this might be a local problem centered around Lake Mikwa. Once you got a day's hiking distance away from the lake, probably you were outside this bear's territory and back to dealing with the usual list of carnivores that wanted to eat you. A person only needed to survive the first day before getting out of range . . . maybe.

Okay, so somebody tries to hike out.

With that question settled, the next question was who should attempt this idiotic task? I already knew the answer. Grace might be pregnant. Grandfather was too old and possibly dying. Nick was too young. So, when the music stopped, the only person without a chair was me.

No matter how logical the analysis, once I decided I should be the one to go, I was frightened out of my gourd. That bear thing out there scared me, wolves scared me, and every other creature that crawled or crept around in the woods after dark scared me. In fact, the prospect of sleeping outside on the ground terrified me. So, I was the best person to go and the worst.

If I meant to do this, *how* would I do it? I could announce my decision to the others, but they would argue with me about it. No one would agree to let me go off alone. Grace would absolutely insist on coming. Nick would demand to come just as strongly. Maybe, Grace and Grandfather would stand behind me in refusing to bring Nick, but I'd never garner any support for leaving by myself.

So, I wouldn't tell them.

"I'll sneak off," I said, "and make sure no one figures out what I've done until it's too late to follow me."

Was this plan as dumb as it sounded? Yes, it was. But, desperate times called for desperate measures. Was this what soldiers said when they climbed out of their trenches to charge the enemy's machine guns? Probably. I liked their survival odds better than mine.

Decision made, I blocked out the basic plan. I usually woke at least an hour before the others, maybe more. Tomorrow, I'd wake even earlier, leave a note, and take off.

Well, that was an easy plan.

In the back of my mind, I told myself that if I ran into trouble and couldn't go on for some reason I could always turn back and return to the cabin, bear be damned. I didn't have to die out in the middle of the unexplored hinterlands, where no one would ever find my body.

I could come back.

This fallback plan was a slender reed to cling to; if I managed to march for a week or two into the woods, realistically, there would be no turning back. Still, this was my Plan B, and it was the only safety net I had. So, I clung to it the way a drowning man at sea might cling to a scrap of wood floating next to him.

Later that night, we all went to bed early. Nick and Grandfather had caught enough fish to provide plenty to eat for two or three days. They probably would have caught even more, but Grandfather had to stop to help Grace untangle her line. She didn't catch anything, of course.

I lay awake most of the night, unable to sleep. Ideas, worries, and fears tumbled around and around in my brain like laundry in the dryer. At four in the morning, I rose and tiptoed around the cabin gathering stuff for my journey. There wasn't much junk to gather, so this didn't take long. By the time the sun peeked over the treetops, I was ready to go, having jammed my supplies into Nick's backpack, which I was technically stealing. No one roused, even when I dropped the plastic container of peanut butter on my little toe and whisper-cursed.

For clothes, I wore jeans and an Exeter hoodie over an apricot T-shirt. I also brought spare underwear and socks, but I didn't bring my tennis shoes or flats. My only footwear would be my boots. If they wore out, then I guessed I'd go barefoot.

For my last act, I left a folded note on the table addressed to Grandfather and Grace. By the time they read it, I hoped to be a couple hours gone. Knives of terror stabbed me over and over again as I headed for the front door, but I forced myself to remain calm and resolute.

A quick glance around the area revealed no large bears pacing about, so I stepped off the porch and headed for the woods.

At 5:35 a.m., I paused for a second at the edge of the forest, glanced back at the cabin, and wondered if I would ever see my family again. Before I had a chance to second-guess my decision, I stepped under the eaves of the towering pine trees and disappeared into the heart of darkness.

CHAPTER EIGHTEEN

I stopped for lunch six hours into my first day out, this according to my Cartier watch I still wore. I should have left it behind for Grace, but I held on to it as a kind of charm; it was my tether to the outside world. I had this irrational idea that as long as I wore the watch I would make it home one day. Sure, I was being silly and superstitious, but, hey, whatever got you through the day.

Sweat from the humid air drenched my clothes, and my thigh muscles burned with exhaustion. Call it a lunch break, but really my body simply refused to go on. For all the hours I had spent hiking this morning, I didn't think I covered more than a couple miles of ground. Three obstacles slowed my progress. The big three.

One, there were no trails. At least, I didn't find any. I'm sure animals were out here, but I saw no tracks and heard no sounds, other than birds and my own huffing and puffing.

Two, the brush. The trees allowed plenty of space to pass between them, but that space was crammed with bushes as high as my head, bushes whose branches were thick and unyielding, scratchy and tangled. Trying to push through them not only tired me, but the effort left my bare skin scraped and, in a few places, bleeding. My body felt as if Mother Nature and I had gone at it for hours in a vicious knife fight.

Three, the dead trees. Like people, trees in the forest eventually died and fell over, and when they toppled, they didn't do it in neat, organized rows. Instead, I confronted a chaotic labyrinth of mossy logs. Tree trunks lay on the ground at all angles, often several crisscrossed on top of each other. This made my passage very hard, as I had to climb over some deadfalls, crawl under others, and go way out of my way to bypass many.

With my backpack beside me, I sat on a rotting log and took deep breaths. A slight breeze stirred my hair, and it felt heavenly. Bending over, I loosened the laces of my boots. Although old and worn in, my left boot had become a problem. My sock slid down to my heel, where the skin burned and teetered on the edge of morphing into a big momma blister. That could become obstacle number four . . . and a big one. So, I removed my boot and sock to air out my smelly, reddened foot.

"So, what's for lunch?" I said out loud, hoping to cheer myself up.

I pawed through the meager contents of my pack searching for the container at the bottom. Besides a map, some matches, and a few other doodads in side pockets, the pack held a blanket for me to sleep on; a compact, travel-size first aid kit; a skinning knife; a fork; food and a water bottle; and some other junk. In terms of food, I didn't have much: a few canned goods and a twenty-eight-ounce jar of creamy peanut butter we'd hardly touched. I planned to forage as much as possible, save the canned stuff for emergencies, and get my protein from the peanut butter. And when the peanut butter ran out? As Scarlett O'Hara would say, "I'll think about that tomorrow."

Hopping on one foot, I picked some leaves from friendly-looking bushes and snapped off a couple handfuls of fronds from nearby fern-like plants. Then I settled in for my meal. Preparation was simple. I dipped my finger into the peanut butter, smeared it on a leaf, and plopped the combo into my mouth. The leaves tasted a bit acidic, possibly from insects peeing on them all day long, but the peanut butter helped mask the bitterness. The fronds tasted like fiddleheads. The nutritional value was meager, but I ate enough to give a hint of a full stomach.

"Time to go," I said after about an hour, rubbing my hands on my jeans.

Once I shouldered my backpack and got my boot on, I started off again. My pace was slow and methodical. I took time to place my feet carefully when stepping over fallen trees and scrabbling over the occasional rocky ridges I encountered. A sprained ankle might cost me days of travel time; a *broken* ankle might cost me my life.

From time to time, I paused to consult the small compass hanging on a cord around my neck . . . I stole it from Nick. My plan was simple. Go south. South was civilization. South was where we came from. And, worst-case scenario, as long as I stayed on course, in four hundred miles, I'd reach Lake Superior.

I had a map, but I didn't think it would help much. The map covered the entire province of Ontario, so it lacked detail, although someone had been thoughtful enough to ink on it an X where our little lake was located. The X did little except taunt me with the distances I had to cover to get to any nearby dot that had a name.

The one point that the map did make perfectly clear was that between our cabin and pretty much the rest of the world were lakes . . . lots of lakes. Rivers too. I had no boat, so I would have to traverse around the lakes. There was no going around the millions of rivers. I would have to ford them and the billions of creeks not shown on the map, and do so daily. My biggest enemies, I decided, would not be starvation and predators, but drowning and hypothermia.

Weary, hungry, and sore, I called it a day at six o'clock in front of a couple of large trees that had fallen against a house-sized rock outcropping, leaving a crawl space under their trunks . . . a nice little lean-to. After clearing away branches and rocks, I spread my throw blanket over damp ground and sat cross-legged on it.

"Now what?" I asked a dangling vine that hung in front of my face.

I managed to find dried clumps of moss, peel bark strips from an aspen tree, and collect dry branches. In short order, I had a small fire going, and it only took me three matches. For dinner, I collected flowers that looked like yellow lilies. Also, I added leaves from the flower stems to my feast, along with the plant's bulbous roots. With a few dabs of peanut butter, it wasn't too bad. Did it fill me up? Sort of. Were the plants poisonous? Well, I didn't throw up, so I guessed they were edible.

The next two hours I spent sitting in front of my twig fire and studying the map until I lost the light. Eventually my body fell over onto its side and my hands volunteered to serve as my pillow. The blanket did little to soften the lumpy, hard ground. Three weeks ago and change, I had four down pillows, one-thousand-count Egyptian cotton sheets, a puffy satin comforter, and a four-poster bed. Nirvana. A pang of homesickness washed through me, along with a feeling of growing despair.

What was I doing out here? I was going to die, and no one would ever know what happened to me. I bit my lip. Hard. If I lacked hope, maybe pain would make a nice substitute.

Not long after the sun disappeared, the temps dropped quickly, and the wind began to blow. Soon, I was freezing my ass off, so I gave up sleeping *on* the blanket and instead used it to cover me. Uncomfortable was too bland a word to describe my makeshift bed. Bumps, lumps, pokes, and wetness afflicted me. So, my feral animal accommodations were . . . tortuous . . . agonizing . . . excruciating.

Then it began to rain.

Then I began to cry.

This was the second time I cried myself to sleep in the last few months. I'd have to go back to Mom's death for the time before that. Tonight, I cried out of a feeling of total abandonment and loneliness. Last winter, I cried over a boy. God, did that ever seem trivial now.

"My parents are looking forward to meeting you," Jack said at the time.

That night was our first night back after spring break, and we were having dinner with his parents before they headed back to the US embassy in Paris. His father was the ambassador to France and rumored vice-presidential candidate if his friend, Mr. What's-his-name Tomkins, won the nomination this summer.

Politics held little interest for me, perhaps because Dad loathed politicians. "I'm an artist," he often said, and he viewed art and politics as the utter antithesis of one another. "Matter and antimatter," he once told me, after several post-dinner cognacs.

Jack's plan was to show me off as his girlfriend, the mysterious Ms. Allie Baylor he had talked so much about . . . or so he told me. The night didn't start off very well. While we waited for an Uber car to take us to the restaurant, I broke the news about my intern plans for August. I knew he was going to be gone for the month, so I honestly didn't expect him to care.

"Are you serious?" Jack asked, sounding both puzzled and annoyed. "Haiti? I mean, my God."

"It's only for three weeks," I countered. "I'll help out at orphanages and schools, help teach English."

"Teach English," he sputtered. "Don't you have to speak Haitian first?"

"They speak Creole and French. I speak French, remember? It'll be fine."

He shook his head and exhaled slowly. "I'm just worried about your safety. It's pretty rough down there. I'm not so sure you can handle it."

I rolled my eyes. "I'm not going to cry if I break a nail or something. I got this. Have a little faith in me."

We argued all the way to the restaurant, not caring that the Uber guy heard it all. However, by unspoken, mutual agreement, we cut off further discussion of my intended Haiti trip when we stepped through the restaurant doors. La Ferme drew large crowds on a Friday night, and that night was no exception. The area around campus didn't have many French restaurants, and La Ferme was the best.

"Mom, Dad," Jack said when the waiter escorted us to their table, "this is Allie Baylor. We met during our class trip to France. She's my girlfriend."

An awkward silence followed for several beats while I smiled and struggled to maintain a relaxed exterior.

"Her father is Paul Baylor. You know, the film director."

"Paul Baylor!" Jack's dad exclaimed in enthusiastic recognition. "Of course. Please, dear, have a seat by me."

Yeah, so I went from strange random girl to esteemed guest of honor in three eye blinks.

Dinner passed by most pleasantly. Jack's dad was quite charming, and he regaled me with stories about Jack as a young child. I enjoyed watching Jack's red-faced embarrassment almost as much as hearing the stories. The conversation drifted along very agreeably as we traded anecdotes. My life to date was really boring and, frankly, mostly trivial, so I related a bunch of stories about Dad and being on set with him almost every summer since I was six years old.

"And what movie is he filming this summer?" Jack's mother asked.

"The working title is *Eternal Sleep*," I said. "It's a sci-fi movie filming in Romania, but I won't be going. I'm interning at a Haitian orphanage in August."

Jack rolled his eyes, and that pissed me off. He exchanged a brief look with his father.

"A waste of time," his father said with a sigh, "but the world needs idealists like you, Allie."

So, was that a compliment or a punch to the gut? I decided to ignore the remark and change topics.

"My stepmother is going to Romania in my place," I said. "She's like Jack, though. She hates flying."

I had no problem throwing Brooke under the bus. I only hoped she got run over by both the front and rear wheels.

"Not me," Jack's mother chimed in. "I was going to mention this later, but this seems like the perfect segue. Evie, my old college roommate, and I are going to skydive. We always said we'd do it before we graduated but never did."

"That's so cool," Jack said.

I grinned and nodded in agreement. I opened my mouth to echo Jack's sentiments, but his father cut me off.

"What?" he asked, unmistakable anger in his voice. "You mean *parachute*?"

His wife nodded. "A tandem jump. We'll take some lessons beforehand and then jump with an instructor. It's supposed to be a real adrenaline rush."

Jack and I fell silent as his father and mother began to argue. It wasn't too embarrassing; they kept their back-and-forth polite and respectful, but it was definitely an argument. I was slightly amused and sat back with a smile on my face, but Jack was tense, and the muscles in his jaws popped as he clenched his teeth.

"I'm only worried about your safety," Jack's father finally said. "I'm not so sure you can handle it."

His mother said nothing, but her face reddened with either humiliation or irritation.

His father's words startled me. Jack's similar remarks were still fresh in my mind from earlier that evening. Thank God the discussion during the rest of dinner and dessert became bland and shallow. I think we were all going through the motions until it was time to leave, and when it came, I exhaled in relief. The four of us left the restaurant together but parted in front of it with waves and promises to meet again.

"I'll catch up with you in a sec," I told Jack. "The waiter refilled my water too many times. I need to go back and visit the ladies' room."

"I'll wait for you at the corner. The car should be here in a couple minutes."

When I emerged once again from the restaurant, I headed down the sidewalk toward the end of the block where I expected to find Jack and our Uber ride. On my way, I passed a couple standing with their backs to me as they waited for the valet to fetch their car. I didn't recognize them in the dim light until I heard their voices. Jack's parents.

"You're not going skydiving, and that's the end of it," Jack's father said, raising his voice at the end of the sentence

"Sam," his mother replied, "it's not a big deal. And this is important to me."

"I said no, and I mean no, Beth. It's not safe. You're fifty years old, for God's sake."

"Sam," she pleaded.

"Hell no," he practically shouted. "That's final."

I picked up my pace and bowed my head in case they glanced over in my direction. As I covered the last few yards to the car where Jack was waiting, I gritted my teeth and tripled my resolve to go to Haiti.

CHAPTER NINETEEN

I woke with the sun, but saying I slept stretched the meaning of the word beyond any reasonable interpretation. My eyes stayed closed, but my mind wouldn't shut down. The rain and the wolf howls didn't help. My body was wet and cold, so I decided to skip fire and breakfast and get to walking. I hoped that strenuous physical labor would warm me up and dry out my clothes.

After squeezing out as much water as I could from my blanket, I repacked my bag and set off, hoping today I would cover more ground. The big three, though, once again rose up in battle against me, making my journey a walking hell. Also, bugs assaulted me in swarms. I didn't remember so many attacking me yesterday, but to-day was a whole new ballgame. Apparently, word had gotten out on the bug grapevine—fresh bag of blood lost in the woods, attack at will.

A cloud of black flies and mosquitoes enveloped my head, con-stantly buzzing in and out of my ears. They nipped and bit at my bare skin, leaving welts on my arms and throat. They were in my hair, too, and I imagined running a comb through it and extracting thousands of bug bodies, as their bug guts stained my hair a grayish-black color. So disgusting.

Hunger eventually forced me to take a break mid-morning, although I tried to stay optimistic by noting that I wasn't as tired as I was at this point yesterday. I didn't want to exhaust my peanut butter, so I ate flowers and fronds again. Besides, I probably inhaled enough flies to give me more than my daily protein needs.

The one item of immediate concern, however, was water. My bottle had maybe a pint left in it. I didn't think finding water would present a problem when I left, given that the entire province was a series of islands among a zillion lakes . . . or so it appeared on the map. Yet, I had not come across a single tiny stream so far this morning.

I pulled the map out of a side pocket of my pack and studied it, as I chomped on white flowers whose petals were dusted with pollen. The taste was bland and grassy, but I hardly cared. I only wanted something to puff out my stomach a bit and make it shut up for a while.

Tracing what I thought was my route on the map, I saw I was heading directly for a small, unnamed lake shaped like a little blue jellybean. I named it Lake Jelly Belly. Using my fingernail and the map scale, I guesstimated that the lake was four to five kilometers from my current position. Call it three miles. Could I cover that much ground today?

Yes.

I can because I must.

Brave words from a teenage girl who took off on a hundred-and-fifty-mile wilderness trek with little more than an industrial-sized jar of peanut butter.

I forced myself to pick up the pace, tossing aside a good deal of the cautiousness I exhibited yesterday. Also, I found new ways to travel in this tangled jungle. When I came across a big fallen tree that more or less toppled over in a southernly direction, instead of going over, under, or around it, I climbed on top of it and used it as a walkway. At first, I had to pause frequently to maintain my balance with spastic arm flapping, but soon my body learned the trick. By mid-afternoon, I practically loped down these bark highways with no problem, deftly sidestepping jagged branches. As the day wound down, I made it a point to search out these log walkways. Still, when the sun reached the horizon, transforming the sky to fiery orange, trees still surrounded me.

"I will walk all night if I have to," I told the forest in no uncertain terms. "So get out of my way."

Walking in the dark was stupid, particularly in this environment, but I had set a goal—a teeny-weeny goal in the grand scheme of things—and I needed to accomplish it. Constant, grinding failure had nearly worn me down. All I asked from the universe was one speck of success. Then it could toss me back into the cesspool of endless failure.

"I am strong—"

The concluding words of the sentence never made it out of my mouth. My right toe caught on a hooky thing—a root maybe—and I lost my balance. The snag caused my body to pitch forward into the darkness surrounding me, where I expected to face-plant in the middle of stabbing branches and scraping rocks. Instead, my hands sank into . . . gravelly sand.

"What the . . ." I muttered as I struggled to my hands and knees.

My sluggish brain put the pieces together. Sand meant beach. Beach meant water. Water meant lake. Lake meant . . . it meant I did it. This must be Lake Jelly Belly.

As beat up, tired, and hungry as I was, I leaped to my feet, tossed my arms into the air, and did the Rocky-climbed-the-stairs dance. Then I pivoted to face the forest and gave it two middle fingers and yelled out loud at it.

"I came, I saw, I kicked your gnarly fir tree butts!"

Such hubris. I would pay a price for it.

Sigh.

In the blackness of a moonless night, I had trouble finding a place to bed down. The best I could do was a nearby tangle of driftwood. As soon as I had a modest fire going from detritus washed up on shore, I rewarded myself with three heaping spoonfuls of peanut butter. I couldn't forage for plants in the dark, so this would have to do for dinner. Before I curled up and tried to sleep, I prostrated myself at the edge of the lake and gulped water until I almost made myself sick. The water had slimy stuff in it, which I guessed to be algae, but I didn't care. I told myself I was drinking organic water. The same stuff probably costs ten bucks a quart at Whole Foods, right?

My blanket was still wet, so I curled up as close to the fire as I could and sought sleep. Surprisingly, my brain shut down immediately, and I fell into a deep, dreamless trance. If bears or wolves wanted an easy kill, I was it, and now was the time.

The sound of waves softly lapping against the shore woke me. The sun had risen well above the horizon, and it was already busy warming me and drying out my clothes. I stumbled to my feet, still groggy from sleep, and stared out across the blue expanse of water before me. It wasn't a big lake; I could make out the trees on the other side with no trouble, but it was too big to swim across. Still, if I had a canoe and knew how to paddle it, the trip across would probably take no more than a half hour or so. Since I had no canoe, I would have to spend the entire day walking around the lake.

Before I began my day of picking 'em up and putting 'em down, I washed my clothes in the lake and set them out to dry on a couple large boulders. Then, I waded out into the water, revealing all of me to the birds, the bugs, and the fish. I had so much grime and dried sweat on my body from the last two days that it felt divine for the water to wash most of it away. The water was cold, but I got used to it after a few minutes and soon dove under the surface to soak my hair. So refreshing. My clothes were still damp when I finished eating my humble breakfast naked, but I put them on anyway and took off.

I made decent time hiking along the lakeshore. Parts of the shore consisted of gravel, which I found easy to walk on, and even where the forest came down to the water, the going wasn't as tough as it was in the heart of the woods. So it was that I made it to the far end of the lake well before I expected, but my way was blocked by a rapidly flowing stream some twenty feet across. I decided to walk along it until I found an easy place to ford, which meant I had to scramble over slick boulders and occasionally slog through swampy ground.

After an hour of fruitless searching for a good spot to cross, I paused to rest on a massive granite dome next to the water, which rose from the ground like the top of a gigantic bald head buried beside the stream.

From the telltale feel of irritated skin on my right heel, I knew I had a blister. Once I took my boot off and peeled down my sock, sure enough, there it was. Poking and prodding it with my fingers, I explored the puffy bubble of skin that sadly was as big as a half dollar.

What was I supposed to do? Pop it? I vaguely remembered being told not to do this, but I had to keep walking and this annoying sac of fluid would make that mighty uncomfortable.

"Screw it," I said.

I took my knife and lanced the thing, and then I used my fingers to pinch it several times to squeeze out all the liquid. Then I extracted my first aid kit and bandaged the wound with a square of gauze and tape.

There. Not as good as new, but my foot was functional. I could walk on it.

The stream shallowed until I came to a spot where it bubbled over a bed of small rocks, thinning to a depth of only a few inches. My boots wobbled a time or two on the slick rocks, but I made it across with no falls. My plan at this point was to follow the stream back to the lake and bed down on a nice sandy spot. Tomorrow, I'd refill my water bottle and turn south again. After consulting the map, I'd pick a new goal a few days away and charge forth with all the determination I could muster. Tomorrow. Not today.

I found an old driftwood log lying parallel to the water with an apron of black sand and gravel stretching between it and the lake. My campsite for the night.

My good mood soured instantly when I removed the boot and sock from my sore ankle, intent on soaking my poor foot in the lake. The bandage had worn off, leaving me to stare at red, raw flesh. Disgusting. My poor sock was stained with blood, and the inside of my boot was soaked with the stuff to the point that it smelled like a dead animal was putrefying inside. The rest of my foot was swollen and pasty gray in color. Not good.

"Shit!" I yelled.

My outburst silenced the forest around me, as the birds stopped their annoying chirps, the bug mating calls petered out, and even the wind seemed to die down. Seconds later, a sound broke the quiet.

Grrrrr, something voiced in a throaty growl.

Not human. An animal.

At the sound, my head snapped up in surprise and panic, my poor aching foot instantly forgotten. I tried to stand but tripped over my boot and fell backward on my butt. I crab-walked sideways a few yards before I managed to stand with one foot bare and one foot with my boot still on.

What the hell lurked in the bushes? Had an apex predator finally tracked me down and now was moving in for the kill? Maybe. But the growl I heard sounded more from distress than aggression. In fact, if I wasn't out here in the middle of flipping nowhere, I'd swear someone was torturing a cat.

Grrrrrr.

There it was again!

My head swiveled over in the direction of the cry, but I couldn't make out anything in the heavy brush before me. Whatever was out there didn't seem inclined to move on me, so the tension in my shoulders relaxed an iota or two, but my breathing shallowed, and my eyes were as wide-open as saucers.

What the heck should I do?

Sadly, I was so paralyzed with fear I could not get my legs to respond to my mental commands to move it and get the holy Jesus out of here. So, I kept standing there like a human popsicle begging a meat eater to come take a bite out of me.

For several long moments, utter silence descended on the forest around me. No more growls came from the brush, and I managed to freeze into a flesh statue, remaining completely motionless even though all my weight was resting on my right leg. The big toe of my decomposing left foot barely touched the ground. In Karate Kid terms, I looked like I was about to spread out my arms, raise my knee, and prepare to launch a crane kick.

Owwrrr.

I blinked. Was that a moan?

Owwrrr.

Yes, it was.

A beast groaned with pain, not aggression. It sounded like keening. What in a horse's patootie was going on here? I no longer felt threatened, so my muscles relaxed a touch and I took a step toward the source of the noise. I didn't know why I was doing this. It was stupid on so many levels, but I felt . . . well, empathy. Whatever was out there was apparently injured, and I was injured too.

Slipping my boot back on, but not bothering to tie it, I walked toward the unknown source of the cries. Eight steps in, my mouth dropped open in complete and utter surprise.

CHAPTER TWENTY

I stared down at a fallen tree that was so rotted it might well have toppled over before Elvis was even born. Next to it, lying on its side, was a gray-brown cat that was much larger than any domestic kitty I ever saw. It possessed a stubby, black-tipped tail and its pointy ears had tufts of hair sticking up as if it came here from the planet Vulcan. I came a step closer, which caused the cat to move its legs as if to rise, but its efforts were feeble, and soon it stopped and began to pant softly.

I advanced two more steps so that I was now a mere yard away from the creature. Then I saw. Two red slashes raked diagonally from its shoulder, across its ribs, and down to her belly. Her leg was twisted aside so that I had no trouble seeing that the cat creature was a girl.

Wow, another thing we had in common.

As I stood still and studied her, recognition woke inside my brain. Not a kitty cat. She was a Canada lynx.

"What happened?" I cooed softly to her.

The cat lifted her head to stare at me for a second before letting it flop down again onto the mulch from the rotting tree. She seemed near death, but what had done this to her? I thought lynxes were alpha predators. Guess not. The gashes were not recent and didn't appear particularly deep . . . it wasn't as if her guts were hanging out. That said, her fur was crusted with dried blood, and the exposed flesh looked angry and swollen. Probably infected. She was also thin, and from the looks of things, she had lain here for some time.

"Someone really did a number on you," I said. "You thirsty?"

She let me approach with only a flick of her tail, and then she twisted her head to stare at me as I extended an arm toward her with a cap full of water from my bottle. My hands trembled when the rational part of my brain whispered this was a wild animal capable of flaying my hand into shreds of flesh and bone with its claws and teeth. Oddly, though, I wasn't afraid. Somehow, as irrational as it was, I knew she would not attack me, that she wasn't a threat.

The lynx must have been severely dehydrated, because she didn't even hesitate before lapping up the water with her pink tongue. I refilled the cap twice more before she finally seemed sated and refused to drink anymore.

"Hungry?"

No response.

I kneeled on the wet earth and rummaged in my backpack for something I could offer the cat to eat. I doubted she would want peanut butter or flowers, but I had no meat. What I did have was a roll of fishing line and a few hooks I brought along in case it came down to starvation or meat. Retreating to the lake, I tied on a hook, attached a small rock as a weight, and baited the hook with the only thing I had—peanut butter. I had to hurry; in thirty minutes or so, the sun would disappear.

To my complete surprise, only minutes in, I felt a jerk on my line. Damn, I actually caught a fish. It was a dinky thing, maybe seven inches long, but I didn't expect to catch whales when all I could manage was to toss my line out ten feet from shore. Gripping the slimy little critter tightly with both hands, I watched the poor fishie's gills rise and fall, as its pathetic eyes begged me to show it mercy.

Sorry, Charlie. Welcome to the food chain.

The water seemed to have revived the lynx a little, because she rotated her head to watch me as I approached with the wiggly fish. I considered cleaning the fish first, but come on, this was nature. Animals didn't clean their prey before munching on it. The prospect of eating a fish was revolting to me, and maybe she thought so, too, since she wrenched her head back when I brought it close to offer to her. Not wanting to force the issue, I dropped the fish on the ground near her and backed away. She made no attempt to clamp her jaws on the wiggler.

"Well, what are you waiting for?" I asked the cat, who eyed me suspiciously. "What? You want me to sauté it in butter and finish it with a beurre blanc sauce?"

I backed away to leave the lynx in peace. I had my own dinner to worry about, so I combed the shore for greens in the remaining light. I collected leaves from weeds that resembled giant dandelions, red berries, and more white flowers. Lacking a pot to cook them, I washed my plants and ate them raw. I allowed myself a single spoonful of peanut butter. Soon, I curled up once again by the small fire I managed to start and let my thoughts ebb and flow over the lynx.

What was her story? I imagined her to be like me—a teenager . . . in lynx years. She was roaming the wilderness, too, searching for her family maybe. She was lost and alone. I was lost and alone. She was injured. I was injured. We were two ships passing in the night possibly, but for now, we could share a campfire and swap stories before going our separate ways. My romanticized image broke and dissolved. She wasn't lost. She could survive just fine out here, unlike me, and, of course, she didn't speak English and I didn't speak meow.

Maybe my fanciful musings grew out of being alone. Some people didn't need human company. They might go most of their life forming little or no meaningful connections with another person. Not me. As I lay on the edge of the lake staring out at the stars, I realized I couldn't do this alone. As big a threat as hunger and lack of water were, loneliness would kill me first.

Eventually, sleep washed over me. My last conscious thought was to check on the lynx first thing in the morning.

When dawn arrived, I woke to find a moose standing knee-deep in the water about a hundred yards away from me, seemingly oblivious to the dumb human sleeping on the beach. Velvet covered its massive antlers. The beast was huge. He dipped his nose down to slurp at the water. Casually, he twisted his head around to stare at my motionless body lying on the ground. He bobbed his furry chin as if he were nodding to me in greeting before pivoting and lumbering back into the trees. He looked like a big brown doofus with a dorky nose and a misshapen hump on his back, but he also looked regal and majestic.

I never cared a wit about animals, but the thought that people hunted Mr. Moose and his brethren for sport made me ill. Couldn't we leave him alone? Surviving out here was already a real bitch without adding hunters with guns into the mix. Yeah, I knew I was a hypocrite at some level; I had no problem with butchers whacking a cow so I could wear leather. Where was my empathy for them? I didn't know.

With these idiot thoughts banging around in my head like a cue ball ricocheting off the bumpers, I went to check on Mrs. Lynx. She was exactly where I left her, but the fish was gone. I guess she got hungry during the night. Her eyes fluttered open and fixed on me.

"Those are nasty-looking cuts you got there," I said. "I don't suppose you'd let me put a bandage on them."

So now I was going to waste some of my meager first aid supplies on a lynx that was probably going to die anyway?

"What is wrong with you, girl?" I whispered in as soothing a voice as I could.

Maybe I should have left the lynx to its fate and continued my journey south, but my foot was too sore to walk very far anyway, and if I left her, I had a hunch she wouldn't last long enough to see another sunrise. And so I decided to kill a few days here helping Miss Meow and giving my infected blister time to heal. The cat seemed to welcome my presence, but I was probably projecting my own desire to feel needed onto her. Still, she continued to drink the water I offered her, and when I gave her another fish I caught in the afternoon, she didn't hesitate to tear into it.

After the cat had eaten, I inched close to her with my little first aid kit, unsure if she would let me touch her wounds. Surprisingly, she did. She seemed to understand I was trying to help her. So, I went to work on her with a disinfectant ointment, cotton, gauze, and tape. I wasn't sure if human medicine would help at all, but I figured it couldn't hurt.

"Time for me to hit the sack," I told my new friend when I finished dressing her wounds. "I'll try to keep the fire alive through the night, but no promises. Don't worry, if any of those damn wolves come sniffing around, I'll knock 'em upside of the head with this."

I held up a softball-sized rock I found earlier. I envisioned it as my wolf projectile weapon. True, I had a knife, but if a wolf got close enough for me to stab it, the monster probably already ripped my throat out with its teeth.

Purrr.

I nodded with a smile at the lynx's half purr, half growl.

"My sentiments exactly, girl."

As I was turning to leave, I hesitated. I couldn't keep calling her girl. My lynx needed a name.

"Mind if I give you a name?" I asked. She blinked three times, which I took to mean "Sure, Allie, please name me."

"How about Tyche?" I suggested. "She's the Greek goddess of chance, fate, and fortune."

I smirked at the memory of motor mouth Riona mispronouncing the name in class as "tike" instead of "tykee" and eliciting chuckles from around the room.

Tyche's response was to glance away and begin to lick her paws. I'm fairly certain that in cat lingo that gesture meant "thanks, best name ever."

CHAPTER TWENTY-ONE

"Oh my God!" I blurted out in the middle of the night.

Abdominal cramps sent waves of pain lancing through my body, and I instantly curled into a fetal position on the beach beside Lake Jelly Belly. One minute ago, I strolled through pleasant dreams; now, I clenched my teeth in sudden agony. It felt like an enemy was jamming a barbed spear point into my guts over and over again. The agony jerked me out of my sleep in the dark; dawn was still far away.

"Shit!"

As I writhed on the ground, the pain shifted to an overpowering urge to throw up. So, I twisted around to get to my hands and knees, intending to try to stand, but I never made it. My stomach squeezed violently, and I vomited repeatedly. My stomach quickly emptied itself, but the convulsions didn't stop. Dry heave after dry heave wracked my insides until every muscle in my torso felt shredded. When the cramps and nausea finally ebbed somewhat, I lay on the ground panting and gasping for air.

What just happened?

After a few minutes, I crawled the five yards to the water's edge intent on washing my mouth out. Then the convulsions started again, long and agonizing, but I had nothing left inside me to vomit up. Eventually, my body calmed down, probably more from exhaustion than anything else. I brought several handfuls of water to my mouth before crawling back up the beach and collapsing on my back. Despite the continued cramping, I fell back asleep.

When rays from the morning sun hit my face, my eyes blinked open. Every muscular fiber above my waist burned from overexertion. My abs felt ripped and torn, leaving me barely able to stand. I staggered over to a clump of bushes I had designated as my latrine area, intent on taking care of my morning business.

A new surprise greeted me. I had diarrhea. *Bad* diarrhea.

Even with my nonexistent survivor knowledge and woodcraft, I had no problem diagnosing myself. Clearly, I ate something really, really bad, and my stomach and intestines were in full-on rebellion.

My appetite nonexistent, I drank several cups of lake water while pondering what might have poisoned me. I supposed the lake water itself might harbor deadly parasites or bacteria, but it was the only water around, and I had no way to boil it.

Mentally, I ticked off the various plants I ate within the last twenty-four hours. The only items I positively identified as new were the white berries I collected for dinner. They hadn't tasted that great, but they were filling. Okay, never eating spherical white things of any kind again.

I fought diarrhea for the rest of the day and didn't dare eat anything, but I did succeed once again in catching two little fishies. Peanut butter was killer bait.

I brought water to Tyche throughout the day, which she accepted, lapping it up while lying on her side. When I brought her the fish for a mid-afternoon meal, Tyche had risen to a sitting position. She looked funny with the white bandages on the one side, but my veterinary efforts seemed to have paid off. Tyche was back from the dead.

I offered one of the fishes to her. Her jaws lunged forward and snapped shut on the fish, yanking it from my fingers. Reflexively, I jerked my hand back, but this was an overreaction. Had she wanted to take my hand off, she could have easily, but she had purposely snagged the part of the fish outside of my grip. Still, I tossed the other fish at her feet.

I spent two more days on the shores of Lake Jelly Belly, letting my intestines regain their equilibrium and allowing my infected blister to heal. On the third morning, I knew it was time to push on. Armed with water, I paid one last visit to Tyche, intending to say my goodbyes and wish her well. We were two injured creatures whose paths crossed while fighting to stay alive out here, and I felt a bond with her. But when I reached the place of rotting wood where she had spent so many days lying on her side, she was gone.

"Stay safe!" I yelled at the trees beyond. "And don't eat the white berries!"

Before I resumed my journey south, I spent a few minutes studying my map, searching for a new goal to head toward. I wanted a location not too close but not too far either. My index finger traced down until it stopped at another small, unnamed lake to the southeast; this one in the shape of a limp penis. I named it Lake Dick. It was perfect for me. I guessed it to be about eleven miles away, which should take me about three days to reach at my current land tortoise rate of speed.

I walked down the shore until I reached the spot where I had seen the moose. Then I turned and plunged into the forest where the moose had gone. Maybe big guy had busted through the brush and left a path for me. If he did, I never found it, so it was back to slogging through unforgiving underbrush and walking logs where available.

The one piece of good news that first day back on the trail was that my blistered foot seemed fine—no pain, no irritation, no burning.

The one piece of bad news was that I checked my compass at the start to identify south, but I didn't refer to it again for hours. Bad mistake.

My internal sense of direction was completely certain it knew where to head as I clawed my way through the brush. Late in the afternoon, I broke through the jungle of trees and vegetation and stumbled onto a lake. What lake was this? It couldn't be Lake Dick, but I was certain there was no other lake nearby. After twenty minutes glaring at my map, I finally figured out the situation. I had spent the entire day walking in one gigantic circle. I was back at Lake Jelly Belly, maybe a half mile down the shore from where I started that morning.

Damn.

Disheartened and weary, I collapsed on the ground, buried my head in my hands, and started to cry. Everything seemed so pointless and absurd. I was completely beaten and gutted. My polite crying quickly turned to hiccups and sobs. A sudden urge came over me to take off all my clothes and simply walk out into the water and let the waves carry me under. Well, there weren't any waves to speak of, so maybe I'd have to wrap my arms around a big stone to weigh me down. Well, there weren't any conveniently sized rocks for this. And like that, the impulse became too difficult to follow through on, so I let the suicide-by-drowning idea drop. In its place, despair and depression descended on me like a heavy blanket.

For an hour I sat staring out over the water feeling as if I had hit rock bottom. Like an idiot, I thought this was as low as I could go. Moron. There was always another depth to which a person could sink.

"I am not giving up," I said aloud finally.

I got to my feet, pivoted, and headed back into the forest. This time, I held on to my compass, determined to check it every ten minutes in order to stay on target. At this late time of the day, I wouldn't be able to walk long before darkness descended, but if I could just get in a half a mile, it would help redeem a total failure of a day. I plowed on for almost two hours before I paused to lean one arm against a tree.

"A half hour more," I announced to the surrounding trees, "and I'll stop for the night."

The light beneath the trees grew dim as I slogged forward, carefully placing each foot as I advanced over a patch of rock scree. The ground waffled under me as I shifted my weight from one foot to the other, but I maintained my balance by grabbing the limbs of a sapling.

Woof.

The deep rumbling grunt of a large dog from directly behind shattered my concentration just as I shoved off my right foot and stretched forward with my left. Startled by the noise, I wavered, and immediately the rocks under my right foot slid out from under me. I flailed wildly with one arm while my other one clung desperately to the tree branch. I had a long second to savor the realization I was toppling over backward and there was nothing I could do to break my fall. My right leg buckled underneath me and tried to bend at an impossible angle. I felt muscles tearing followed by the ugly sound of a pop. My teeth dug into my lower lip as I landed on my side and half rolled, half slid, down the modest rock ridge I was traversing. I managed a glance back at the source of the noise that started this chain reaction.

It was no dog.

At first, I saw a large black boulder at the crest of the hill I had slid down the face of moments ago. That was puzzling, since it wasn't there minutes ago when I hiked over that ground.

My confusion melted away and reformed as shock when the rock unfolded itself like a Transformers car, growing limbs and rising upward. In two blinks, the dog-slash-boulder became a towering monster with thick, clawed arms attached to a massive torso.

I stared up, mouth agape, at the giant bear Grandfather, Nick, and I had seen that one day on our fishing trip. Either the same bear or its brother. I guessed the former, since I didn't want to think about a world in which there were more than one of these things.

The beast had risen to stand erect on two legs, and it pointed its nose up in the air and began sniffing. The most astonishing and simultaneously frightening aspect of this monster was not its massive bulk, but its height. The crown of his head was easily as tall as the top of a basketball backboard. He made Chewbacca look like a puny little, midget runt in comparison.

For several seconds, the creature and I simply stared at each other. He made no move toward me at first. Having watched my ungraceful, klutzy tumble downhill, perhaps he was as surprised at my collapse as I was.

For a moment, I wondered if this encounter would be benign. Maybe this thing was like BFG. That wistful thought evaporated in an instant when the bear bellowed out a really angry growl that seemed to shake the ground with its ferocity.

Then . . . he charged me.

I screamed, first in utter terror and then in pain.

The bear came at me impossibly fast, covering the rugged ground between us in mere nanoseconds. I tried to get to my feet and run but only managed to crawl on my hands and knees. I might have covered a couple of feet of ground when a huge weight flattened me onto the forest floor on my stomach. My face slammed into a rock, and all my muscles went slack. I could feel consciousness draining out of me, and all sound faded to a dull ringing in both ears.

An instant later, a massive force lifted me off the ground as if I was a ragdoll and shook me back and forth while I hung suspended several feet off the ground.

A snap and rip tore through the air like gunshots, and my body fell back to earth like a dropped sack of groceries. My brain was still functioning enough for me to realize what happened. The bear had picked me up off the ground with his jaws clamped on my backpack and shaken me until the straps broke.

Knowing it was run or die, I scrambled forward in a spastic crawling motion as fast as I could make my limbs move. I felt like I was trying to escape by swimming through a vast sea of mud. I made some progress but couldn't resist glancing back over my shoulder to see what the bear was doing. The beast was standing on two legs with the corner of my pack hanging from its mouth. Then the bear released the backpack and let it slip to the ground. The thing actually locked eyes with me for a moment before dropping back to all fours.

This was it. I was going to die, but I would be alive when it started to eat me.

The bear advanced toward me, but it took only a couple of steps before a streak of gray came flying out of nowhere in the dim light and crashed into the side of the bear's massive head.

It was a huge cat.

It was Tyche.

Her blow caused the bear to stumble sideways, and Tyche immediately followed up her body slam by attacking the bear's face with a blur of slashing claws and snapping jaws.

For a second, I lay frozen on the ground staring dumbfounded at this kamikaze feline trying to save my stupid human life. Then I realized she was buying me time. Time to get out of there. It wouldn't be much, but maybe it would be enough. It had to be. If Tyche was putting her life on the line to give me a shot at escaping, then I was going to make her sacrifice worth it.

I stumbled back to my feet, ignoring the searing pain in my knee, and lurched forward as fast as I could manage. Heedless of direction, I simply followed the path of least resistance, turning this way and that to avoid as much as possible any obstacles that would slow me down. After what seemed like hours, the pain in my knee became unbearable, and when my foot caught on a gnarly root and sent me sprawling, I didn't try to get up. I lay on the forest floor panting like a thirsty dog.

How long had I been running? Where was the bear? Was it still pursuing me?

I had no answers, except that over the next ten minutes or so as I lay like a dead animal on the ground, I didn't hear any noises of pursuit. The forest was eerily quiet. And . . . it was dark. Night had come.

My knee throbbed in pain. My backpack was gone. I had nothing but the clothes and boots I wore, and I began to shiver as the temperature dropped rapidly and my sweat turned clammy and then cold.

But I was alive. I was fucking alive!

I used that last thought as a sword to fight off my pain, slash aside my fear, and beat down my despair. Then I closed my eyes, and sleep instantly overwhelmed me, a sleep I wasn't sure I'd wake up from.

I didn't care. There was nothing I could do.

My body shut down.

CHAPTER TWENTY-TWO

The next day, gray morning light filtered through the trees and hit my eyes, and I blinked rapidly. My brain quickly booted up memories of snapping bear teeth and ripping sounds, and I jerked up into a sitting position. The sudden movement made me wince at the painful stiffness of every single muscle in my body, particularly my knee. Two squirrels in a nearby fir tree chittered noisily at each other like a husband and wife arguing over taking the garbage out.

"Shut up!" I blurted out.

The little tree rats went silent and scurried away.

So, remind me again what happened? Oh yeah. A bear attacked me. No, more than attacked, that thing tried to *kill* me. So very strong. It lifted me off the ground like I weighed next to nothing.

How had I gotten away?

Then I remembered Tyche. She had to be dead. That poor, brave, fierce cat died helping me escape from a big black ball of fangs and claws. I should be dead too. I wasn't worth anybody sacrificing their life for.

My head slowly swiveled about to take in my surroundings. Trees. Trees. Trees.

I hate trees. I didn't before, but I sure did now.

A flicker of movement out of the corner of my eye caught my attention. I twisted around to search for the cause, hoping—no, praying— it wasn't that monstrous bear.

It wasn't.

Tyche sat on her haunches a few yards away from me, watching me and flicking her ears every time I made any movement. Relief flooded into me.

"Hey," I said softly. "Thanks, girlfriend. You okay?"

The cat raised a paw off the ground and began to lick it. She seemed unharmed and obviously was not intimidated by me in the slightest. And why would she be? She just fought off Godzilla's bear child. Who was I for her to be afraid of?

"I'd give you some water, but I lost everything, girl."

The reality of my situation sunk in with those words. My compass had been ripped from my neck. My backpack was gone. So I had no map, no food, no water bottle, no knife, no anything. And the whipped cream on top of this miserable mocha Frappuccino? I had absolutely no idea where I was.

"I'm so screwed," I muttered to Tyche, who stared at me, as if waiting for me to do something. "You might want to take off before my bad karma infects you too."

She didn't respond but began casually grooming herself again. Apparently, she wasn't as concerned about my impending death as I was.

With a grunt of effort and the help of a tree trunk, I managed to stand after inching my way up by putting weight on only one leg. It was time to test my bum knee, but I hesitated for several seconds. I was flat-out scared at what I would find.

When I was eight, I freaked when the dentist showed me the needle he was going to jab into my gum to numb my mouth. As frightening as that was, the prospect of what I would feel when I tested my knee was worse.

"Just do it," I finally said. Tyche glanced up at me and paused her licking to stare at me with her searching, yellow-green eyes.

Okay. No more delay.

So, gritting my teeth, I eased my weight onto my gimpy right leg . . . and almost passed out from the pain shooting up from my knee. The pain receded some as I took a few halting steps, but the realization I would have to walk on this knee for God knew how many days terrified me. Like air escaping a deflating balloon, my body sagged, and I slid down to the ground.

The nearest injury I ever had to compare with this was a bad sprained wrist I received skiing at Lake Placid. I lost an edge and used my arm to break my fall, and my wrist bent the wrong way. Mom whisked me off to Dr. Feldman, our family doctor, who took X-rays and an MRI, wrapped my arm in an elastic bandage, and gave me pain meds that made me wish I could injure myself more often.

My knee was much worse than a sprain. Maybe I screwed up my ACL or tore a meniscus. If I survived and made it back to civilization, I imagined Dr. Feldman grimly telling my mother I would always be a cripple . . . or I needed knee replacement surgery . . . or he had to amputate because of the gangrene.

I shot my fist up at the sky and yelled, "What do you want from me!"

Then I fought to hold back the tears. I should simply be thankful to be alive at this point, but I fixated on what I had lost and how I was utterly screwed. I swiped at my eyes, but dirt and grime covered my hands, which I smeared all over my face. With no mirror, I could only guess at how filthy I was. My mind jumped to the facials I would need to restore my skin, but the fleeting thought quickly dissipated. I was going to die out here. Plain and simple. It was over. Why bother trying? I should give up, lie down, and let the end come.

Then I asked myself, *Why are you so weak?*

I had no answer. I just was. Maybe it was genetic.

Tears threatened. I tried to fight them off but failed.

Yet again, I was degenerating into a blubbering idiot. When the going got tough, the tough got going . . . while Allie sat on her butt and bawled like a baby.

The last time I felt myself losing control like that was when I cried at the reception after my mother's funeral. Mom's death left me numb and speechless for days and days, unable to talk to anyone or to cry. All I wanted was for people to leave me alone, so I withdrew to my bedroom, hid under the blankets, and slept.

"Honey, you have to get up," Dad told me the day of the funeral after gently shaking me awake. "It's time."

A week had passed since the horrific accident, and the morning of my mother's funeral had arrived. I didn't want to go. I wanted to curl up into a ball in total darkness and sleep. In a way, possibly I wanted to die too. Death would be an escape from the searing pain of loss, maybe sort of a way to follow Mom and join her.

"Please," Dad insisted. "I need you to be strong today, Allie."

I nodded silently and climbed out of bed. Maybe five words escaped my lips the entire time from when I came downstairs in my black silk funeral dress until the reception afterward. Dozens and dozens of people I didn't know flooded our house, eating and drinking and talking. I sat in our living room in Mom's favorite wingback chair, ensuring none of those strangers who didn't belong here could use it. My hand held a glass of root beer someone handed me earlier, perhaps thinking it was balm for the soul. I ignored it as a steady stream of people came up to tell me how sorry they were for my loss.

"Thank you," I told each one in a flat, robotic voice.

The conversations during the reception were somber at first, but as the booze flowed, the mood shifted. More laughter and lighthearted banter filled the house as men loosened their ties and joked about how bad the Mets would be this year. All these people invading Mom's home, my home, made me, in turn, angry and sick. Grace stood near me with a plate of food, talking with a couple of our cousins about getting a butt tattoo of all things. Jesus God.

Moments later, Grace strolled over to me and said, "You should get something to eat."

"Why? You're eating enough for both of us."

Grace didn't hear me and prattled on cluelessly. "These sandwiches Patty made are really good."

I stared at the plate she held with one hand, which had a mound of potato salad on it and a small, slider-sized sandwich roll. My eyes focused on the meat, the half raw chunk of beef tenderloin. Blood stained the bread and trickled out to form a tiny puddle. The sight of it tore open the seals holding back all the emotions I had locked away inside since Mom's death.

"Get away from me," I told Grace through clenched teeth. I rose from the chair, wanting to grab a fistful of her hair and punch her.

"What?" she replied, totally shocked.

"Never speak to me again."

Then, I threw my root beer in her face and slapped the plate out of her hand, sending Patty's yummy sandwich of ultra-rare beef tumbling through the air. All conversations came to an instant halt, and heads swiveled as everyone stared at me. It was time to leave, so I ran to the stairs and vaulted up them without a glance back. Moments later, I lay on the floor of my walk-in closet and let the volcano of grief explode. I sobbed uncontrollably for what seemed like hours.

Everyone left me alone.

One thing to come out of that day was that I swore off meat forever.

Meanwhile, when my wilderness crying jag wound down, I scolded myself for losing it.

"I am not weak!" I yelled at the nearest lodgepole pine.

Then I glanced about for Tyche. She hadn't left. She still sat about ten yards away and watched me, maybe with amusement or disgust or simple curiosity. The best part of an hour passed when Tyche rose and padded over to me, where I leaned against a tree with a hand on the ground to maintain my balance. I tensed. Not out of fear, but out of uncertainty. She stopped a foot away and blinked a couple times at me. Then, with the same speed I saw her display with the bear, she raked the claws of one paw across the back of my hand.

"Ow!" I cried out, jerking my hand up to hold against my chest. "Shit, that hurt."

I held my hand up to see the damage. Three two-inch lines of red slashed across my flesh, each oozing a tiny rivulet of blood. Tyche apparently didn't intend the attack to hurt me. If she wanted that, I suspected her razor-sharp claws could have ripped deep enough to sever tendons and major blood vessels. Or worse, she could have easily sliced my neck open before I even had a chance to say, "Get back, honky cat."

Tyche retreated a few feet and resumed sitting.

"What did you do that for?"

She responded by rising to her feet and ambling off into the brush.

"Wait."

She didn't.

Maybe she wanted me to follow her? That seemed completely impossible. However, I probably should put away my self-pity, get back on my feet, and start walking. My mission to head south had failed. With my backpack and compass gone, I couldn't possibly go on. All I could do was return to the cabin, and the journey back meant a long, impossible hike north. Yet, what else could I do?

I rose to follow Tyche.

My pace was earthworm slow; I not only had to navigate around fallen trees and unyielding underbrush but do so on one-and-a-half legs. As for Tyche, every hour or two, I would see a flash of her disappearing into the brush or shooting under a log. I sensed she was showing herself to me purposely to give me a target to aim for or maybe just reminding me she was there.

As I struggled along, I relived the bear attack several times, considering whether I should have done things differently. If I had heard the bear sooner. If I hadn't lost my balance. If I had only brought along an assault rifle and grenade launcher . . . If I had only stayed at the cabin.

The fact was, if I could go back in time and relive the attack, ninety-nine times out of a hundred, I probably ended up dead by bear mauling. I wouldn't call it a miracle I survived the attack, but it was akin to winning the lottery. So why was I so depressed and disconsolate? Probably because I felt like I hadn't escaped death, only delayed it.

The one thing that struck me, though, was the conviction the bear that attacked me was the same monster Grandfather, Nick, and I saw out on the lake. I would also wager it was the same bear that left tracks all around the cabin. And lastly, I would also bet this bear had followed me.

Wonderful.

I had an obsessed animal enemy on my trail. My own personal Lord Voldemort.

But wait. Why did bear behemoth hold off until days into my hike to attack? Why now? Why here?

I had no idea, and this scared me even more.

This I knew. The monster and I would meet again, and the thought made goose bumps ripple across my skin.

CHAPTER TWENTY-THREE

I limp-walked for three days, using the morning sun to gauge where north was. If I faced the sun, then I should turn left to go north. Or, was it right? Or, should I hop up and down twice, pirouette thrice, and then go whatever direction my left eyebrow was facing?

Oh, shut up and just walk in a straight line in some direction, I told myself.

My knee improved, but at the end of each day, it was stiff and throbbed with pain. By the third afternoon, my stomach had a dull ache from hunger, even though I constantly ate flowers, greens, and berries as I hiked. Worse than the hunger by far, though, was the thirst. As the afternoon aged, all my mind could think about was a cool energy drink . . . an iced lemonade . . . a wild cherry Slurpee. I hadn't drunk any water since the day before, so my throat was parched and sticky, as if I swallowed pine sap.

As for Tyche, she'd gone MIA the last couple of days, so I guessed she finally got tired of the stumbling, feeb girl and went off on her merry way. I couldn't blame her.

With a defeated sigh, I lowered my butt onto the ground and took in several deep breaths. Bugs buzzed around my head and, as always, got in my hair and ears. Waving my hand to shoo them away was a futile gesture, but I did it anyway. Besides, bugs were not my biggest distraction. My body sweated away gallons of fluids as I hiked, but my water bottles were gone. Probably the bear had claimed them as his new chew toys. With nothing to drink but my own spit, not only was my throat a desert, but my lips were so scabbed and cracked I had no time to worry about bugs.

"Please, universe. I need water."

To my utter surprise, my pathetic plea drew an immediate response from Mother Nature. Within minutes, it began to rain. At first, the drops were sporadic and light, but the rain quickly became torrential. The downpour drove away all the black flies and mosquitoes, washed the sweat off me, and did a fair job of sluicing the grime out of my clothes. Even though I was soaked to the skin, the water was so refreshing I didn't want the rain to stop.

Sadly, the rain did little at first to slake my thirst. Trying to drink the rain as it came down was like eating rice one grain at a time with a toothpick. A lot of work for little gain.

I didn't need to worry. Soon after I got to my feet and continued my journey, I came across a small depression in the land where the rain had collected in a puddle some five feet across and a few inches deep. Without hesitation, I flung myself onto my stomach, plunged my face into the cool water, and gulped furiously. Never mind the leaves, sticks, and other unidentifiable stuff floating in it. I didn't bat an eyelash. I was drinking out of a large mud puddle, and I utterly didn't care. The water tasted wonderful. A tiny voice in the back of my brain reminded me this puddle was likely filled with malicious microbes, but better sick and hydrated than desiccated and dead . . . or something like that.

I lifted my head after downing at least a gallon and noticed Tyche on her stomach like me lapping at the water on the other side of the puddle. I grinned at her. She flicked her ears at me in answer before she rose to leave. I interpreted it as her way of telling me, "Get on your feet, you big baby. It's time to move out."

The next two days passed in a blur of walking, resting, eating berries and plants, and sleeping in hollowed-out areas under fallen trees. I no longer had any clear idea of what direction my legs took me. Each morning began with the sun to my right and me heading north, but inevitably, I got turned around during the day, and Big Bird only knew what direction I ended up going by the end of the day.

Usually, I spotted Tyche a couple times a day, but she kept her distance. Surely, she had something better to do than haunt my steps, but I was too busy keeping alive to think much about it. The forest held an abundance of food, but it didn't matter how many leaves or berries I ate, the hunger inside grew stronger every hour and seized my full attention every second I was awake.

I fantasized about Ellie's, a takeout place near Exeter, and their almond milk, banana-chocolate milkshakes with a dollop of whipped cream and crumbled vanilla wafers on top. I also hallucinated about salty french fries and onion rings, but I had to be careful. If I savored the dream too much, my stomach went into a food hysteria.

I reached the end of my rope in a small grove of aspens interlaced with large rocks. Maybe I was hiking, if you use the word very broadly, but in reality I was merely stumbling along like a zombie from the old school . . . the ones who can't run or move fast. When I stopped to lean against a white-barked tree, a wave of vertigo washed over me. I shrugged it off and tried to keep going, but no mas. More dizziness came over me, my nose began to run, and I felt a distinct tickle in the back of my throat.

On top of the hunger and the thirst, I now had a freaking cold . . . the start of a bad one. My sinuses rapidly became stuffed up, and I started to cough. After a restless night curled up in a ball on a bed of dried leaves, I woke the next morning with a fever

My body went into a fetal position, and a sheen of sweat coated my skin. Touching the inside of my wrist to my forehead confirmed the obvious—I was burning up. I drifted in and out of consciousness for I don't know how long. Sometimes it was dark as black ink around me, and other times the rays of the sun heated my face. Each time I woke, I craved water and my belly cried out for food, but there was none of either, and I couldn't move to search for any.

At one point, my eyes fluttered open, and I found clumps of half chewed leaves in my mouth. Apparently, in a stupor, I tried to eat a nearby bush. I spat the bitter-tasting stuff out and promptly threw up. The fever still hadn't broken; I was being burned alive from the inside. My only escape was to descend back into the oblivion of sleep and what pathetic escape my murky dreams offered.

The next time I regained consciousness for more than a few minutes, my fevered brain struggled to identify the lump of flesh lying on the grass inches from my face. From the fur on it, my best guess was that I was staring at the haunch of a snowshoe hare. My stomach threatened to turn itself inside out again, but instead I sank back into sleep. Sleep was about the only thing I was capable of.

In my dreams, I became a monster like the bear that attacked me. At first, I was a vampire. Then I became a crazed bigfoot creature who squatted over a recent kill, an animal I couldn't identify. I picked up the raw flesh with my hairy fingers and brought it up to my mouth. After pushing aside the soft fur, I bit down on red muscle, my teeth ripping off chunks of raw meat. I swallowed bite after bite with only a minimal amount of chewing until my stomach cried out it had had enough for now. I howled at the moon and then woke.

My fever had broken.

Then my eyes narrowed at a disturbing sight. Only bones and bits of fur remained of the rabbit leg, and I felt full in a way I hadn't since my last night at the cabin. This was slightly disturbing. Understanding dawned on me about what I had done in my fever delirium.

I had eaten a bunny leg sushi style.

Oddly, I felt no urge to throw up. My body wanted the protein and was not going to give it up without a fight. I sat up, telling myself what was done was done. If God was a vegan, surely, he'd forgive me my sin given all that had happened to me.

Rising to a sitting position, I took several deep breaths and assessed my body. I knew immediately that my cold had eased because, for the first time since I began this suicide march, I craved a toothbrush and toothpaste. The inside of my mouth tasted rank, and they didn't make breath mints nearly strong enough to mask the stink radiating out of me when I breathed. In lieu of the above, I'd take a creek to push my face into and drink until I filled my hump.

I spent three more days in that aspen stand, drinking what I could find in hollowed-out areas at the foot of trees or logs. Also, in desperation, I licked the dew off leaves each morning. I didn't have much choice. I needed to heal completely before I could walk for any meaningful period.

On the morning of the third and last day, I found a fat squirrel lying on the grass where the rabbit leg had appeared earlier. Another present from Tyche although I hadn't actually seen her in days. I reached for it. This dead animal was food, and I needed food.

Worming my finger into a hole in the hide where Tyche's teeth had bitten, I widened it until I was able to grab a handful of fur and strip the skin off. I had no knife, so I used a shard of rock to gouge open the stomach and let the guts slide out. I would have liked it if all the intestines and gooey slimy stuff just fell out onto the ground, but they hung there dangling. So, I had to reach a few fingers into the body cavity, grab the innards that felt like wet spaghetti noodles, and yank the mess out.

Then, I lifted the carcass to my mouth and began to rip off chunks of raw meat with my teeth. I picked the squirrel clean, leaving only fur and bones, which I tossed into the bushes. When I rose to my feet, the last bits of the meal squirmed down my esophagus, and I burped. A drink of water to wash the food down would be nice, so I shuffled off heading north to find a puddle, stream, whatever.

Who was I? *What* was I? Wherever the line was between human and animal, I crossed it. Every second of my waking existence focused on staying alive; finding something, anything, to eat; and living completely in the moment. Didn't that make me an animal? Getting back to the cabin remained the goal, but it shifted to a vague, abstract goal, a goal subordinate to finding a place to sleep each night. Most telling . . . I ate raw meat from that squirrel and liked it. Or was I confusing need with like?

One good thing about getting sick was the downtime helped my knee recover. My limp was gone. I wasn't ready to do deep knee bends or run sprints, but I could hike just fine. My spirits rose around noon when I broke through the underbrush and beheld a stream that was almost a small river.

"Thank you, gods above," I said, as I rushed down to the water's edge.

Easing my body down to the ground and stretching out on my belly, I lowered my face into the cool, lazy flowing water and drank. After a couple minutes of frantic guzzling, I had to stop or get ill. Surviving out here meant feast or famine. One minute, you gorged yourself, and then you went without for days.

Feeling revived, I decided to explore the stream and find a place to bed down for the night. Within minutes, I spotted a recently downed tree upstream that had dammed the water, resulting in a modest little waterfall flowing over the bark. That must mean a small pool had backed up behind the log. If so, maybe I could take a bath. The prospect of immersing my body in water and escaping the ever-present swarm of bugs, if only for a few minutes, seduced me. I clamored over a series of boulders until I found what I hoped for: a nice, deep pool of still water.

I stripped out of my clothes, tossed them on the stream bank, and waded tentatively into the water, sucking in a breath through clenched teeth as the icy-cold water sloshed against my skin. My feet shuffled forward, and gradually more and more of my body disappeared below the calm surface. When I reached the deepest part of the pool, I was disappointed that the water only came up to my first rib. So, I crouched down, allowing the gentle waves to slosh around my neck. I had no soap, shampoo, washcloth, or brush. Instead, I scooped up handfuls of sandy gravel off the streambed and scrubbed my skin with it. This mostly worked. The grime came off, and the abrasive material left my body pink and tingly.

There was nothing to do about my hair; if I had a knife, I would have hacked it off. By this time, it had become tangled, matted, and greasy. My once smooth legs and armpits were as hairy as a sasquatch.

After I washed myself, my eyes fluttered shut, my arms swung lazily back and forth under water, and I allowed myself to enjoy the rays of the sun on my face. My body adjusted to the water temperature quickly, and my impromptu bath became a tiny slice of Elysium . . . for about five minutes.

A slick object brushed against my leg.

"Shit, what was that!" I cried out.

A dark shape, visible in the clear water, glided away from me, apparently as startled by me as I was by it.

A fish.

But what a fish.

The little beastie had to be at least a couple feet long. And it wasn't the only uninvited guest at my pool party. A school of a dozen fish congregated near one end of the pond, hugging the underside of the bank where the water had eroded a small pocket.

The glare from the sun reflected off the surface, but if I shielded my eyes just so, I could peer deep down into the depths of the pool. The fishies were big suckers, but they were big suckers in a small bathtub. The pool I stood in the middle of was shaped like an ellipse that was as long and wide as the lines of a tennis court, and the end opposite the log dam was narrow and shallow. The water at that end rippled for several yards over a bed of rocks that poked up above the surface. The poor fishes were trapped in this pool quite literally between a rock and a hard place.

Could you say dinner?

I walked toward the fish, slapping the surface of the water with my hands and arms. The commotion worked. The fish panicked and rushed for the narrow end of the pool where the stony, shallow water barred their escape. I slogged after them. Most of the fish swam past me in a panic as I drew close, but one big guy was so scared he tried to leap over the rocks blocking its path. Bad move. The lunker landed on the rocks flapping frantically but in vain. I grabbed the Incredible Mr. Limpet by the tail with both hands and tossed him high into the air where he arced up and landed on the bank in a thicket of weeds. Then I scrambled up after him with probably the same leering expression the bear had for me, not even noticing I had no clothes on.

I bashed the fish's head on a rock several times until he stopped moving.

Next . . . I ate it.

I didn't bother to clean it; I simply tore into it with my front teeth, careful to avoid the guts. As I ate, blood trails snaked their way down my chin and over and between my breasts. Plus, I had scales and fish mucous on my chin. So, when I finished, I jumped back into the pond and scrubbed the goo and gore off.

As if any doubt existed, I was officially a meat eater.

I had become a predator.

CHAPTER TWENTY-FOUR

The next few days passed in a blur as I roamed the forest mostly heading north. The fact was, I had covered enough ground to walk back to the cabin six times over. For all I knew, I had passed right by Lake Makwa and now headed for Hudson Bay. Not a comforting thought. At least, water now abounded. I encountered small ponds and streams several times a day, so I had plenty to drink. The air became mighty cool at night, and I had no ability to make a fire, but I was never in danger of hypothermia. Thank God it was summer up here, and a warm summer at that.

Food was another matter. Without any weapons but my bare hands, hunting wasn't an option. Catching fish sucked without a hook and line. I tried my trick of searching out fish trapped in small pools, but that worked only one other time. So, I became an herbivore who eats shoots and leaves.

As for Tyche, on a few occasions, I caught sight of a blur of movement, but I had no confirmed sightings of her. I remembered bobcats and the like were night hunters, so that probably explained why I never saw her during the day.

My inability to get meat frustrated me. My body craved it now. Yet, I couldn't do anything about it. That changed late in the afternoon when I came upon a tiny brook only a few inches across. No fish in this ribbon of water, but it bubbled in and out of enough clean puddles that I enjoyed drinking my fill. Only as I rose to continue my eternal march did I see the prints embedded in moist soil. The claw indentations were a dead giveaway that a really big bear passed this way . . . maybe this morning or late yesterday.

In all the days of walking since my attack, I thought I had put miles and miles between me and my stalker bear. The tracks said otherwise. Even now, he could lie in ambush in the next tangle of underbrush.

The gigantic paw prints might belong to a different prehistoric bear, true enough, but a visceral reaction inside me said that this was the same bear I had encountered before. Panic tried to seize my mind. This damn bear was never going to leave me alone until it ate me.

I needed a weapon.

I resumed walking, but slower and quieter, pausing frequently to listen for the sounds of a great lumbering beast. I heard none. I also used the time to think about weapons. Unless I stumbled upon an abandoned military arsenal with bazookas and machine guns, I could count on little help beyond sticks and stones. Not too promising.

"What about cavemen?" I burst out at one point before quickly slapping a hand over my mouth.

Great, Allie, I thought. *You just alerted the entire ecosystem for a mile around that a human stalked the woods.*

I stopped walking to think about this revelation. Cavemen. They had nothing but sticks and stones, yet they were able to take down wooly mammoths, right? Of course, they had a whole tribe to help, but still they had to have weapons. The bow and arrow was out. Too complicated for me to construct.

What about a spear?

Yeah, a spear.

I could do that.

It took some searching, but eventually, I found a straight branch, an inch-and-a-half around and about six feet long. Two branches actually. Why make just one when I could have a spare as well?

The next step took longer. I hunted for an edged rock I could use to shape and sharpen my spears. Eventually, I found what I wanted at the foot of a granite outcropping. Pieces of the rocks had flaked off and some were quite sharp. With the branches positioned on my lap, I spent the rest of the day whacking and smacking until I managed a decent taper. A sharp point was the key. I had the arm strength of an al dente linguine noodle, so if I threw or jabbed with the spear, the key to penetration was a needle-sharp point. I now had that.

I finished the job by using the rock to remove the remaining bark and smooth the shafts. By the time I crawled into the hollow spot beneath a log to sleep, I had two fine spears to hunt and defend myself with.

Back in the civilized world, I frequently had trouble sleeping or staying asleep, so much so that I took OTC sleep meds, and on those occasions when I returned home from school, I was guilty of swiping Brooke's Lunesta pills every so often. Didn't need them out here. By the time I curled up to rest each night, exhaustion overwhelmed me. So, I fell asleep fast and stayed asleep. Frequently, it rained during the night, but I shrugged it off, rolled over to my other side, and went on sleeping.

So, tonight was a surprise. My eyes sprang open not long after I had dropped off, hardly able to see amid the pitch blackness surrounding me.

I rose onto one elbow, wondering what had woken me. A sudden scratch on my bare forearm answered the question. Tyche sat on her haunches mere inches away from me. Her eyes were luminous in the starlight. I sensed something was very wrong, so I bit back the impulse to cry out at the pain from her claws. She hadn't really hurt me. Like before, she wanted my attention.

"What is it?" I whispered.

She raked my skin again. I think she was saying, "Shut the hell up."

I did.

I lay back down, clutching the rotting leaves and dirt that served as my mattress tonight. My breathing shallowed, and my ears went on high alert. Moments later, I heard the clatter of snapping limbs and rattling bushes. Whatever was out there, it didn't care about making noise. As for me, I ceased my loudmouth breathing and went completely still, taking care not to even twitch a single muscle.

A very large animal passed in front of Tyche and me, not more than fifteen yards from our hiding place. The beast didn't slow up, and I couldn't see more than a dark outline stomping by, but its guttural coughs and huffs left no doubt what it was. A bear. No, *the* bear. The bear that supposedly went extinct back before humans ever came to this land, but for some reason still survived here.

I continued to lie unmoving on the ground for at least an hour; Tyche sauntered off immediately after the bear disappeared. Not one to fear bears, she.

One puzzling thought I had while I lay kissing dirt was Mr. Bear's nose. Maybe he couldn't see me, but couldn't he smell me? As close as he came to my hiding spot, wouldn't my human stink light up his olfactory mechanism? Maybe I was so covered with grime and surrounded by rotting wood I smelled like part of the forest? Another mystery of the animal kingdom.

With the bear long gone, I rose from my bed, brushed myself off, grabbed my spears, and crept as quietly as possible in the opposite direction that the bear went. If he was going one way, I was going the other. The sooner I began putting distance between him and me, the better, even if it meant stumbling around in the dark. Luckily, I always slept with my boots on.

I took eight quiet, cautious steps when a deep-throated growl erupted behind me. No, call it a roar. Two nanoseconds passed before realization hit me—the damn bear had been waiting for me to come out of hiding.

That fucker!

I took off.

My legs scrambled pretty fast even in the dark, leaping over logs, shimmying under them, and crashing through bushes that whipped at my body. I couldn't outrun a bear on open ground. I knew that. But this wasn't open ground. My hope was that he just wasn't that into me tonight; I was too much trouble, so let the poor human female go. For this to work, though, I had to keep moving as fast as I could. The main problem confronting me? The night. The blackness made it challenging to move quickly without stumbling over a root or tripping on a rock.

I entered a small clearing, and the starry sky above came into full, unobstructed view. My feet picked up speed as I raced across the tiny meadow, not daring to waste a millisecond glancing over my shoulder. When I plunged into the forest again, my sight went totally black moments before the ground disappeared beneath my feet. Apparently, a sizable depression had opened up in front of me and I ran straight out into space.

"Shit!"

A sickening sensation of falling twisted my stomach as my arms windmilled helplessly. I braced for impact, which came an instant later when my feet smashed onto the ground, sending me cartwheeling forward. My forward momentum ended abruptly when my torso slammed into a tree trunk, and every bone in my body shivered from the collision. I lay in a heap, stunned, but only for the seconds needed to catch my breath and confirm I wasn't paralyzed from the neck down.

Muscles and joints ached like hell, but I shoved aside the pain and listened to the forest around me. At first, my ears picked up nothing but silence, but then I heard heavy paws sliding on rock scree as colossus bear descended into the bowl I had fallen into. Running was no longer an option. Miraculously, I still clutched my spears, but even with them, I was hardly capable of fighting back.

The bear approached me on all fours at a seemingly leisurely pace, as if he knew the chase had ended. I read somewhere that one option for dealing with an angry bear was to stand your ground, make a lot of noise, and throw rocks or sticks at it. Yeah, right. But . . . what else could I do? So, I stood, waved my arms, and yelled curse words at the beast. He stopped and stared at me, his nose sniffing the air. Then he stood up on two legs about five yards away and bellowed at me. Well, maybe I bought myself an additional ten seconds of life with my idiot actions.

From the left side of the bear, a blurry ball of angry fur flew and crashed into the bear's leg. The monster roared in anger and swiped one of its big mitts at the attacking creature but missed. It was Tyche again. She was helping me once more, just like before. This time, though, she went for the bear's legs and flanks instead of the head. What is with this cat?

Don't ask questions. Take what she's giving you.

Tyche's slashing claws and nipping teeth did no real damage to the bear, but she annoyed the hell out of him. He couldn't pull his attention away from her. That was what she wanted.

What followed was a chaotic squall of bear bellows and cat attack screams. After slashing viciously at the bear's gluteus maximus, Tyche leaped out of range to avoid the swinging bear paws. I knew from before what she was doing. Tyche was buying me time to get away. As I pivoted to run, tuning out the cuts and general trauma from my pell-mell leap into this crater, I saw Tyche fling herself at the bear for another assault.

I froze in my tracks. I couldn't run away and leave Tyche to fight my battles alone and probably die doing it.

"No!" I yelled with all the fury I could muster.

Neither the bear nor Tyche paid any attention to me. Instead, that crafty, evil bear anticipated Tyche's follow-up onslaught perfectly. His paw slammed into Tyche's ribs as she soared at him, and the blow sent her flying, the way a baseball player blasts a homerun ball out of the park.

"Tyche!" I screamed.

Still standing on two feet, the massive black bear roared a challenge at me.

"Eat this, fuzzball!"

I ran at the bear with my hands tightly grasping one of my spears, the other one left behind on the ground. The bear seemed momentarily puzzled by my sudden offensive move. This was all the time I needed to plunge my weapon into its unprotected gut. The spear point was as sharp as a needle, and it sank into the monster's flesh almost effortlessly. I released my grip and backed away to stay out of range of his raking claws. The bear dropped down to all fours, shaking its head furiously. I heard the spear snap like a twig.

I turned and ran. Well, more like floundered, lurched, and careened. Yet, I covered ground and moved about as quick as any human could out there.

Climb a tree! one part of my brain shouted.

Seriously? What tree? another part of my brain hollered back.

All I saw as I stumbled forward in the dark were shadows of skinny pines, and none of them had ladders helpfully propped up against them. Instead, I made my feet keep pumping up and down with my arms up in front of me to shield my face from the slap of branches. Gradually, my mental state ratcheted down from panicked rabbit mode, and I tried to concentrate on what to do. Eventually, a plan formed in my mind as I kept moving: I wouldn't stop until I reached safety or the bear stopped chasing me. Yes, thank you, brain, for a dose of the obvious.

Next, once I lost the bear, I would circle back for Tyche. Unless she was hurt bad, she'd hole up nearby. If she *was* hurt bad, the bear might well make a meal of her. Unwelcome tears flooded my eyes and overflowed down my cheeks as I ran. Then I paused, hands on knees, to gulp air into my heaving lungs.

"Stop it," I said out loud to myself. "Focus, Allie. Escape if you can; fight if you must."

The sounds of a large animal crashing through the brush a couple hundred yards behind me snapped my attention back on the moment. The damn bear wasn't giving up; it was still chasing me. The tiny sliver of good news, though, was that it didn't sound like it was running. My spear must have wounded it badly enough to slow it down.

I'd heard all I needed to. I hurried away from the noise, plunging farther into the darkness beneath the trees.

Gradually, over the next hour, the sounds of pursuit petered out. I slowed my pace, allowing my racing heart to calm and the adrenalin in my system to drain away. No way was I relaxing, but my body couldn't stay at DEFCON 1 any longer.

As I gulped air and my pulse slowed, I came to one fundamental conclusion. This bear was never going to leave me alone. I hurt him. His dander was up, and he was spoiling for a fight to the death. We had another showdown coming all right, but not tonight. I had to lose him and then go back for Tyche.

I resumed walking but did so as quietly as possible.

Hours passed without me even noticing when dawn's first orange glow appeared on the horizon. My thighs burned from the night's exertion. I had little gas left in the tank. My body screamed for me to stop and lay down, but I numbed my brain to the pain and kept moving forward. Full daylight remained a ways off when I finally did come to a stop.

I didn't want to pause, but I had no choice. I couldn't walk any farther. My feet had brought me to the edge of a lake, but in the dim light, my eyes couldn't see much more than fifty feet out into the watery murk.

"Where am I?"

Birds chirped in response, and a squirrel chittered angrily at me from a nearby tree. I ignored them. Then all the little creatures around me shut up the way they did when something scared them. I whirled about.

A booming roar exploded from the brush not fifty feet behind me. My enemy emerged from the blackness of the trees as the first rays of the sun shot outward over the horizon. The bear rose on two feet once again. Now that I could see him up close in daylight, I guessed he had to weigh a couple tons at least, if not more.

Not only was this guy sumo wrestler fat, but he was smart. I thought I lost him, but he was simply letting his prey exhaust itself before moving in for the kill. How he got so close without me hearing him, I had no idea.

This time, I had no weapon. I had lost my second spear, and the lakeshore all around me was sand and turf. No rocks bigger than a pebble. As soon as the bear dropped to all fours, I raced out into the lake until the water lapped at my thighs. Then, I prepared to dive under the surface, but the instant I raised my arms over my head, hot pain shot through my body. Sharp razors slashed across my right shoulder blade just as my body plunged forward under the water. When I surfaced ten yards farther out, my arms and legs went into action, and I swam freestyle as fast as I could make my limbs move. I wasn't sure if the bear might be swimming after me, so I was determined to keep going until either the bear caught me or I passed out from sheer exhaustion and blood loss.

Turned out, there was a third option.

Land.

My hands scraped the sandy bottom of the lake, and I realized I had swum all the way across to the opposite shore. No accounting for what the female body would do when loaded up with panic and adrenaline.

My legs gave out as I attempted to stagger out of the water onto shore, and I fell onto all fours gasping for oxygen. The sun had climbed enough above the trees to force me to shield my eyes. Dawn had officially arrived.

Unable to go on, I rolled over onto my back and stared up at the sky overhead. My head spun with dizziness. My shoulder burned. I felt consciousness begin to slide out of me.

"Allie?"

I blinked at the sound of my name.

"Holy shit, is that you, Allie?"

A curtain of blackness descended as I plummeted into the deepest depths of hell.

PART III

"You had the power all along my dear"
  —Glinda, The Good Witch of the North

CHAPTER TWENTY-FIVE

My eyes fluttered open long enough to see the familiar log beams of the cabin's ceiling before falling shut again. My brain processed the fact I was lying on a soft bed rather than the forest floor I had become accustomed to. Before anything else registered, I drifted back into sleep for how long I didn't know.

Later, words floated into my mind.

"Why won't she wake up?"

I recognized this voice. It was Nick. But, as hard as I tried, my eyes simply wouldn't open. Instead, moments later, everything faded to blackness again. The next time consciousness returned, a hand gripped my wrist and tugged on my arm. Metal dug into my skin, and my eyes opened and stayed open. I still had my watch wrapped around my wrist. Someone's grip squeezed the watch band into my flesh.

"You're hurting her," Grace said.

"We have to change her bandages," Grandfather replied. "Help me turn her."

"She's awake!" Nick said with a gasp.

A face appeared about two inches in front of mine. I wanted to jerk away from it, but my entire body felt paralyzed. I blinked several times, and Grace's delicate scoop nose came into focus. Her gray eyes stared into mine.

"Allie," Grace whispered. "Stay with us. You're going to be fine."

"Water," I croaked in a raspy, barely audible voice.

"Nick," Grace said, not taking her face away, "give me the glass."

Moments later, the cool rim of a glass tumbler pressed against my lower lip, and a trickle of water flowed into my mouth. My tongue was swollen, and the rest of my mouth and throat were dry and raw. The water soothed my parched skin, but the flow stopped suddenly.

"More," I said.

"Not too fast, Grace," Grandfather said from somewhere behind me. "She'll get sick."

I wanted to object, but all I could manage was several painful swallows. For the next several minutes, Grace dribbled water into my mouth, and gradually, I felt my body revive like wilted lettuce after a summer rain. My brain, however, remained fuzzy and confused.

"What happened?" I managed to say in a husky voice.

"You almost died is what happened," Nick answered from somewhere nearby.

"She didn't almost die," Grace said. "The wounds weren't that deep."

"We found you," Grandfather chimed in. "You've been out for three days. How did you get all those cuts on your back?"

"Fight," I answered. "A fight."

Nick's face came into view over Grace's shoulder. "A fight? With who?"

"Bear."

"Jesus," Grace murmured.

My vocal cords felt almost normal, so I added, "I gave as good as I got."

"I'll bet you did," Grace replied. She grinned down at me. "No one messes with my sister without getting their ass kicked."

"I've got to go," I whispered to Grace.

She helped me sit up in the bed, which was when I realized I was in her room. The guys cleared out while Grace helped me to stand.

Surprise, surprise. I was wearing an undershirt ten sizes too big for me and my bikini bathing suit bottom. There was a story here, but I was too preoccupied with my bladder to ask about it. When I exited the bathroom minutes later, Grace wanted to help me back to bed, but I insisted on sitting at the table in the kitchen. My body had had enough of lying down for this side of a lifetime.

"Are you hungry?" Grace asked as I eased myself down onto a wooden chair.

"Starved."

"We don't have much except the fish Nick catches. We're out of everything at this point."

"Fish is fine," I said.

"Eating fish without complaining? What happened to my sister, and why have you taken over her body?" Grace deadpanned.

I gave her a half-hearted shrug, too stiff and sore to do more. "Let me see what you got."

With a long drawn-out sigh, she retrieved a large ceramic bowl from the refrigerator filled with walleye portions cut into chunks and set it down on the table. Her eyebrows arched upward in total surprise when I casually reached in, grabbed a couple one-inch cubes, and plopped them into my mouth. Mostly fresh, the fish had a silky, soft texture with a mild flavor. Passable. I grabbed a few more and chewed mechanically as if simply going through the motions. I was. I didn't care about taste at all or the pleasure of eating. I needed fuel—fuel to heal, fuel to jump-start my muscles, fuel to rejoin the human race.

"Raw fish?" Grace said with an arched eyebrow. "Uh, disgusting much?"

"I've eaten worse," I replied. I wouldn't tell her about the time a few nights back when I was reduced to eating a toad.

I studied Grace as I ate a couple more chunks of fish. She stood by the sink, hands on hips, wearing baggy gray sweatpants and a loose-fitting pink blouse. I paused my chewing to stare at her belly. She sensed what I wanted to know.

"Nick," Grace said, "fetch the first aid kit. We need to change Allie's bandages."

Once Nick departed, her face relaxed into a smile. "I'm not pregnant."

I smiled back. "You had your—"

"Yes," she cut me off. "I had my period. My very, very *late* period. So, false alarm."

Good. Because we would never make it out of this place if Grace was pregnant. Relief flooded into me but nothing close to the relief Grace must have experienced.

"I guess you dodged a bullet," I said.

"I was pretty scared," she admitted. "I never felt so alone in my life."

"Not alone," I said quietly. "I would have helped."

She chuckled at this for some reason. "And give up your summer at all those exotic places you always visit? I don't think so."

"Maybe not before, but I would now."

When Nick returned with the red bag, Grace snatched it from his hands and shooed him off again. Then she helped me out of my shirt before bending over to probe my wounds with her fingers tipped with nails polished in green. I winced when she squeezed my skin and sucked in a quick breath through my clenched teeth.

"How's it look?" I asked.

"Infected," Grace said. "A lot of pus is draining out."

"Yummy."

She swabbed a rank-smelling disinfectant on my lacerations and applied new bandages. Grandfather reappeared and helped hold new gauze squares in place while Grace taped them down.

"What happened to you out there?" Grandfather asked.

"Everything," I answered, then added the one word that summed it all up. "Lost. What about you guys?"

Grace shook her head. "Nothing. No plane. No bears. No moose. Just the three of us . . . and lots and lots of fish."

"How are you feeling, old man?" I asked Grandfather.

He exhaled slowly before answering. "I have my good days . . . and some *not* so good days."

"Your hair is a giant clump of dirt," Nick observed. "You look like one of the walking dead."

"Yeah, I don't know how we're ever going to fix it," Grace added.

"Don't," I said. "Help me cut it off."

"If you want to get rid of the entire mess," Grace said in a rising voice, "we'll have to take it all off. You'll be as bald as a bowling ball."

"It's the least of my concerns," I replied. "It's my punishment for sleeping rough for a couple weeks."

"A couple weeks?" Nick repeated.

"Sorry?" Grace said, sounding a little incredulous at my remark.

"Honey," Grandfather cut in, wiping his hands on a dish towel, "you've been gone for a month and a half."

CHAPTER TWENTY-SIX

Eight days have passed since I washed up on the shores of Lake Makwa. My shoulder mostly healed, but Grace said I would wear the scars from the parallel slashes to my grave. Before I came to this place, the prospect of ugly scars on my back would have mortified me enough to never wear a bathing suit or strapless top. I would have gone to great lengths to hide my torn skin. Now, I really didn't care. This was me. Take it or leave it.

That night, as we gathered at the table with a Coleman lantern set in the middle, we ate our fish in silence. I wasn't sure how long a person could live eating only fish morning, noon, and night, but the answer didn't really matter. Fish was all we had. I still foraged plants, but nobody else but me was interested in eating them.

"We have to get out of here," I announced to the group. "No one is ever going to come for us. It's been almost three months since they abandoned us here. If someone was coming back, they would have showed up by now."

"I don't disagree," Grandfather said. "But from what you've told us, hiking out doesn't seem feasible. It almost killed you."

Gazing at my grandfather's face, I saw he was afraid. Grace was too. Leaving the safety of the cabin and launching out into the great unknown scared them. I got that. But cringing inside this building meant giving up and waiting for certain death. I didn't get that.

"Aren't you frightened at the idea of going back out there?" Grace asked.

"No. Not all. I've already been there and survived. Trust me, we can do this."

"Yeah, well we're not all as strong as you," Grace objected.

I spent a lot of time since I came back thinking about this point. Whatever doubts I had about Grace's and Nick's stamina, clearly, my grandfather was in no shape to endure the grueling daily regimen we'd have to follow for weeks and weeks. Food would be scarce. Shelter nonexistent for the most part. Grandfather would never make it.

We weren't leaving him behind.

But Grace was right. Hiking was out.

What then?

I had an answer to this question.

"We leave by boat," I said.

"Boat?" Nick repeated, turning it into a question.

"The province is dotted with thousands of lakes and rivers," I explained. "They're all interconnected."

"Are you serious?" Grace asked.

"We boat from one end of a lake to the other," I went on, "and then we find a river that leads us to another lake. Rinse, repeat."

"But these rivers," Grandfather said before pausing for a second, "they'll have rapids—"

"Waterfalls, shallows, and other impassable spots," I interrupted. "I know. That's where we'll have to get out and hike. We'll portage around the obstacles, but most of the time, we sit in a boat."

Grandfather scrubbed at his chin in thought. "I don't know, Allie. The boats aren't exactly lightweight."

"One boat," I corrected. "And no motor. Just oars."

"We have to row?" Nick said. He sounded like I asked him to chop off a finger.

"That's right," I confirmed. "Motors need gas, and they weigh a ton."

Silence descended over the room. No one met my eyes. Then Grandfather spoke.

"Not to rain on anyone's parade, but what you're suggesting sounds like a mighty dangerous undertaking."

"It's *outrageously* dangerous," I agreed. "But we don't have any choice. And we need to leave right now."

"What's wrong with staying here?" Nick protested. "We can survive here. We have plenty of fish."

"For now," I said. "In six weeks, we could see snow flurries. Next, it's winter. How's the fishing going to be when it's twenty below zero and the ice on the lake is a foot thick?"

"I can ice fish," Nick pushed back, sounding defensive.

"What about fire?" I pointed out. "When winter comes, that puny pile of firewood outside won't last a week. Even if we started chopping trees right this minute with our pathetic little hand ax, no way we're able to put up enough firewood to get us through six months of winter."

"And let's talk about clothes," Grace jumped in. "First, mine are gone, of course. Second, you all brought summer clothes. There isn't a winter coat among us, not to mention gloves and heavy socks."

"I like our chances with the boat better," I summarized. "If we leave now, we can avoid the cold."

"Sounds very desperate and very risky," Grandfather said. "Maybe I should stay behind. I don't want to end up being a burden."

"No," I shot back, perhaps too sharply. "We do this together, or we don't do it at all."

No one said anything, and no one would meet my eyes.

"Guys, just do what I tell you, and I'll keep us alive. I promise." Then I gritted my teeth and added, "Trust me. I know what I'm talking about."

I gazed into the eyes of each person in turn. Grace quickly nodded. Grandfather grimaced at first but then nodded agreement as well.

"What about Morgon?" Nick whispered in so soft a voice that Grandfather had to lean forward to hear better.

Everyone trained their eyes on me to answer that question. They looked to me because I was now the leader of this motley group, and the others now looked to me for all the answers. Before, I would have run from the responsibility like a scalded cat. Today, I embraced it. I felt like all my life was one long build up for this day, this moment.

So, what about Nick's question? I took a couple of breaths, ran my hand over my bald head, and cleared my throat.

"He's out there," I said. "I'm sorry, Nick, but I think I brought him with me. And the road home leads through him. But this time, we finish what we started, and we don't back down."

Then Nick slowly nodded his assent.

So that was it. Everyone was on board with the plan. As the others rose to go to bed, I stayed at the table, shaking my head at what I had just gotten us into.

What the hell are you doing, Allie?

Over the next two days, we planned out our journey. We had no map or compass; Nick was not very forgiving about me stealing his and then losing it. We did have a hand ax and several knives, as well as a first aid kit. I hoped we wouldn't need it, but deep down, I knew we would.

One fortunate thing was that we didn't have to bring water or food. My plan was to spend most of our time on lakes, so we would have all the water we needed, and we would fish along the way as necessary. The one thing we had in abundance was fishing gear. In addition to the poles and well-outfitted tacklebox Grandfather brought, the cabin came with a lot of stuff too. So, we had plenty of poles, hooks, lures, sinkers, doodads, and thingamabobs.

When Nick returned from fishing the next day, I took him aside and showed him the hand ax.

"What?" he asked, puzzled.

"I need your help," I explained. "We're going to make some spears."

While we searched for four poles that were straight enough

and long enough, I told Nick about the bear. I explained that our only real weapon against him would be the spears we were making.

"Aim for the gut," I told him. "You'll only get one shot at him, though."

"But your spear didn't stop him," Nick pointed out. "He still came after you."

Yep. I skewered him good. I thought I killed him. But he kept coming and nearly took my head off with his paw. For a moment, I wondered if he *could* be killed.

"If he attacks," I said, "it won't be easy to stop him. Before it was only me and a single spear. Let's see how he does with three or four jammed into him."

One intractable issue we discovered in assembling our gear was space. The worn aluminum skiff we would use didn't have enough room for everything once you took into account the space the four of us would take up. We didn't have nice compressible sleeping bags, only thick, heavy wool blankets. So, we had to make some choices. Leave the cast iron frying pan; take the medium-sized cook pot we used to boil water. Leave most of our clothes; take the dirty, beat-up tarp Nick found. For my part, I fell on my sword and agreed to leave behind my useless smoothie maker.

That evening, preparations complete, we gathered for a final meal in the cabin. Making dinner, like all our meals, was simple: chunk the fish fillets, salt the fish, fry the fish, and eat the fish. So, I was happy to break the routine.

"I got us a treat for dinner," I said

Moving past Grace and Grandfather, I unhooked the canvas bag hanging from my belt and emptied the contents onto a placemat sitting on the kitchen table. A couple dozen black-skinned creatures spilled out.

"What *are* those?" Grace said with a groan of horror.

"Salamanders. I chopped their heads off and gutted them. They're ready to fry up and eat."

"I think I'm going to throw up in my mouth," she said and stalked away.

Grandfather had the same reaction as Grace, crinkling his nose in disgust at the little nuggets of protein after I sautéed them in some rancid bacon fat we still had lying around. Nick, however, was willing to try them, and after chomping down a few, he pronounced them edible, if a little gamey. I just plopped them in my mouth and swallowed.

Protein was protein was protein.

Don't ask, don't tell.

"Get some sleep," I told everyone when dinner ended. "We leave at dawn."

"When did you become so strong and bossy?" Grace asked after Nick and Grandfather had retired to their rooms. "You're like a general ordering his troops around."

"Somebody has to."

"Yeah, but—"

I cut her off. "Look, I'm not going to die out here, Grace. Not without a fight. I will do *whatever* I have to in order to survive, including kicking your butt up between your ears if necessary. Are we clear?"

"Yeah. Jesus."

"Okay then. See you in the morning."

CHAPTER TWENTY-SEVEN

Fog hung heavy over the surface of the lake when we shoved off the dock at first light; our collective mood was somber as the muted gray light surrounding us. I was anxious, but the others were flat out scared. For them, this venture was a giant leap into the great unknown; for me, it was "been there, done that."

The oars plopped rhythmically into the still water as Grandfather rowed us out into the center of the lake. We left the cabin closed up and battened down for winter as best we could.

I gazed back at the wooden building as it receded into the mist, trying to remember the day we first arrived. What I recalled best were the arguments and fights with Grace and, to a much lesser extent, that Trevor dude. I snuffed out the trip down memory lane; the mere thought of Trevor Lasley made my blood boil.

"Remember, we take turns," I told everyone. "When Grandfather tires, I'll take over. Then Grace."

"I can row," Nick complained.

"Then Nick," I agreed.

"Aye, aye, Captain," Grace said with a mock salute.

Two hours slid by before we reached the east end of the lake, all of us having taken turns with the oars. The fog had burned off some by then, but it still limited visibility to about a hundred yards. From Grandfather and Nick's many fishing trips, we knew there was a river inlet nearby. This would be the first test of my plan. Could we navigate up this river and through to whatever other lake it connected to? If not, then we were bottled up in Lake Makwa and we'd never leave this place. My teeth clenched at the possibility.

We couldn't stay here. Not an option.

"I'm hungry," Nick said, as soon as he finished his rowing turn.

"I fried up the last of the fish," Grandfather said. "It's in a Ziploc bag inside that box."

Nick rummaged through the contents until he extracted the gallon-sized bag. "Anybody else?"

"Sure," Grace said. "Pass me over a happy meal."

Grandfather was at the oars now, and he reduced speed as our boat advanced toward the mouth of the river. The water was completely still, like a pane of glass, and an eerie silence greeted us from the nearby forest. In the fog, I had trouble seeing where the water ended and the shoreline began, so I couldn't gauge how wide the inlet was.

Besides obstacles blocking our passage, I worried about charging up a river that gradually narrowed to a small creek or petered out altogether. Backtracking would be a bitch. Fortunately, this river appeared to be quite broad at the mouth, which was a good sign we would not run out of water anytime soon.

"Go slow," I told Grandfather and then addressed Grace and Nick. "Everybody keep their eyes and ears open for trouble."

We hit our first obstruction a half hour downriver while I was at the oars. Two massive fir trees had fallen into the water, clogging most of the river. On the far side, however, a narrow gap of some twenty feet swept pass the half-submerged trees. This was our out, but a scary one. The water flowed mighty fast through the bypass route; the slightest mistake could flip the boat and dump us and all our shit into the drink. Good news? We only needed to go fifty yards before we got past the logjam area.

I pulled in the oars, gripping one of them with both hands. I would use this oar to push off against the riverbank as needed to keep us in the center of the current.

"Everybody scoot to the middle as much as you can and hold on," I said, pitching my voice loud enough to be heard over the rushing water.

The current strengthened, grabbed hold of the skiff, and sucked us ahead with a jolt that yanked all of us backward a smidge. The shore was lined with rocks, which caused the water to spray up in our faces as we shot by. The bottom of the boat banged on something, a rock I guessed, but no apparent harm came of it. If we sprang a leak, our trip ended. We had no way of repairing tears in the boat's aluminum skin.

"Look out!" Nick hollered.

"Watch it!" Grandfather echoed.

I glanced over my right shoulder and saw we were rushing into a head-on collision with a boulder the size of a garden shed that lay half submerged in the river. I stabbed my oar into the water and made contact with the rock bottom. With every iota of strength I possessed, I shoved off against the bedrock. I barely managed to turn the bow enough that the boulder hit us with a glancing blow as we rocketed past, but the oar twisted in my hand as I pushed.

"*Merde!*" I cursed in French, as a mother effing sliver from the oar sliced into the palm of my hand.

Within seconds, the boat slowed almost to a standstill, as the churning rapids ended, and we spilled out into a stretch of placid water. For the first time, I noticed the morning sun had burned off the fog, showing me how wide the river was—about fifty feet. Then I held up my hand for my eyes to study. A steady trickle of blood snaked over my wrist and down my forearm. A slender, three-inch piece of wood was jammed under my skin with about an inch protruding.

"We should pull ashore and take care of that," Grandfather said, pointing to my palm.

"No time," I answered.

"If that gets infected," he said, "and you can't row, it'll really slow us down."

Made sense.

"Okay."

We wrestled the boat up onto a sandy spit that jutted out in the river and secured it. Grandfather led me to a massive tree root exposed by erosion and sat me down. With tweezers from the med kit, he yanked the sliver out while I bit back a cry of pain. Like water flooding out after the collapse of a dam, the removal of the sliver triggered a gush of blood, but it quickly reduced to a trickle.

"That should do it," Grandfather said when he finished dressing the wound. "We have a pair of gloves you can use while rowing."

Meanwhile, I realized Nick had wandered off on a mini-exploring mission, and then I heard him yell my name. He didn't sound panicked or frightened, but I detected an edge of concern in his voice.

"Nick," I called out.

"Over here" came the reply.

We found Nick a hundred yards downriver, standing near the water's edge in a grassy area dotted with a few small saplings. He waved us over.

"What is it?" Grace asked.

We formed a rough semicircle behind him.

"There," he said, pointing to the ground in front of him.

The sod was torn up, and splotches of blood were plainly visible. Something died here.

"Those are bear prints," I said, gesturing at several sets of paw impressions clearly visible on exposed areas of soft earth. "Not today, but maybe yesterday or the day before."

What I didn't say, and probably didn't need to, was that the paw that left these prints several times the size of your plain vanilla bear. This was *the* bear, *my* bear.

Grandfather also gestured at the tracks and said, "Looks like it's heading in the same direction we are."

"Of course it is," Grace muttered while rolling her eyes.

Nick began to tremble. Crap. I moved over in front of him, wrapped my arms around his shoulders, and drew him into a hug. He swallowed hard twice and moaned, the way he did before a bad episode.

No . . . no . . . no. Not here. Not now.

"Sir Captain Captain," I whispered to him. "You must protect the queen. Remember?"

I felt my thirteen-year-old brother nod vigorously against my shoulder. He cleared his throat. The incident was passing. Thank the gods.

"Get one of the spears, and keep it by your side at all times," I told Nick. "If Morgon shows his ugly face, cram it down his effing throat. Got it?"

"What are you guys talking about?" Grace asked.

"Monster stuff," I answered.

"We better get moving," Grandfather interrupted. "Party's over."

Minutes later, we shoved off with Grace taking her turn rowing. She wore a blue Exeter sweatshirt of mine but soon stripped down to her pink sports bra as the exertion beaded her skin with sweat.

The river surrendered. It gave us no more trouble that day—no rapids, no more downed trees, no boat-killing boulders. The current was lazy and slow to the point that those not rowing fought to stay awake in the warm air. All we had to do was keep to the middle of the river and drift along with the muddy waters. Grandfather and I kept our eyes on the track of the sun, both of us agreeing we were headed in a southeasterly direction. Good. My plan was to head south at all times, if possible; go east if necessary; and never travel north or west.

When the sun finally fell toward the horizon, nobody argued when I suggested we stop for the day and make camp. Without a map, we had no idea how long this river was or where it was taking us. All of us chose to see the river as a highway bringing us home, but I wondered whether home even existed anymore.

"This is the last of the fish," Grandfather said as he passed out chunks of lukewarm walleye. "We'll have to restock first thing tomorrow if we want to eat."

"You and Nick can troll as we travel," I suggested.

We gathered around a small fire, each of us sitting on the moist sand beside the river. Our camp wasn't much to look at. Besides the fire, we made a large lean-to with our tarp and spread out our blankets beneath it.

As night descended, I ate my fish in silence from my position close to the fire, where I welcomed the smoke that wafted my way. It kept the mosquitoes out of my face and off my neck. Thank the gods the bastards didn't carry malaria this far north, or I'd be writhing on the ground by now with the disease. Still, the constant buzzing and biting nearly drove me crazy.

"What's the first thing you're going to do when you get home?" Grandfather asked us.

"Eat something other than fish," Nick said.

"Amen," Grace agreed. "And buy clothes. Lots and lots of clothes. What about you, Allie? Still going to France?"

Rather than answer immediately, I stared into the flames and thought back on my last face-to-face conversation with Jack. We had taken a break from making out in my dorm room when he spoke.

"Sorry, if I was too pushy about Haiti," Jack said. "I just want to be with you."

"I know. But I signed on for this weeks ago. Backing out now would make me a douche bag. It's only for a month."

"I've already talked to my parents," he said. "They're so jacked to have you. Mom really wants to spend time with you."

CHAPTER TWENTY-SEVEN

My resolve weakened.

"Jack, I—"

"So, let me tell you what it's all about."

He proceeded to describe Château d'Amour Fou, the place his family would be staying at, and the neighboring town of Limoges. No question, it sounded amazing, but I bristled a tiny bit at having my arm twisted.

"I don't know," I said. I wanted out of this conversation, but Jack wouldn't let it go.

"I got the feeling you're not into me as much as I'm into you."

"What? No!"

"I mean, we've been treading water for, what, three months now? It's time to sort out what's going on between us."

So, I was a water treader? New one on me.

"I want to be honest," he continued. "Allie, I'm in love with you."

Boom. There it was. No dodging and weaving around that statement. You either hit the ball back over the net or . . . game, set, match.

"I love you too."

"Then . . ." He didn't finish whatever he was going to say, but I knew what it was. He wanted to say that if I really loved him I would abandon this stupid Haiti trip, but he stopped himself.

Instead, he said, "This is important to me, Allie."

Yes. I was in love with Jack. No getting around that fact. And the boy I loved was pleading with me to give up what I wanted and join him in France. Wasn't that what you did when you were in love with a guy? Wouldn't you toss aside what you wanted and do what he wanted?

"Okay," I finally said. "I'll come."

He kissed me to cement the deal . . . maybe he should have tossed thirty pieces of silver at me instead.

A few days later, I hung around the classroom to talk to Ms. Ashley. She taught a seminar called Just Wars: Theory and Reality, and she was the faculty member sponsoring the trip to Haiti. I wanted to explain why I was backing out.

She beat me to the punch.

"I heard you're withdrawing from our Haiti trip," she said casually, as I approached.

She was young, maybe ten years older than me at most.

"Yeah," I replied. "I think so."

"It's probably none of my business, but what's the problem, Allie?"

I paused in the middle of fiddling with the clasps on my messenger bag and took in a deep breath. It wasn't her business, but she was my friend, and she deserved more than a simple brush-off.

"My boyfriend wants me to spend August with him and his family in France," I said with a shrug. "It's kind of a big deal."

"Jack Carter, right?" She smiled playfully at me. When I lifted a questioning eyebrow at her, she added, "Oh, I have my sources."

"My friends think France is a no-brainer."

"Why isn't it?" she asked.

Yes. Why wasn't it? I had asked myself some version of this question for days and days. Why was I so hesitant about going?

"Scared," I said in a hushed tone. "Nervous."

"Why don't you have lunch with me?"

Fifteen minutes later in the dining hall, my fork stirred a bowl of kale topped with pomegranate seeds. Ms. Ashley sat to my right and lifted a turkey sandwich to her mouth. I began to regret agreeing to lunch; the silence between us was awkward.

"You're heading north to Dartmouth in the fall, aren't you?" Ms. Ashley finally asked me around half a mouthful of turkey.

"Yes. I'm going to major in French language and literature."

She nodded and took another bite. I rearranged my salad leaves some more, but I had yet to eat any of it.

"Where does Jack Carter fit into things?"

I tossed my fork into the bowl and slumped back in my chair, crossing my arms over my chest.

"I don't know," I confessed. "It's not that . . ." A long, slow exhale drained out of me. I didn't know what I was trying to say.

"What?" she pressed.

"Things are getting a little too serious, you know?" I said. "It feels like we're moving too fast."

"So slow it down," she replied, as if it was as obvious and easy as turning off a light switch.

"Yeah," I agreed half-heartedly.

"Do you have reservations about Jack?"

Her question touched the center of confusion inside me and I blurted out, "I don't know. Yeah . . . no . . . I . . ."

"Which is it—yes or no?"

"I have things I want to do," I said. "I want my own life, you know. I'm not sure what he expects of me. His parents . . ." My voice fell off into silence. I didn't like Jack's dad, and it disturbed me that I saw a lot of him in Jack.

"And this trip to France, you—"

"I think he's going to propose to me," I interrupted. "I don't want to hurt him."

"Wow," she said dryly around another bite of her sandwich. "Can't help you much there. No one ever proposed to me . . . at least, not so far. Why don't you just tell him you're not ready yet. If he truly cares about you, he'll understand."

"Yeah, but I'm not sure I'm *ever* going to be ready."

She nodded thoughtfully. "That does make things more complicated. What is it about Jack that you're not sure you want, Allie? What's really bothering you?"

To delay having to respond, I leaned forward and finally took a forkful of my salad and chewed slowly and thoughtfully.

"I feel like he wants to put me on a shelf, like a decorative prize or ornament, and show me off." I stuffed another bite of kale into my mouth and continued, "I don't want to be some useless trophy gathering dust on somebody's mantel."

"So don't be."

I shook my head in a hopeless attempt to clear my head of these memories. They were a distraction I didn't need.

"Earth to Allie," Grace said. "Turn off the mute button."

"Sorry," I replied, clearing my throat. "What did you say?"

"I said, are you still going to France?" Grace repeated.

My answer came immediately. Decisively.

"No. Never."

And with those words, I said goodbye to Jack Carter forever.

CHAPTER TWENTY-EIGHT

The stars blazed bright enough that I blinked several times when I awoke in the middle of the night to answer the urgent call of nature. The gentle gurgle of the river provided soothing background music as I crept away from the others and into the brush. Wolf howls broke out minutes later, loud and excited. The pack hunted a couple miles away at least, but the wind carried their jarring yelps to me as if they prowled a few hundred yards away from us. In another life, they would have scared me senseless, but tonight, they were simply part of the landscape, like a stump or a lake.

I had a bad feeling about tonight, even though morning wasn't far off, so I went to the boat to fetch one of the spears. Although I urged Nick to keep one at his side at all times, I hadn't followed that advice myself. I wished I had.

I reached the bar of sand where we parked the boat and swiveled my head back and forth searching for it.

No boat.

The frigging boat was gone.

"What!" I shrieked.

The wolf howls went silent. The others sprang out of their blankets in an instant. Soon, all four of us stood on the wet sand in the light of a half-moon staring at the void where our boat once rested.

"What happened?" Grandfather asked, sounding half asleep.

Ignoring his question, I asked, "Did anyone hear or see anything?"

"Not me," Nick replied.

"Me neither," Grace concurred.

"Shit," I muttered. "It must have dislodged and floated away."

"I tied it to a huge rock," Nick protested. "It would take a tidal wave to dislodge it from that big mutha clucka."

I lifted an eyebrow at him in the dark. Somehow sensing my surprise at his unusual expression, he shrugged. Then I glanced about and pointed to a potato-shaped rock lodged in the sand that was as big as a refrigerator. It had no rope wrapped around it.

"That rock?" I asked Nick.

He strode over to it, bent to examine its surface with his hands, and then straightened.

"The rope's gone," Nick said in an apologetic tone. "I don't understand."

"Then it floated away," I repeated. "Nothing we can do about it until morning."

"But the boat has all our supplies," Grace protested.

"We'll find it," Grandfather said. "Not all who wander are lost."

"Please don't start with the *LotR* crap," I said. "Not tonight."

None of us could sleep the rest of the night. I lay on my side with my mouth hanging open, speechless . . . or maybe so full of speech I couldn't settle on any one sentence to shriek into the darkness. The boat was everything. No boat, no escape. Losing it brought on a despair so deep I understood for the first time why a person might want to end it all to be free of the misery.

Why had my life gone so far off the rails? What did I ever do to anyone in the universe to deserve this shit? Dying in the wilderness was what happened to idiot losers who had nothing better to do with their existence than play Russian roulette with their demons. Me? I didn't have any demons. I had servants, I had a Beamer, and I had a thirty-thousand-dollar Cartier watch for eff's sake.

Funny thing I was learning about life. It slapped you around and knocked you to the ground until you were curled up in a ball begging for mercy. But there *was* no mercy. Instead, my so-called life kept kicking me in the head, the stomach, the throat. Anywhere it could slip a blow in. The only way to make it stop was to get off the ground and fight back.

Teeth clenched, I rolled out of my blankets and did just that. I rose to my feet and lifted my middle finger in the air and shook it at the sky overhead.

"You're going to have to do better than this!" I yelled at the canopy of stars.

"Allie, what the hell?" Grace said, propping herself up on one elbow.

"Can you wait until the morning to have a psychotic meltdown?" Nick said drowsily.

"You're one to talk," I muttered to myself.

Grandfather snored on through my outburst without missing a beat.

We climbed quietly out of our blankets in the morning, but the residual shock and fear from last night hung so heavy on us that you could spread it like peanut butter. We were miles and miles from the cabin, too far to return, and yet we could hardly push on with nothing more than the piddling few things we had.

"It must have drifted downriver," I told everyone, as we crouched around a fire Grandfather had made. "Maybe it washed ashore downstream a ways."

"Or overturned and sank," Grace offered, ever the voice of hope and comfort.

"Well, let's go see," I said.

"And if we don't find the boat?" Grace asked.

"We—" I started to say.

Nick cut me off. "We die." Then he shrugged as if it was no big deal.

Grandfather carried the folded tarp, and the rest of us took the blankets with our few remaining items split up among the four of us. Our mission was simple: walk downriver until we found the skiff. I bit back the urge to blame Nick; I didn't have to voice a word. He felt awful, and it showed.

After several hours slogging through the underbrush and searching along the river's edge, our spirits were lower than low. We hadn't found a shred of evidence of our boat's passage. Grandfather tried to cheer us up.

"Lot of our stuff floats," Grandfather said. "If the boat had capsized, we'd be seeing debris washed up all over the place."

Grace suddenly moaned as if having labor pains, and her shoulders slumped.

"What?" I asked.

"I just remembered I left my wallet back at the cabin," Grace said. "On the nightstand. Crap."

"Damn," I said. "Replacing that student ID is going to be a real bitch."

"I had five hundred dollars in it," Grace replied, sounding a little whiny.

"Fat lot of good that does you out here," I said with a snort of laughter.

"Start a fire with it," Grandfather observed. "Better than bark and pine needles."

"Toilet paper," Nick offered. "It would make good toilet paper."

"Oooh, good idea," I agreed. "Getting really tired of leaves and grass."

The words hardly left my mouth when we broke through the trees and each of us gasped. The river came to an abrupt end, and stretching out in front of us was a gigantic lake. If only we had the boat, this would be a moment of triumph, celebratory hoots, and high-fives all around.

Instead, the four of us stood quietly on a grassy promontory gazing out over the water. We saw no sign of our boat, no sign of debris. Yet, my spirits actually lifted a touch. My hope of finding the boat climbed a few notches. The prospect of the boat smashed or sunk seemed to lessen as I gazed out over the serene surface of the lake.

"I'll bet the skiff washed up somewhere along the lakeshore," I said. "We just have to find it."

"We split up," Grandfather said. "You three go that way. I'll swim across the river and go the other way."

"No," I protested. "We shouldn't split up."

"Don't worry about me," he said. "If I find the boat, I'll row your way and pick you guys up. If you find it, you come get me. Search till noon tomorrow, then head back here if you don't find anything."

Reluctantly, I murmured my assent. Grandfather's plan made sense. We could cut the search time in half, but it made me uneasy. The old saying was that there was safety in numbers, and boy, did I believe it out here.

Grandfather set down the tarp he carried, took off his shoes, and tied their shoelaces together. Slowly, he waded out into the river, his shoes dangling from around his neck, while the three of us watched his progress. The mouth of the river was easily the length of a football field wide, but I perceived no current to speak of. Once in up to his gray-haired chest, Grandfather started swimming using a form of the sidestroke, which kept his head above water. We watched him in tense silence, each of us anxious about what might go wrong. I worried that an undertow would tug him below the surface and bit my lip at the prospect. If he got into trouble, there wasn't much any of us could do to save him.

"He made it," Grace said a short while later. She let out a ragged exhale.

She was right. We watched our grandfather climb out of the water on all fours on the other side of the river, much like a muskrat or beaver might waddle up the bank with its fur slicked back. He waved at us before sitting down to put his shoes on. I knew all too well what it was like to walk for miles in wet boots and socks and what his feet would feel like at the end of the day.

"Come on," I said to Grace and Nick. "We're burning daylight."

Without a glance back, I marched off to cover as much ground as we could before we lost the sun. The area around the river's mouth was flat and muddy, pocked with marshy areas, and dotted with skinny pines. Soon, however, the land rose, and much of the forest and brush faded away. In their place, we strode over a vast table of rock. Beyond lichen, tufts of grass, and resilient bonsai-sized trees, the granite expanse was barren.

The rock sloped straight down into the water, gradual in some places, steep in others. Not only was the land easy to walk on, but visibility was excellent. We didn't have to worry about impenetrable stands of trees and underbrush obscuring our sight of the lake shore.

Gazing over at Grandfather's side of the river from time to time, I saw he didn't have it so easy. There, the forest came right up to the water's edge. We would probably cover three times the distance he would.

"What do we do for food?" Nick asked late in the afternoon.

"We find the boat," I said.

"Yeah, but what about in the meantime?" he went on.

"We starve," I replied. "Get it together, Nick. It's all mental at this point. Your body can handle a few days without food no problem."

"But I'm going insane," Nick persisted. "I need to eat something."

"Hey," Grace said, "if I die later today, which seems very possible, you guys can cannibalize my arms and legs. My treat."

"Disgusting," I murmured.

"Just taking one for the team," she said with a smile.

We trudged on, occasionally stopping where the lake was easily accessible to slurp up water using our hands as cups. A couple of times, I saw good-sized fish scatter and flee from the rock shore where they were hanging out. If we could only get our hands on the fishing gear, catching some of those beauties would be easy. My stomach grumbled at the prospect.

The afternoon light was fading, and I began to think about where we might sleep for the night out here. Perhaps we could find a cave or crevasse to crawl into, where we'd likely have to share a bed with only a few bugs and newts. I could deal with those. Snakes? Nope. I drew the line there.

Grace blew up my thoughts.

"There!" Grace squealed in a half yell, half banshee screech.

She jumped up and down in excitement while pointing ahead of us. Sure enough, in a small cove lined with floating driftwood, I saw our boat sitting pretty as you please, bobbing up and down with the gentle swells. And just like that, I went from *kill* me now to *kiss* me now.

We found it! Hot damn, we found it. Unbelievable.

Grace and I spontaneously tumbled into an embrace, squeezing each other tightly for several long moments. Meanwhile, Nick did a little jig and thrust his hands in the air in a "we are the champions" pose. His redemption was complete. Grinning, Grace and I both mussed his hair, and we jog-walked side by side toward our salvation. Inwardly, I sang "we're out of the woods, we're out of the dark, we're out of the night" from *The Wizard of Oz*. Odd how utter despair can flip in the space of a couple heartbeats.

Retrieving the boat took little time. Beyond some scrapes and a couple new dents, we found no damage. All our gear remained exactly as we last saw it, and the inside of the boat was dry. After striking out most of the day, we finally got a hit, and a homerun at that. I couldn't have asked for a better outcome, other than not losing the boat in the first place.

I took the first shift at rowing, fully intending to go all the way to our destination—the promontory where we started. By then, it would be too dark to go on to find Grandfather. Unfortunately, he'd have to spend the night in the bush.

The shoreline we traversed today curved in a giant arc, so my plan was to steer the boat in a straight line for the promontory, thereby taking the diameter route rather than the longer circumference path. I rowed hard, intent on making as good a time as possible. With each backward pull on the oars, I stared at my biceps. Modest bumps rose and fell as I retracted my arms before extending them outward again. I had some serious guns on me now. They certainly weren't there before in Scarsdale, where the extent of my arm exertion was dragging a brush through my tangled hair in the morning.

"Catch us some dinner," Grace told Nick a few minutes into our cruise.

Nick obliged by kissing his favorite lure, tying it on, and casting a line far out into the water beyond. Whether it was the kiss, the lure, or simply a lake full of ravenous fish, I didn't know, but Nick reeled in four biggies in less than a half hour, more than enough to feed us dinner and breakfast.

I hadn't fished with Nick since that one day weeks and weeks ago, so he surprised me with how efficiently he handled the catch. He yanked them up into the boat, bashed their heads on the gunwale, and then used a knife to clean them lickety-split. He made it look easy, holding the fish over the water by the gills, while slicing open its belly. Then he immersed the fish in the lake, shook it, and voilà. I worried the fish would slip out of his hands, but no probs. None did.

At the start of the summer, Nick wouldn't have been able to harm any animal, not even a centipede, and I never would have trusted him with a sharp knife. And here we are.

Dusk descended, and a tiny remnant of the sun glowed like a smoldering fire on the western horizon when we came aground at the promontory. I rowed the entire way, so my arms were numb with exhaustion by the time we climbed out. Grace took charge of attempting to start a fire while Nick and I went about foraging limbs to use in setting up our tarp lean-to. Getting the semblance of a shelter erected didn't take long. It wasn't like we were constructing Frank Lloyd Wright's Fallingwater here.

We also collected several armloads of fir tree boughs to give us some ground cover so our butts didn't sit directly on the moist earth when we slept.

"That's not a bad fire," I told Grace once Nick and I were done.

"Like it?" she replied. "It's my first . . . unassisted by lighter fluid, that is."

The August night hung a curtain of warm, humid air about us, so Nick sat shirtless with an orange bandana wrapped around his head. It was his *Lord of the Flies* getup. Grace and I had stripped to our sports bras earlier; it was our Brandi Chastain getup.

My biggest discomfort tonight wasn't the bugs, the heat, or the sweat and grime. No, it was my lack of hair. With only fuzzy bristle, the back of my neck and the top of my head itched and stung from sunburn. It would get worse, I knew. And to think back in the day I regularly spent sixty bucks a bottle for Alterna Ten shampoo to use on hair that didn't even exist anymore.

As night settled over us, we dangled strips of walleye impaled on small tree-branch skewers a couple feet above our fire. I was fine eating my portion raw, so I didn't waste much time with cooking. Grace, on the other hand, insisted on roasting her pieces until they were almost charred. Probably something psychological going on there.

"Any new ideas about what's happening back in the real world?" Grace asked when we finished eating. "Allie?"

"People must be looking for us," I answered after reflecting on the question for several moments. "Probably hundreds and hundreds, but they're searching in all the wrong places. They don't know where we're at. I have no idea why."

"So, Trevor the tool simply forgot where he dropped us off?" Grace countered, a hint of amusement in her voice.

"Yeah, that's the big problem with my theory," I acknowledged. "How could he lose us?"

"Maybe his plane crashed on the way back," Nick offered. "No one else knows where he took us."

"Maybe," I said. "His operation didn't inspire a lot of confidence that they knew what they were doing."

"No," Grace said. "I could see them misplacing us for a week tops, but three freaking months?"

"Zombies," Nick solemnly told Grace. "That or the EMP thing you said before."

"Pandemic?" I tossed out.

"What about a comet?" Grace suggested. "I saw a movie where a comet blinded everyone and man-eating plants took over the world."

"Man-eating plants took over the world," Nick repeated in a mocking tone.

"I thought the comet turned everybody into powder," I said.

"That was a different comet movie," Grace clarified.

"Turned everybody into powder," Nick said in the same deadpan voice.

"It doesn't matter," I finally said. "The reality is we're totally on our own. Unless we stay alive and make it back, we'll never know what really happened out there."

"What if we get back to civilization and everybody is gone?" Nick asked.

Grace and I exchanged sideways glances.

"Then I have dibs on Mall of America," Grace said. "I'm moving in and calling it home."

"Cold winters," I noted. "Nick, how about you and I head south and take over Disney World? We'll have the whole park to ourselves."

"Universal Studios," Nick said with a smile. "That would be awesome."

"With no one around, traffic would be light," Grace observed. "We could pick up a couple Ferraris and zoom down the interstates. I'll race you, Allie. First one there gets to sleep in Cinderella's castle."

The return of wolf howls cut short our banter, reminding us we had a long way to go before we escaped this wilderness and enjoyed unlimited Space Mountain rides. Also, the howls brought to mind the bear tracks we saw yesterday. Until we put a couple lakes and some long rivers between us and those tracks, I wasn't relaxing.

"Let's get some sleep," I said. "But we should take turns keeping watch. I don't trust that bear."

"I'll go first," Grace offered. "Then I'll wake Nick. You go last, Allie. That should give you most of a night's sleep."

"Sounds like a plan," I said, rising to head to my blanket. "Remember. Hear something, yell something."

Nick woke me a couple hours before dawn with a slight push on my shoulder. My eyes flew open. I expected to hear bellows from a charging bear, but the night was quiet but for the sounds of a million insects and their chaos of mating noises. Wordlessly, I rose, accepted the spear Nick offered, and strode over to the glowing embers of our fire. With nothing better to do, I hunted up some branches and revived the flames until I had a nice blaze going. Then I paced about trying to find a pleasant memory to dredge up and entertain myself with.

I never found one.

Pleasant daydreams were cowards. The slightest bit of adversity and they ran for the hills and let the nightmares take over.

An odd sound came from the distant tree line, one I never heard before. Definitely an animal, not a bug. A bird? No, it had a husky, snarly tone. Also, it almost sounded like the thing was in distress.

Maybe it's dying.

Since it wasn't coming closer, I stood my ground on high alert, spear gripped tightly in my right hand. Whatever made the noises, it didn't advance, so I decided to leave it alone. If the strange snarly thing didn't want to bother me, then I didn't want to bother it. Just two lost and lonely souls passing in the night.

When dawn finally arrived, and with it wisps of yesterday's fog, I stared intently in the direction of last night's funny animal sounds. More than an hour had passed since I last heard anything, so I assumed my whiny companion had said its peace and moved on. Still, I didn't relax.

When I was at Exeter, I felt safe, protected, insulated, and mostly exempt from harm. I spent most of my time calm and un-concerned. Out here? It was eat or be eaten. You could never let your guard down.

I was wrong about my friend in the dark. It hadn't left at all.

Out of the morning mist, a moving shape resolved. It walked toward me but at a slow pace. I saw four legs, but one was held off the ground; only three limbs were working. This was no bear. This was no wolf. It's tan-gray fur rippled in the breeze as it drew closer.

Wait.

I sucked in a breath and held it. I recognized those ears.

It was her.

CHAPTER TWENTY-NINE

"Tyche!"

Yelling might have scared her off—she didn't like loud noises—but it didn't. She stopped and sat on her haunches waiting for me as I sprinted to her. My outburst did, however, wake my companions, whom I heard scrambling out of their blankets behind me.

I covered the fifty yards between Tyche and me in seconds although the tussocky ground threatened to trip me up a couple times.

When I reached my friend, I collapsed to my knees, inches in front of her, thrilled to see her after so long, but the smile on my face vanished in an instant. I clenched my hand into a tight fist, jammed a knuckle into my mouth, and bit down. Tears erupted and stung my eyes at the sight of her in front of me.

Tyche was horribly emaciated. Her fur hung loosely on her bones with the bumps of her ribs plainly visible. Worse, her right eye was gone. In its place was a crusted mat of dried blood and fur. She held her left paw a few inches off the ground, as if to offer it to me as a gift. From the way I had seen her walk just now, clearly it caused great pain for her to put any weight on it, but I couldn't tell what the injury was.

"Oh God," I said with a moan.

My tears and sniffling lurched toward sob territory, but I swallowed hard to keep a grip on myself. I couldn't lose it out here. Not in front of the others. Not in front of Tyche.

My girl let me wrap my arms around her and give her an awkward embrace. She never wanted me to touch her much before, but it was different this time. Maybe she thought my embrace could heal her.

Sorry to disappoint.

Then I noticed how dirty her fur was. Mud spatters covered her legs and hips. Caked-on dirt was on her muzzle and in her ears. Before, she always kept herself groomed and clean, the way a housecat washed itself with its tongue.

I heard footsteps approaching from behind me.

"Get back," Nick said in a half-excited, half-scared voice.

"Allie!" Grace shouted.

Tyche tensed. If she were healthy, this would be the point where she sprang backward and hightailed it back into the forest. Not this time. She didn't have the strength to break out of my grip and I wasn't even holding her that tightly.

"Back off!" I yelled over my shoulder.

Both Grace and Nick had a Cheerio mouth as I lifted Tyche up and held her in my arms. She was a skeleton of her old self.

When Tyche and I had gotten separated during the bear attack, I doubted I'd ever see her again. I knew the bear had injured her bad, so bad I worried he had killed her, but I never had a chance to go back and see. Well, she survived the attack obviously. Barely. She probably hadn't eaten anything since that night by the looks of her; her frail, starved body broke my heart. The tears I held back came cascading down my face as I carried her over to our campsite and laid her down on my blanket.

"What is that?" Grace asked, pointing to Tyche, who lay on her side.

"A lynx," I said. "She saved my life twice. Get me a water bottle, Grace."

When Grace returned with one, I dribbled water into Tyche's mouth a few drops at a time. Her swollen tongue slurped it up. I gave her more.

"She looks like she was run over by a Humvee," Nick said.

"Close," I agreed.

After she drank as much as she wanted, I fed Tyche bits of fish that was to be my breakfast. She accepted the food but hardly ate with any gusto. Her jaws worked slowly, and her throat muscles constricted noticeably as she labored to swallow.

"So, what's the story with that thing?" Grace asked, pointing a shaky finger at Tyche.

Haltingly at first, I related my friendship with the cat, pausing several times to wipe my nose and give into a few sniffles. If I had told them the story before, they wouldn't have believed me. Not completely. But seeing Tyche lying with her head on my lap made them believers.

"She's coming with us," I said. The tone of my voice made it clear that anyone objecting to this would be left behind.

"Any other friends we should know about, Dr. Doolittle?" Grace said with a smirk.

"Fine by me," Nick said.

I nodded and went to work seeing what I could do about Tyche's injuries.

After observing me minister to the lynx for the best part of an hour, Grace asked, "Now, what about Grandfather?"

"Stow the tarp and blankets in the boat," I answered, without taking my eyes off Tyche. "We shove off in thirty minutes."

Grace nodded, but made no move to leave. "Where do we put . . . it?"

"She won't take up any room," I said in a level voice. "She can sit on my lap."

"Is she going to attack us?" Grace went on. "I mean, when she's recovered."

"If you keep sneering and calling her an 'it,' she might," I said. "Come on, let's hurry."

Once the sun edged up over the trees, giving us good visibility of the lakeshore, we shoved off. Grace volunteered to row while I sat on the back bench gently stroking Tyche, who lay on my lap half awake. Staring down at the remains of her eye made my heart squeeze. With only one eye and a gimpy leg, she'd never hunt again . . . at least, not very successfully. No matter. I would nurse her back to health. And win, lose, or draw, we would face the rest of this journey together; we wouldn't be separated again.

"How'd you tame her?" Nick asked at one point.

"She's not tame," I snapped. "We help each other. That's all."

"Oh," he replied, but I could tell he didn't understand.

Nick and Grace rowed the first shifts. We had no idea where Grandfather was, only that he was supposed to stick close to shore and keep the lake in view at all times. We rowed slowly within fifty yards or so of the land, pausing every so often to call out to him. Judging by the terrain I was seeing, I doubted he made it more than a couple miles at best yesterday. We should find him quickly.

We didn't.

After two hours of rowing, covering who knew how many miles, Nick retracted the oars and slumped forward, breathing heavily. No way Grandfather could have hiked this far along the shore.

"We missed him," Grace said, stating the obvious.

"How?" Nick wondered. "We yelled for him all along the way."

"I don't know," I said wearily. "We have to circle back and try again. Only this time, I'll walk along the shore parallel to the boat. He might be injured."

"What about your pet?" Grace asked. The alarmed expression on her face was what I would expect if I asked her to babysit a ten-foot anaconda.

"I'll set her down on the bottom of the boat," I said. "On the tarp. She's not going to hurt anyone."

"I'll guard you, sis," Nick proclaimed, half facetiously. Then he launched into a poorly rendered version of the Mighty Mouse chorus. "Here I come to save the day."

"Mighty Nick is on the way," Grace and I sang in unison.

We laughed for several moments, which helped revive our spirits. Not finding Grandfather weighed on each of our minds, but even worse was the dark thought of what we might find if we did locate him.

We brought the boat close enough to shore for me to slide out and slosh the last few feet to land. With a wave, I took off hiking the shoreline, keeping as close to the water as possible.

I found Grandfather three hours later.

He lay at the bottom of a V-shaped crevasse between two rock outcroppings, stretched out like he was sleeping, except that his body was rotated to a forty-five-degree position. My desperate cries for him to talk to me brought no response. Blood stained the rock surface by his head.

I flagged the boat down by frantically waving my arms.

"Grace!" I shouted, cupping my hands around my mouth. "Up here!"

Once Nick steered the boat up against the land, Grace disembarked and scrambled up the rock slope to where I lay on my stomach with my hands extended down into the crack. I couldn't reach Grandfather, who rested a few feet beyond my grasp. She kneeled beside me.

"What happened?" she asked.

"Not sure," I said. "Looks like he fell maybe."

"Is he . . ."

I shook my head. "Don't know. He hasn't moved since I found him. Can't tell if he's breathing or not."

In the end, I had to shimmy down into the narrow space and wrestle a rope around his chest and under his arms. His body was limp and warm, so he had to be alive. Plus, I thought I detected a pulse, but it could be my thumb sensed the pounding of my own frightened heart.

He remained unconscious as Grace and I pulled, tugged, yanked, and heaved on the rope. Grandfather had a lanky, stooped build, but he was tall and had to weigh at least two hundred pounds. We progressed slowly until we raised him enough to free his arms. Then both of us grabbed a wrist and slid him up and out. The effort left us sitting on the granite surface, our lungs heaving for oxygen.

The blood on the rocks came from a gash above one eyebrow. The cut wasn't deep, but it bled like an artery had ruptured. I debated whether to administer CPR when he began to tremble and groan. Good. Since I didn't actually *know* CPR, trying to give it to him probably would have resulted in me smothering the life out of him.

When Grandfather's eyelids finally fluttered open, Grace hastened to fetch the first aid kit from the boat. In minutes, I bandaged his cut while he lay on his back staring up at the sky. I didn't see any other obvious injuries . . . no broken bones or other cuts. Of course, when it came to fractures, we didn't bring along an X-ray machine, so unless the bone was actually sticking out of his flesh, I really wouldn't know.

"Oh my," Grandfather said breathlessly.

"What happened?" Grace immediately blurted out.

"Grace, give him time to wake up," I chastised. "Jeez Louise."

We offered him water to drink, but he pushed it away.

"Just need some air," he gasped.

Today seemed like the lead-in to a *Twilight Zone* episode. First, I was giving water to Tyche and now to my grandfather. Who was next?

"Can you sit up?" I asked.

He nodded weakly. Grace and I helped him prop himself up on his arms. Red splotches mottled one side of his face. Drool and blood trailed together on the other side.

"Where is it?" Grandfather gasped.

"Where is what?" Grace answered.

"The bear," he replied. "Damn monster just about took my head off."

"A bear?" I repeated. "Here?"

He nodded. "I was about to settle down for the night when I heard this beast from hell screaming at me. I couldn't see it at first, but I didn't have to. I took off running across these rocks but fell into that seam."

He pointed at the chasm we dragged him out of minutes ago.

"Last thing I remember was tumbling ass over teakettle into the darkness."

"Sounds like you knocked yourself out all night and most of the morning," I said. "Come on, we found the boat. Let's leave Mr. Bear to his domain and get out of here."

Grace and I arranged Grandfather's arms around each of our shoulders, and with him heavily leaning on us, we eased him down the granite slope to the water. Nick stood on shore waiting for us, his arms outstretched to help us hoist Grandfather into the boat. I noticed Tyche was still lying on the tarp where I left her, but she raised her head to study our approach with her one eye.

"You okay, Gramps?" Nick asked once we reached him.

"Not really," he answered, grimacing in obvious pain. I suspected he had a headache that transcended the worst migraine. "I just need to sit down."

Grace and I started to help Nick ease Grandfather into the boat when an explosive roar thundered from the crest of the slope where we stood only minutes before. The bellow cracked like an artillery shell going off.

The enormous prehistoric bear I kept encountering stood on two legs snarling down at us from the top of the rise, snapping his jaws at the air. The dark area of fur on his right side—blood, I thought—told me all I needed to know. This was indeed the same bear I had hurt with my spear, the same bear that had it in for me, the same bear that had stalked me for days all over this godforsaken wilderness.

"Oh my God," Grace gasped. Her hands trembled. She had never seen this monster before, and no amount of description can prepare a person for the sight of it.

"In the boat!" I yelled at everyone.

Poor Grandfather. I shoved him backward over the gunwale so that twice in twenty-four hours he found himself falling ass over tea-kettle. Grace had one foot in the boat and one in the water, but I couldn't wait any longer. I gripped the back of the skiff with both hands and pushed with all my strength, hoping to shove it as far out onto the lake as possible before the bear attacked. Grace tumbled into the boat, exhaling a string of curses intermixed with panicked meowing sounds from Tyche.

"Start rowing, Nick!" I shouted.

I kept advancing into the water, pushing the boat, until the water reached my armpits. Then the boat pulled away from me as Nick's steady strokes kicked in. I dove after it and swam freestyle as fast as I could manage for ten yards until I caught up. Grace took my hands and helped drag me out of the water.

I glanced back at the shore, half expecting to see the bear in the water dog paddling after us. Apparently, he wasn't hungry enough today to go swimming. Having waded out on all fours, the bear stood silently in a few feet of water and watched us glide away, his vast bulk towering out of the water like a massive pillar of fur. If bears have facial expressions, I couldn't read his. Did he hate me? Was I merely a potential meal that kept stumbling across his path? Or was this personal? Mano a mano.

"Keep going that way," I told Nick, pointing over his shoulder at the vast expanse of water behind him. "That's our way home."

As we rowed roughly parallel to the shore, but a few hundred yards out, I watched a black lump lumber back into the forest until it disappeared from sight. Goodbye and good riddance . . . except, deep down inside me where the monsters hid, I knew we'd meet again.

Don't know where . . . don't know when.

CHAPTER THIRTY

"That's the only way out of this lake," I said, pointing to the distant inlet.

The very long day was coming to an end, and each of us slumped on the hard boat seats, exhausted, hungry, and dirty. I pulled in the oars and watched the others as we drifted on the still water, each of us withdrawn into our own thoughts and worries. Tyche lay on the bottom of the boat at Grandfather's feet; he had accepted having a wild lynx in our boat as a perfectly normal thing to bring along on a desperate survival trek.

"The stream doesn't look very big," Grandfather finally noted. "We could go in a couple miles and get stuck."

"Then we carry the boat," I countered. "Our choice is simple. Either we venture up this waterway or we try to go back to the cabin. We've rowed and rowed around this end of the lake. There is no other way out."

"What about the bear?" Grace asked. "It attacked Grandfather only a few miles back. It could have easily followed us along the lakeshore."

"Maybe," I agreed. "But, again, what other option do we have?"

With various expressions of reluctance, each of my family nodded agreement about proceeding. They didn't necessarily believe that this was the right thing to do, but they trusted me and trusted that I knew what the best course of action was. Pressure much?

We would need to stop, set up camp, and make dinner in an hour or so, but I wanted to make some progress down this small exit river before we stopped. It meant that when we woke tomorrow morning we were committed—one mind, one path.

I wasn't sure why everyone listened to me and did what I asked. No one elected me leader. I certainly didn't have any special knowledge of where we were or where we were going. What I did have was conviction and determination. We had to follow the water wherever it led, however grueling the journey might be, or we'd never get out of this jungle. This I knew with certainty . . . the way a person knows that corn flakes left in milk too long get soggy.

Also, I think they followed me because I didn't show any fear. Not that I was never afraid, but out here, you controlled it or it killed you.

With a weary sigh, I gave up rowing for the day about a mile up the small tributary, where the route turned in a big bend, leaving a nice, gravelly area exposed. We put up the tarp, spread out our blankets, and made a fire. Surprisingly, Grandfather and Tyche took to each other as if they were long-lost siblings separated at birth. He held her on his lap all night, giving her food and water while softly stroking her fur. I dipped an old sock of mine in the water and gave it to Grandfather. He used it to dab away some of the dirt caked on Tyche's fur.

While the others prepared to turn in, I withdrew a little ways away from them and plopped down on a fallen tree. I tilted my head back to stare up at the moonless sky studded with so many fiercely bright stars that it almost hurt my eyes, and I smiled. Three months ago, this world was scary and alien and brutal. Not today. I wasn't an invader or a trespasser here anymore. Somehow, I felt as if the land welcomed me as one of its lost children come home.

"You like the wilderness," Grace whispered as she sat down beside me. I hadn't heard her approach. "I can see it on your face."

"It's not so bad."

"Are you serious? What, you like the misery of it all?"

"No," I said, shaking my head slowly. "I like the *clarity* of it all."

Each of us took turns standing watch, but the night passed without incident or unusual sound. When we climbed back into the boat the next morning, after a breakfast of cold fish and pine needle tea, a chill hung in the air.

No one kept track, but I guessed the end of August had passed and the land around us was making the turn into a brief autumn before plunging into a brutal winter. We didn't want to be here when that happened.

"The river is definitely narrowing," Nick said after we were underway for some time.

At its mouth, the inlet was as wide as a four-lane highway, but Nick was right. Our water highway had shrunk to the width of a two-lane country road. It had also shallowed, judging by the occasional jolts we felt when the aluminum bottom struck a rock.

We officially hit a dead end just after lunch. Our river had reduced to a stream and then a creek and then a trickle hardly big enough for us to float a folded paper boat down.

"Now what?" Grandfather asked.

"We follow the water," Nick said. "We can drag the boat along the creek bed."

"Well, we've come this far," Grace said, not exactly oozing enthusiasm. "I guess we push on."

The unknown in front won out over the emptiness of our back trail, so Grandfather rigged up shoulder straps from the rope we had and attached them to the prow. Two of us at a time would slip the straps over our shoulders and pull the boat along. Following Nick's idea, Grandfather and I took the first shift and slogged forward along the creek bed. The water flowed slowly over rocks and into small pools, and at its deepest, it covered the tops of my boots.

Made of aluminum, the boat wasn't too heavy, and our pathetic mishmash of supplies didn't weigh much either, so we made pretty good progress. Tyche initially tried to climb out of the boat, but she still could barely walk, so gradually, she gave up and lay back down inside.

I expected this undertaking to be only slightly easier than Sisyphus pushing his boulder up a steep hill, but not so. The flat bottom slid along quite nicely, thank you very much, and only occasionally did our slog require special effort overcoming downed limbs and inconveniently placed boulders.

After a time, when Grandfather and I could barely stand, Grace and Nick took over with the hauling straps. I trudged along behind the boat, from time to time giving it a shove when the going became rough. This was our routine for days and days. I waited for someone to tell me I screwed up and going this way was a mistake, but no one did.

It helped that we had spectacular weather for a week—mostly blue skies, sun, and only a few wisps of clouds.

Our run of good weather luck ended mid-afternoon one day. Ominous black clouds rolled in, darkening the sky, and soon rain began to fall. None of us had any raingear, so within minutes, we were soaked. The rain also drenched our blankets and everything in the boat that wasn't in a Ziploc bag, including Tyche, who lay on the bottom of the boat looking forlorn and wet.

"Let's hole up until the rain stops," I told everyone.

No one argued with this. Finding a hole to hole up in proved difficult, though, as in we found nothing resembling a natural shelter. In the end, we huddled against the trunk of a massive spruce tree, using its hundreds of radiating branches to block as much of the rain as possible. Some drops got through, of course, but a lot less than standing out in the open. With my clothes drenched and a slight breeze rustling through the forest, I quickly went from cool to chilly to cold. I began to shiver, which triggered nightmares of hypothermia. Grandfather was the only one who seemed unaffected by the rain, which was fine, since he held Tyche on his lap and focused his attention on keeping her warm. Tyche needed what only humans could give—love—and Grandfather was giving it to her.

Meanwhile back at the ranch, the pounding raindrops made it difficult to hear anything, but Grace sat jammed up next to me so close I heard her teeth chattering. She looked utterly wretched. Then the wind picked up speed, and sideways rain lashed us like knotted rawhide whips. I curled into myself to escape the stinging downpour, but my efforts did little good.

To put an exclamation point on the monsoon rain, the skies darkened further. Then deafening cannonades of thunder exploded all around us. Crackling bolts of lightning followed. As nasty a storm as I have experienced rolled over us. I remembered reading that sitting under a tree was risky during a lightning storm. I didn't care. I would roll the dice. The alternative was to step out into the open and most certainly catch pneumonia from exposure.

"Are we going to die out here?" Grace asked me at one point.

She might have been crying. Hard to tell in the rain. I pulled her head tight against my shoulder and held her.

How to answer her question?

"I don't know," I finally answered. "Maybe, maybe not."

I wasn't going to lie to her. As much as Grace and I didn't get along prior to this trip, she always knew if I fibbed. And what was Grace to me now? I only knew things between us were different. Mom's death had torn a gaping, unbridgeable chasm between us, but I think maybe we had moved past that breach. It wasn't healed, but possibly it now lived on only in my rearview mirror.

"I'm sorry," she said. Now I had no doubt she was crying. "I know you blame me for Mom. I—"

"Shhh," I cut her off. "We don't need to do this. Not today."

I fought to stay in the moment, but the past sucked me backward into its embrace. What really happened that day I had buried deep inside myself and swore I'd never dig up. Now it unfolded in my mind. I couldn't completely avoid remembering the day Mom died, but I had an abbreviated, sanitized version that my brain pulled up when I had to face her death.

This time was different. The *real* version of what happened flooded into me, not my abridged construct. In seconds, the full, uncensored edition of that horrible afternoon emerged from the depths of my memory like an old rusty ship rising from the bottom of the ocean to float on the surface once more. I didn't want this, but it was sort of like a theme park roller-coaster ride. The ride guy strapped you into your seat and you were locked in for the duration—with all the ups, downs, twirls, and swirls. No getting off halfway through; no skipping over the scary parts.

"Dylan gave me a couple joints," Liv said, as we walked off the field from lacrosse practice.

"Why? I thought you hated each other."

"We do. He gave them to me because I promised to say 'yes' if Peter asked me to the dance."

My eyes scrunched together in an "uck" poison face expression. "You should get at least a key for that."

"Want to smoke them tonight?" she asked, batting her eyelashes several times.

"I think I can get Frederick to drive me," I said coyly. "We have to study together for next week's English final, remember?"

"Oh, we are going to study the shit out of English," she said with a laugh.

After I showered and dressed in the locker room, our black Mercedes sedan lurched to a stop two feet away from me in front of Scarsdale Middle School, but when I tried to open the passenger's side door to enter, it was locked. After two impatient raps of my knuckles on the window, the door lock clicked open. I expected to see Frederick, our usual driver, but instead, it was Mom, who had her phone plastered to her ear talking rapidly to someone. She gave me a quick waggle of her fingers in greeting.

"Okay, call me tomorrow," Mom said. "I have to run. Allie is here." She dropped her phone haphazardly into the cup holder and smiled warmly at me. "How was lacrosse practice?"

"Could you not ask me how lacrosse practice was every single day? I'm tired of saying 'fine.'"

"Are we a little grouchy this afternoon?"

"No, we are a little *starved* this afternoon," I answered tartly.

"We have to make a slight detour—"

I interrupted her, "Mom, please. Take me home first."

"I have to stop at Dalby's for your father, and . . ."

She paused mid-sentence. Another shoe had yet to drop, so I swiveled my head around to stare expectantly at her.

"Grace needs a ride home from Sasha's house," she blurted out in a rush.

My mouth fell open in shock, and after two gulps I said, "But she's grounded."

"She is. She was supposed to come straight home after school, but Sasha accidentally took Grace's notebook home with her. I told her she could stop by and pick it up."

"Yeah, right," I muttered. "And you fell for that?"

"It's none of your business, Allie. It's between me and Grace. You stay out of it."

With an exasperated sigh, I slumped into the front passenger seat and began shaking my head. Mom and I drove in silence. Since Mom was listening to a radio channel playing nothing but smarmy, lame-ass nineties songs, I inserted my earbuds and scrolled through my phone until I found my favorite playlist. As the first song began, Liv texted me, confirming all the rumors around school today that her ex-boyfriend, Evan, had indeed hooked up with Victoria. I texted her back.

Me: ***Sleepover my house Friday? Chocolate party.***

Olivia: ***Yes!...U coming tonight still?***

Me: ***Dipshit little sister issues...stand by.***

When we reached Sasha's house and pulled to a stop in front of a stone walkway leading from the curb to the front door, there was no Grace. Of course not. She was supposed to be waiting out front, but she was MIA. Even Mom clucked her tongue in frustration.

"Hop out and get Grace," Mom said. "Say hello to Mrs. Heller for me."

"Why bother? She's an alcoholic, you know."

"Allie!"

"It's true," I protested. "You shouldn't let Grace come over here."

"Well, say hello anyway. And while you're getting Grace, I'm going to run to Dalby's. It'll only take fifteen minutes, so kill some time with Grace and Sasha until I return."

"I'm not going in there! It's a dump. Sasha's baby brother has his toys littered all over the place. Last time I went in to get Grace, his diaper needed changing. Their house is disgusting."

"You sound like a spoiled brat, Allie."

"So what if I am?" I challenged.

"Nobody likes rich, entitled white girls," she replied. "Except other rich, entitled white girls. Don't be one of those."

"Please," I begged, ignoring her comment. I really didn't want her to leave. "Can't we send Frederick to Dalby's when we get home?"

"Allie, it's only a few minutes."

"Well, I won't be here when you get back," I replied, arms firmly folded across my chest. "I'll walk home."

"That's ridiculous," she said. "It's over five miles."

"I'll hitchhike," I answered, sounding nonchalant. "Who knows, maybe a registered sex offender will give me a ride. I'd rent my body out for a few lines of coke."

Mom tilted her head back against seat rest and exhaled dramatically. "Fine, you *enfant terrible*. I'll wait. Now go fetch your sister."

I smiled at her, and she punched on the car's hazard lights. Then I jumped out and jogged toward the house. Once on the porch, I tapped the electronic doorbell and stepped back to wait.

Thirty seconds later, my mother died . . . incinerated in a horrific car crash. She'd be alive if only I had let her go to Dalby's. I spent all these years blaming Grace because I couldn't face the truth. If anybody was to blame for my mother's death, it was me. But really? If I learned one thing out here in the hinterlands, it was that life was life and death was death. They happened when they happened, and they were matters too big for me or Grace to take the blame for. And with that realization came acceptance and absolution . . . both of myself and Grace.

The memory of that day faded away. I was back to holding Grace in my arms under the limbs of the spruce tree.

"Mom was never your fault," I whispered to her. "I'm sorry I haven't been there for you the last few years."

She snorted a couple times as she tried to get her sobbing under control.

After a wasted attempt to wipe her eyes dry with the back of her hand, she said, "I'm sorry that it felt so nice punching you in the eye."

We both laughed, and I squeezed her tighter against me. As if on cue, the wind blew stronger and the rain came down harder.

CHAPTER THIRTY-ONE

The torrential downpour stopped around midnight. I knew because I still had my Cartier watch, it still worked, and I couldn't sleep. All of us were cold and miserable; we huddled as one against the spruce tree for hours and hours, smooshed together to share body warmth.

I disentangled myself and stood shortly before dawn, every inch of my skin and all of my clothes soaking wet. Grandfather uncurled from his sitting position and rose to his feet too.

"Thinking we should stay here another day," I told him. "Get a fire going, dry out our clothes, rest up. We can start off again tomorrow."

I shivered and prayed for a warm day today to bake heat into my bones and get the blood circulating again.

"Same path as before?" he asked.

"Maybe," I answered. "I'm going to scout ahead and see what's in front of us. No sense stumbling ahead blind any longer."

He nodded. "Be careful. That bear is still roaming the woods."

Tyche came over to me with her damaged face and sat on her haunches in front of me, staring up at me with her single eye. In the days since I found her, her strength seemed to have revived significantly, but she was still a bag of skin and bones. She might not be the fierce hunter she once was, but her hearing was scary good. Nothing would sneak up on us with her around.

"I'll take Tyche," I told him. "Her foot seems better."

"We've got enough fish for one meal," he said. "Just FYI."

"No probs. If I pass a McDonald's on the way, I'll get us some takeout . . . with the wads of nonexistent money I have."

I started to smile but froze when Grandfather banged his fist against his chest and his cheeks went crimson red. The grimace on his face said it all; tremendous pain wracked his body. He bent over, hands on knees, and coughed violently before slumping to the ground. Grace and Nick didn't rouse.

"What is it?" I asked, kneeling beside him.

"It hurts," he replied, as his chest heaved to gasp in air. "God, it hurts."

"Where are your meds?" I asked.

"Gone," he said. "I ran out weeks ago."

"What can I do?"

He shook his head. "Nothing. He said it would get like this even with the meds."

"He?"

Grandfather gulped twice, his Adam's apple moving slowly up and down. "My doctor."

I nodded in understanding. However bad things might be with his cancer, I wasn't going to let him die out here. Not like this. We were all walking out of here together. That was the deal—united we stood or divided we fell.

"Let's find a dry spot for you to lie down," I said.

"It's passing," he murmured. "You go on. Find us a way out of here, granddaughter."

Once I helped him back to the tree where the others drowsed, I turned my back on my family and strode away with Tyche at my side, her injured leg no longer a problem. We followed the stream-bed but tried not to walk in it. I suspected my boots were never going to dry out, but maybe today I could at least attempt to keep them from getting soaked again. As for my clothes, if I managed to get my body heat back to where it should be, I could walk them dry.

Tyche and I marched for several hours through the jungle of fir trees and underbrush in search of navigable water for the boat. As bad as Tyche looked with her matted fur, I knew I looked worse. My body was disgusting. My skin had ugly rashes, scratches, welts, and too many scabs to count from prior cuts and scrapes. Plus, I was fairly certain I had a yeast infection . . . and the hits just kept on coming.

Thank God we didn't have a mirror; I wouldn't want to see my face. My head had a bristly stubble of hair on it, as my brown locks began to grow back, but my scalp was sunburned and covered with itchy bug bites, some of which I had scratched until they bled.

My heart sank when I came to a point where the stream picked up volume and plunged down into a steep ravine. The sluggish water gained speed as it raced downhill, tumbling over a bed of large rocks. No way would we ever drag the boat past this point, at least not following the stream.

I reached a dead end and couldn't go any farther this way. Part of me wanted to collapse on the ground and cry. Hopelessness and despair descended over me . . . or, I should say, they *tried*. I refused to let them anywhere near me.

"Come on, Tyche," I said, gritting my teeth. "It ain't over till the fat lady sings."

The obstacles in front of me became a dead end only if I gave up and stopped trying. So, I turned aside from following the stream and dove straight into the forest. There had to be a way out somewhere.

Tyche and I clawed our way ahead for about a half a mile when I froze in my tracks staring up at the sky through a break in the trees. A big bird flew over us. I started to say something to Tyche when another one glided by. At first, I thought I was seeing eagles, but that couldn't be. The birds appeared large enough to be an eagle, but their white and gray feathers nixed that idea.

"Seagulls," I finally said to Tyche. "What are a bunch seagulls doing out here?"

I answered my own question. There had to be a major waterway they followed into the interior from the sea.

A river?

Must be. And not just any river; it had to be a big sucker.

The nearest body of saltwater was Hudson Bay. Although we had covered a lot of ground, there was no way we had come close to walking all the way to Hudson Bay. Encouraged, I tramped onward with the confidence and renewed strength a person gained when staring up from the bottom of an abyss expecting to see only blackness and instead spying a tiny spark of light.

Within minutes, we broke through the trees and emerged into a clearing at the edge of a bluff that stretched as far as I could see to my left and to my right. In front and below me, a vast forested plain extended out to the horizon, but I didn't care about any of these things. My eyes focused instead at what lay at the foot of the hundred-foot-high bluff I was standing on. A brown river. A beautiful muddy brown river. And not your ordinary, plain vanilla brown river either. This momma had to be at least five hundred feet wide. It was freaking huge!

I gawked at the ginormous ribbon of torpid water that meandered like a slithering snake. If a tugboat rounded one of the bends and chugged upriver it wouldn't surprise me in the least . . . or maybe a couple of bright yellow float planes following the water like a boulevard leading them to remote settlements around the next curve. I had to settle for squawking seagulls and a pair of bald eagles that glided effortlessly above the land below.

"That there is our way home," I said to Tyche. "There have to be settlements along a river this big. All we need to do is float down the river until we find one."

Tyche glanced up at me and blinked several times.

"Slap me some skin," I told the cat, holding out one hand for a high-five.

Instead, she backed up a step and stared at me, perhaps thinking I'd finally gone zonkers.

"Booyeah!" I shouted to the surrounding forest, fists raised in the air. Nature went silent.

Then I started dancing the Dougie, shuffling my feet from right to left while my arms swayed back and forth to a make-believe rap number. We were going home!

My return journey to the boat went a heck of a lot faster than the journey out. I was jacked. My mind ran through fantasy after fantasy of reuniting with Dad and seeing Liv again, of eating chocolate ice cream until I threw up, and of sleeping in a real bed. I decided I'd delay going back to vegan long enough to binge on a couple dozen hamburgers and milkshakes.

When Tyche and I reached our makeshift camp at dusk, I found Nick and Grace sitting on a log in their underwear by a fire. Their grubby, dirty, grimy clothes hung near the fire on a length of rope strung a few yards off the ground. I had a moment of envy that their clothes would soon be dry while mine remained positively sopping wet from busting through the waterlogged brush all day.

My eyes searched for Grandfather. I found him lying on the ground nearby with his forearm covering his eyes.

"She's back!" Grace said playfully. "Did you find an interstate with a Mercedes on the side of the road, keys in the ignition?"

"Close," I said, smiling broadly at her.

"Really?" Nick said.

"I found a river that will take us home," I announced. "We just need to drag the boat to it."

Grandfather sat up at this news. His face was ashen and pinched. I could only imagine the pain he was in. Yet, he managed to calm his expression so he didn't betray to the others the cancer eating away inside him. As far as I knew, Grace and Nick had no idea how sick their grandfather was. I had debated several times since I found out whether to tell them or not. Not only was it not my story to tell, but what good would it do? None.

Nick and Grace bumped fists. I joined in the celebration but paused when I saw an ugly red lump directly above Grace's belly button. I pointed at it.

"What's that?" I asked.

"Spider bite. Big ugly thing. He got under my shirt yesterday and fanged me. Stung at first, but it doesn't hurt now."

"Let's keep an eye on it," I said. "Shame if you died just as we're about to get out of here."

"Or I could develop spidey abilities," she said. "Might come in handy."

She pivoted her wrists up as if to shoot webs out of them.

Nick started to sing, "Spiderman, spiderman, does whatever—"

"*Woman*, jerko," Grace interrupted.

"Right," Nick said with a grin. "I knew that."

Not much of the day remained, not enough to pack up and head out, so we stuck with the original plan of resuming our trek tomorrow. Although I was so excited I could have hiked for twelve hours, a good night's rest would serve me better.

Sadly, the fish was gone, so we ate an air dinner . . . I had waffles with strawberries and whipped cream.

"I'm eating a bacon cheeseburger right now," Grace said. She moaned in ecstasy. "Grease and melted cheese are dripping off my chin. The pickles are crisp and scrumptious, but the killer is the bacon. Oh my God."

"Even though I will have faux heartburn all night," Grandfather said playfully, "I'm still going to finish every last bite of my twenty-ounce porterhouse steak, including all the gristle."

"Just a steak?" I chided.

"Oh no," he said, chuckling for the first time in days. "I'm also working on a loaded baked potato, Texas toast, and a fifty-year-old bottle of Château Margaux."

"Nick?" I asked.

"Fried chicken, extra crispy," he said. "My teeth are ripping into a drumstick. Also, I'm stuffing hot buttermilk biscuits in my mouth, soon to be followed by apple pie."

After each of us was sated by our food orgasms, I passed around my pine needle tea. The taste was bitter as usual, but at least it was hot.

"No offense," Grace said, "but I never want to drink this shit again."

"Don't knock it," I replied. "It's full of vitamin C, and that is what's keeping you from getting scurvy."

"Since when did you become a wilderness plant lady?" Nick asked.

"I didn't. One of the girls in our dorm, though, is Jeremiah Johnson's granddaughter. She'd probably love to be doing this right now."

Grace sighed. "Happy to swap with her, but there's never a teleportation machine around when you need one."

We went to bed after that. I climbed into my mostly dry, but grimy, blanket, dragging Tyche in alongside me. I shamelessly used her fur and warmth as my personal body heater device. She didn't seem to care.

My last thought before sinking into sleep was that we did it. Our journey was almost over. I just wanted it all to end.

Be careful what you wish for . . . be *very* fucking careful.

CHAPTER THIRTY-TWO

Dragging a boat through virgin forest land with ropes and shoulder straps ranked a notch above cleaning out septic tanks, but a person wouldn't know that by watching us. We sang and joked as we wrestled our banged-up and dented little boat over the mostly dry streambed and toward our liberation. For the first time in weeks, hope flared inside us beyond the tiny ember that was there before. I told and retold all the details of the river I could remember. While I wished I could say I saw a cruise ship at anchor with a big sign reading "stragglers and lost folk welcome," finding the river itself was enough of a discovery. A body of water that big had to lead to something, and something meant people, and people meant rescue.

"Maybe Dad will direct a movie about this," Grace suggested. "I can costar as me."

"Vain much?" I replied.

"Hey, I've earned it."

Although our spirits were high, the work was grueling. The boat with our gear didn't weigh that much, but we had to negotiate rocks and downed trees that constantly blocked our path. In some cases, the four of us would lift the boat up over our heads and carry it over an obstacle, and in others, we had to unload our stuff and slide the boat sideways to get it past narrow areas. Nobody complained. No one wanted to rest for more than a few minutes. We all wanted to cover as much ground as possible.

"How ya doing there, G?" I asked my grandfather at one point.

"Other than feeling gut shot, run over, and left for dead, I am fine and frisky."

I bit my lower lip. I knew he was in pain, and we had to stop frequently for him to catch his breath and get through one of his coughing sessions. His distressed condition was the only dark cloud hanging over our day.

"This is as far as we go," I told the others when we reached the place where the stream disappeared down into the steep gorge. "Now we keep to the left side of the stream and head overland."

"How far?" Nick asked.

"A few miles maybe," I said. "We can make it before dark."

The stream at this point broadened, but it was only a few yards across. It went from barely covering my boot tops to knee-deep, almost big enough for us to use the boat. Almost, but not quite. The water then cascaded over one set of jagged rocks after another as it cut a path downhill to the river I now knew lay below. Over the years, the centuries maybe, the gravity-aided stream eroded the soil so the water eventually rushed downhill through a giant gorge with steep, unclimbable walls on each side.

After we slogged for a few hours on the left side of the gorge, the distance between the side we were traveling on and the other side of the chasm expanded to fifty yards at least, and the gap continued to grow as we drew closer to the edge of the butte overlooking the river. At that point, our little stream became a small river and the gorge became a tiny canyon.

"Let's take a short break," I said after a few hours of nonstop hauling.

I rubbed one hand over the top of my bristly head, which was slick with sweat. Nick, Grace, and I wordlessly agreed hours back that we would not include Grandfather in the boat-pulling rotation. He was doing all he could to stand and walk.

"We're almost out of water," Nick said, handing a bottle to Grace. "Hope your river is close, Allie."

"Couple more hours," I said.

One worry that nagged at me was getting the boat down to the river itself. Soon, we would break out of the trees and stand on the lip of a bluff overlooking a flat tableland below. How were we going to drag a boat down the slope? My only answer to this question was we'd figure something out when we got there. After all we had been through, we weren't going to let some stupid cliff stand between us and going home.

I sat cross-legged on the dead-leaf-covered ground, leaning back on my hands. My designer jeans, once so new and trendy, were torn and slathered with dirt, but who cared? We all looked like we'd spent the last year sleeping inside a refrigerator box in a filthy alley somewhere.

Comme ci, comme ça.

Various discomforts attacked my body; it itched, burned, or ached, depending on location. No matter how cold the water, I resolved to plunge into the river and baptize away all my scum and dirt sins.

My lips parted to tell the others to get their tushes up and moving again when my eyes caught a flicker of movement on the other side of the gorge. Not a squirrel. I was too far away to pick out an animal that small. Deer? Moose? Hard to tell through all the underbrush. It stopped moving, and leafy green bushes screened its silhouette.

Tyche, who sat next to me, sprang to her feet and began to hiss. She only acted this way in the face of a bad-ass predator. It was all the warning I needed. Dread trickled into me.

"Guys," I said, rising to my feet.

Nick and Grace were arguing over who got the left tow strap versus the right.

"Guys," I repeated in a louder voice.

All voices went silent, and Nick, Grace, and Grandfather turned their heads toward me to see what I wanted. I lifted my hand to point across the chasm. As I did so, the obscuring brush across the canyon parted, and dino-bear stepped out into full view. It knew we were over here, whether by sight, smell, or hearing. Immediately, it began bellowing in seeming outrage at us, tossing its snout around in the air and baring it vicious teeth.

The bear.

My bear.

"Shit!" Grace gasped. "That mother humper followed us!"

"That extremely *angry* mother humper," I clarified.

"A balrog," Grandfather murmured. "Durin's bane."

"Huh?" Grace and I said at the same time.

Then Nick started to convulse.

Oh God, not now!

I grabbed Nick under the arms as he slumped, desperately fighting to keep him on his feet. Grace rushed to help me. Nick's eyes rolled back in his head.

"Nick, we need you," I pleaded. "Stay with me. Please."

"Morgon," he whispered.

"You're stronger than him," I said through clenched teeth. "I can't fight him alone, Nick."

This confession helped. We eased Nick to the ground, where he sucked in deep breaths and fought to stay in control. After a few moments passed, he glanced up at me, and our eyes locked. Then I exhaled slowly and nodded at him. After he rested for a few minutes on the ground, we helped him back to his feet.

Nick would not give into his demons today. I needed his spear. We all needed his spear.

"I don't think he can get to us from over there," Grandfather observed.

"Not from there," I agreed. "It's at least a fifty-feet drop to the bottom of the ravine. And it's way too steep for him to climb up this side."

"Tell him that," Grace muttered.

"Let's move back from the edge," I suggested, "and get out of here. Maybe if he can't see us, he'll forget about us."

As soon as I said this, the bear stopped his roaring and carrying on. Instead, he silently stared at us, as if waiting for a bridge to materialize for him to cross. Then he turned and ambled upstream following the edge of the gorge.

"What's he doing?" Grace asked, her voice etched with anxiety.

"I think he's backtracking to where he can cross the stream," Grandfather said. From his whispered tone, he sounded incredulous.

"Are you kidding me?" I burst out. "What is with this guy?"

"How far?" Grace asked, referring to the bear. She sounded flat-out scared.

"A few miles before he could cross," I answered grimly. "Then another few miles to here. He can't run in this jungle much better than we can, so I'd guess he could be where we stand now in three hours."

"He might give up," Grandfather suggested. "It would be a lot of work chasing after us."

I shook my head. "He doesn't seem like the giving-up type."

Tyche nipped at my leg and swatted my ankle with her paw. I had no trouble interpreting her actions. She wanted us to get our bums out of here *pronto*. I completely agreed.

"Well, what are we waiting for?" Grace cried out, practically shrieking. "We need to leave!"

Yes, we certainly did.

We picked up our pace well beyond what we were doing earlier. Before bear, we were like galley slaves on a Roman trireme ship methodically pulling on the oars in no particular hurry to get anywhere. After bear, it was ramming speed.

Grace and I shouldered the tow ropes, Nick steadied the boat, and Grandfather pushed from behind. Tyche sat on one of the bench seats as if the boat was her personal palanquin.

With Grace, my fellow groaner and moaner, beside me I marched ahead with my body bent forward at almost a forty-five-degree angle. The labor was monotonous, draining, and our backs and shoulders throbbed with pain, but Grace and I didn't let up. With our legs pumping up and down like pistons, we moved twice as fast as before. With a bad-ass apex predator chasing us, Grace and I reached down within ourselves and found energy reserves we didn't even know we possessed.

To keep our minds distracted from the physical abuse our bodies were suffering, we made up a little ditty as we stomped along, which we sang to the tune of "The Battle Hymn of the Republic."

"Glory, glory, got to march until we cry," I sang

Grace followed with "Glory, glory, got to haul this boat or die."

I sang, "Glory, glory, got no feeling in my thighs."

And together, we sang, "But we're not weak girls anymore."

After we finished our song, Nick yelled, "Sing it again!"

And so it went refrain after refrain. Yeah, dumb . . . but effective. The rousing tune pumped us up enough that we felt strong enough to take on both Godzilla *and* Mothra.

We reached the bluff late in the afternoon, whereupon all of us promptly collapsed to the ground, our chests heaving from the exertion. Grace and I did all the towing, deciding not to stop to alternate with Nick. The grinding strain on my shoulders turned my muscles into hamburger, and they began to swell like a puffer fish from the contusions.

I didn't know about Grace, but I also had a serious case of Quasimodo syndrome; my shoulders hunched forward, and I could barely straighten my back. I gazed over at my baby sister, who lay on the grass like a felled tree, arms and legs outstretched the way they would be if she was going to make a snow angel. She had stripped to her sports bra before doing her best imitation of a dead animal. Her shoulders were heavily bruised and already turning dark shades of purple and red. Judging from the pain, my shoulders were the same.

"Now what?" Nick asked. He was the least tired of all of us.

"Grandfather," I began.

"Yes."

"Your mission," I said, still breathing heavy, "is to save our butts by figuring out how we get the boat down the bluff."

"I'd help," Grace said, "but I'm still fighting off cardiac arrest. I need at least a fifteen-minute blow."

He nodded and strode to the edge to survey the problem.

After Grace and I recovered, we rose and stretched. We stood in the middle of a grassy clearing that lay between the forest and the edge of the butte overlooking the river. The ground was mostly flat. In another part of the world, you might call it a meadow. The space wasn't big, maybe the size of the infield grass on a baseball diamond.

I walked over to my grandfather, who still stood at the brink of the cliff staring out at the land beyond.

"Any ideas?" I asked.

"It's too steep to drag the boat down," he said. "I say we lower it by rope. The slope is mostly dirt and sand. So, the boat should slide down nice and smooth until we get to the rocks at the bottom. We'll have to portage over those."

I gazed down at the ground below and shrugged. Why not? I got nothing better.

He was right. We should be able to lower the boat smoothly. The slope wasn't perpendicular. We faced maybe a seventy-degree incline. And it was pretty much all sand, except the car-sized boulders that lay at the foot of the cliff. Basically, we stood on top of a giant dirt pile that rose a hundred feet above a jagged rocky floor.

"Sounds like we have a plan," I said. "Time to try it out. We may not have much time."

Grandfather's plan worked perfectly. We spent about an hour attaching ropes to the prow and gradually lowering the boat down the cliff. We took it slow, not wanting to risk the boat flipping over and spilling out our meager supplies. Tyche stood next to me supervising the work, perhaps wondering "what in the name of all that was feline were these humans doing?"

Now it was our turn to follow. The grade wasn't so steep we couldn't inch our way down it, provided we went slow and careful enough not to lose our balance.

Before we could start, though, we heard the sound we dreaded . . . the unmistakable snarl and growl of a bear. *My* bear. He crashed through the brush and paused to stare at me, his nose sniffing the air.

"Go!" I yelled to the others. "I'll hold him off."

I grabbed my spear off the ground, held it with both hands, and crouched in a defensive position. I knew I had no chance of defeating this monster, but that wasn't my plan. All I wanted to do was buy my family time to scramble down the cliff, get the boat to the river, and take off.

Me? I saw no scenario where I was making it out of this alive. Escape was not in the cards. When we first arrived at the cabin, I would have run screaming in mindless fear from this encounter. Not today. I wasn't that person anymore.

"What are you waiting for!" I screamed at the bear. "Bring it, fatso!"

He roared in response and charged.

CHAPTER THIRTY-THREE

"Allie!" Grace yelled.

"Get out of here!" I shouted back.

The bear covered the space between us in a couple seconds, working his jaws up and down and flashing his teeth at me. I jabbed with my long spear, hoping the pointy end might stab a sensitive area and prompt the beast to back off, but my spear made no contact, and he didn't back off. Instead, he drew up a few yards short of me, bawling out angry growls.

Jesus, even on all fours this thing stood at least six feet off the ground at the shoulders. His eyes actually stared down at me like an adult frowning down at a little child.

The size of his voice matched the size of his body. His roars were guttural, primal, and piercing. The ground shook from them. Also, he was so close to me I felt spray droplets from his mouth. And the bad breath? Good God in heaven. And I thought *I* smelled bad.

He was wary of my spear, though. It hurt him once. He remembered. That emboldened me a little.

"Yah, yah, yah!" I shouted at the bear while thrusting my spear at him.

Bearzilla tried to clamp its jaws down on my weapon, and when that failed, he swiped at it with his mammoth paws. So far, my timing was perfect; I managed to yank my spear back out of his reach each time he attacked it. This tiny little impasse couldn't last; either he drew blood or I did, and I wouldn't bet the farm on me.

I lunged at him, hoping to surprise him and stab his eye out.

He dodged.

I thrust again.

Missed.

Again.

Hit!

Sort of.

The spear impaled the part of the skin alongside his jaw. That had to hurt at least a little, but it wasn't more than a mosquito bite to ugly fur face.

Then it was his turn to go on the offensive. He sprang forward with surprising agility and speed for a giant, hairy lard ball.

I leaped back, careful to keep my spear leveled at him.

He stopped and boomed out a howl of fury and maybe annoyance that his puny prey was fighting back. I jabbed several times at him to remind him that if he came at me I'd ram this stake down his gullet.

On my sixth jab, he swatted at the spear with his right paw. I jerked my weapon upward to avoid his attack, but a machete-sized claw caught the spear and snagged it sideways, almost wrenching it from my hands. I managed to hold on, but just barely.

How long could I keep this up?

As long as I have to, I told myself and gritted my teeth.

Once the others were safe, maybe I'd stop, hold my spear up, and let the bear have me. You know, do the Obi-Wan thing. Or, more probably, I'd turn and run. Possibly I'd make it five or ten yards before my enemy dragged me down. What he did next when he caught me would set off an exploding supernova of pain, and I would be alive when he started feasting on my body. Well, that was going to suck.

Strangely, I accepted the inevitability of my imminent death; I wasn't afraid of it. Wow, this was new . . . and quite possibly stupid.

"Everybody dies," I muttered to myself, gripping my spear tighter. "It's not about when; it's all about how."

I wanted to glance over my shoulder to see if the others managed to escape, but if I took my eyes off the bear for even a microsecond, his claws would take off one of my arms.

So far, each time my enemy lumbered forward with his mouth screaming bear obscenities at me, I danced back and jabbed my spear at him to blunt his advance.

The next time when he came at me, I charged him. He paused and woofed a couple of grunts. Aiming for his eyes, I ran at him. My spear missed his eyes but skewered an ear. Not exactly a mortal injury, but it had to hurt, and it surprised the hell out of him. He backed up several yards and rose to stand on two feet. God, was he tall. I heard bears did this to see better what was in front of them, rather than as an attack posture. Yeah, tell him that.

I hesitated. Should I run at him and go for broke, thrusting my spear straight into his guts again? I might not get a better shot at burying my weapon in his vital area. But charging him likely would be a one-shot deal, winner took all. As I took a few seconds to decide, I detected movement out of the corners of my eyes . . . on both sides of me.

Grace came up alongside me on my right.

Nick joined me on my left.

Each held a spear and directed a steely-eyed glare at the bear.

"Nick, get to the boat," I ordered. "Run!"

"Not today," he said calmly.

I locked eyes with each of them in turn, saw that it was all for one and one for all, and nodded solemnly. This would be the Baylors' last stand.

Then I raised my spear in the air and shook it with a whoop.

Grace and Nick rattled their spears and yelled in answer.

The bear, still standing on two legs, clamped his jaws shut and stared at us with WTF eyes.

"Ahhh!" I screamed and charged the bear with my spear pointed outward.

"Ahhh!" Grace and Nick joined in. They charged alongside me.

The bear tilted his head to one side, perhaps confused by our attack.

I reached the target first. My spear impacted the bear on the side, but his hide was tough as leather. Still, I had sharpened the point into the shape of a long tapered needle, so it would get some penetration on even the toughest of skin.

My spear slid in on impact, but the bear twisted at the last second, so I stabbed him high up on his torso and over to one side.

My point hit a rib and deflected in alongside it. The wound was nowhere near serious enough to really hurt him, let alone force him to give up the assault and retreat into the forest.

Grace and Nick followed up my attack a moment later with their own. Grace imbedded her spear in the beast's shoulder; Nick thrust his into the monster's stomach. None of our weapons penetrated more than a few inches. We couldn't generate the newtons of force needed to shove our spears in one side and out the other. I doubted any human could. So, far from maiming the creature, we merely quadrupled how pissed off it was.

The bear fought back viciously. The result of my attack left me vulnerable and only inches away from the beast. His jaws lunged at me and clamped down on my right arm like a titanic vice. He bit down, hoisted me up, and shook me like a doll. A crack erupted, followed by a volcanic eruption of pain beyond anything I ever experienced. One of the large bones in my forearm—the ulna, I think—snapped like a piece of kindling, as enormous incisors sank deep into my flesh. I tried to holler at Grace and Nick to run, but the sound that came out of my mouth was little more than an unintelligible shriek of agony.

It didn't matter what I said.

With hardly more than the effort it would devote to swatting at an annoying insect, the bear tossed me to the side, and I landed on the ground in a heap of searing pain. Then he turned his attention to Grace and Nick.

"Fallayrow!" I shouted hoarsely at Grace, forcing my vocal cords to make words rather than barbaric grunts.

Grace never stood a chance.

Nick never stood a chance.

Two swipes of the bear's massive paws picked my brother and sister up off their feet and sent them flying backward.

Game over.

We were not going home.

I fought to keep my eyes open and hold on to consciousness. Not easy. Blood pumped out of my gash wounds in time with my heartbeat. Were there arteries in the arm? Bizarrely, my brain flashed back to my human biology class for an answer . . . Yes, there were. So, I was going to bleed out onto the grass.

We gambled and lost.

As for the bear, he ignored me for the moment and advanced on the limp bodies of Grace and Nick, who lay unmoving at the edge of the butte. With no enemies left standing, I guessed the bear was going to take things nice and slow and savor his kills. As much as I wanted to rise and fight on, I only managed to get to my knees, and even that expenditure of energy just about caused me to pass out. With its back to me, the bear took no notice of my movements.

The beast opened its mouth to bury its teeth in the back of Grace's neck when it suddenly stopped, pivoted, and stood on two legs again. Something caught its attention.

A noise.

A scream of rage.

From my left, a blur of movement exploded out of the brush. It came out of nowhere.

Grandfather.

He ran at the bear with arms outstretched yelling and screaming. He had no spear. He had no knife. He had no weapon of any kind other than his body.

"Elbereth Gilthoniel!" he hollered.

Him and his damn *Lord of the Rings*.

Still poised on two feet, the bear spread his arms apart to welcome in his newest attacker. Grandfather did the same. He slammed into the bear at full speed, and the monster swallowed him into his arms and gave him . . . well, gave him a bearhug. Then I saw Tyche leap into the air from behind Grandfather and land on the bear's face. I'd seen this reckless move before from her.

My grandfather screamed as the bear began to crush the life out of him, but the bear also bellowed as Tyche raked his face with her razor-sharp claws.

I wanted to avert my eyes. The outcome was ineluctable.

Or so I thought . . .

When Grandfather collided with the bear, I had not counted on two facts. One, the bear stood inches from the edge of the cliff. Two, the law of conservation of momentum.

The bear tottered backward in reaction to the force of Grandfather crashing into him. Not a lot, but just enough. One big bear step in reverse was all it took. The edge crumbled beneath the weight of the two-ton brute, and gravity, sweet fucking gravity, took over. The bear, along with my grandfather and Tyche, toppled over the cliff toward the boulders at its base.

I half expected him to yell back to us, "Fly, you fools."

He didn't. Instead, a couple seconds of awful silence descended before a horrible *thunk, thunk* came from far below moments later.

I crawled over to Grace, who rolled over onto her back and was already shaking her head to get the cobwebs out. She had a four-line slash across her upper chest that made her entire torso slick with gore. Nick, on the other hand, remained unconscious. He took a blow to the head that left a small flap of scalp hanging loose. Blood soaked the ground around him. With my one good hand, I grabbed a fist full of his shirt and shook him violently.

"Sir Captain Captain!" I screamed at him. "Who said you could lay down! On your feet, soldier!"

Tough love.

Sometimes it worked.

Nick's eyes blinked open, a thick trail of blood oozing into one of them, and he struggled to sit up.

CHAPTER THIRTY-FOUR

"Goodbye," I said, blinking back the water in my eyes. "May your next journey end better than this one."

"Farewell," Grace said, tears snaking down her cheeks.

Nick went last. "We'll miss you both."

I dropped the burning stick onto the mound of wood shavings, dry tree moss, and the few scraps of paper we had. They caught fire immediately. Soon, the larger chunks of wood would burn too. Then the fire would spread to the driftwood limbs and logs we gathered and stacked into the rough form of a pyre— Grace and Nick had done all the hauling. In the center of the giant tangle of wood lay Grandfather with Tyche clasped lovingly in his arms.

We assembled enough wood that the bonfire should blaze away on the sandy beach for hours and hours. When it was over . . . well, from dust to dust, ashes to ashes.

I would have preferred a burial, but we had no shovel.

Almost a full day had passed since the battle. All of our clothes were covered with dried blood. Each of us was weak to the point of exhaustion. In addition to our wounds, we had black and blue bruises over most of our bodies.

"Let's go," I said quietly to the others, who stood staring at the flames.

Grungy, beat up, and looking nothing like humans, we trudged over the sand and gravel toward the boat, which sat half in the water. Not far away lay the carcass of the evil bear, all fourteen and half feet of him stretched out on its back with his jaws frozen open in a snarl. I hope he knew fear and terror in those last seconds of freefall before the rocks bashed in his skull.

The tumble from the cliff onto the rocks killed the cursed bear, as it had Grandfather and Tyche. Part of me wanted to mutilate the monster's body, maybe cut off the head, but what would be the point.

No, let the corpse rot in the sun.

The edges of my mouth inched up in a grim smile when I saw a bunch of ravens pecking away at the body.

My favorite orange shorts encircled my forearm as a makeshift bandage. Grace tied two thick tree branches, chopped to size, on either side of my injured arm to function as makeshift splints. One of my sweaters was repurposed as a sling. My wound hurt like a mother, but if Grandfather could endure all the pain he had to suffer after his meds ran out, then I could bear my pain too. So, I bit my lip and shoved aside the throbbing ache, remembering a line I once heard that pain is weakness leaving the body.

As for Nick, he had one of Grandfather's white shirts wrapped around his head like a turban. A rust-colored spot stained the fabric where blood seeped through and dried. Fortunately, the bleeding had stopped after Grace made a primitive attempt to suture the wound shut with a small fish hook and nylon leader line from our tackle box. My brave little brother didn't flinch, cry out, or even grimace much as she stabbed the hook in and pulled the line tight again and again.

Grace looked the best, as usual. The bear claw gashes weren't that deep, but the beast had inflicted ragged tears in her skin that needed stitching too. I couldn't sew her up with one hand, and Nick didn't have the dexterity for it, so Nick and I MacGyvered the wound by closing it up with duct tape and gauze from the first aid kit. The bandage wasn't very attractive, but damn, if it didn't work.

"At least he missed my boobs," Grace had remarked as I finished up.

"Your boobs are safe," I agreed.

"Boob on, girl," Nick added.

We would all carry vicious scars from the battle to our grave, but we'd wear them as badges of honor, not as ugly imperfections to hide or be ashamed of.

No one spoke as we shuffled over to the boat while reflections of the orange flames from the pyre danced on the water's surface. I paused at the river's edge and glanced down at my uninjured arm. I still had my idiot Cartier watch on. It was wet and dirty but ticking. The diamonds sparkled in the sunlight as if to say "ain't life great?"

It was a struggle, but I undid the clasp and hefted the watch in my hand for a couple seconds, and then I tossed it as far out into the river as I could manage. It hit the water with the barest hint of a splash and sank like a rock.

"Your watch," Grace said, her voice hoarse.

"My watch," I agreed.

She raised an eyebrow at me in question, waiting for an explanation.

"It doesn't fit anymore."

She nodded, as if she understood perfectly what I was trying to say. Maybe she did. Then she took my good hand, and we stepped into the boat together while Nick hung back to shove us off. Within minutes, we drifted down the center of the huge river while Nick rowed with deliberate, unhurried strokes as we paddled north with the current.

From the fragments of memory I had of my map before I lost it, I thought—hoped, really—that we were on the northern stretch of the Severn River. If so, there were communities on this river. I remembered that. Not many, not big, but something. All I really prayed for was a radio or, even better, a sat phone. My insides twisted at the memory of our sat phone that fell into Lake Makwa the day we arrived. So stupid. So long ago.

All of this ordeal could have been prevented if Grace and I hadn't gotten into that fight. But I refused to let regret worm its way inside of me. After all, the person I was on that day months ago didn't exist anymore. She died somewhere in the forest of the lost and found.

Good riddance.

The journey downriver took four days. During this time, we fished, we slept on sandbars, and we conversed about what we would do when we got home. One thing that worried all of us was that we wouldn't fit in. We had seen what lay beneath the thin veneer of what people call civilization. Our experience here in the wilderness was ugly at times, but it was real. Our life back home—the money, the credit cards, the spending—it was fake, shallow, and a poor imitation of what life is actually all about. Did I want to go back to that? Did I have a choice? The answers lay somewhere down the river . . . our new best friend.

"I think I'm going to attend public school," Nick said one night around the fire. "I'm done with homeschooling. I'm not afraid anymore."

"What about Morgon?" Grace asked.

"Morgon is dead," he replied. "Right, sis?"

"We killed him," I agreed.

So, in the end, Nick defeated his demons. What all that meant for him, we'd have to see. Already I saw the kind of strength and confidence in his eyes that come from having gone into battle, stared death in the eye, and survived to fight another day.

And then there was Grace. I didn't know what all changed inside her, but I was certain she was going to blossom into someone uber strong and very special. She had become as tough as the cracked, never-say-die leather of my boots. She made me proud. *Nick* made me proud.

When everything seemed hopeless, we stood together and fought back. Not everybody does.

And what about my grandfather and Tyche? Someday, I'd be able to string together words to express who they were and what they did, but not for a long time. Grandfather wanted to be remembered for who he really was. He would be . . . he would be.

I wrestled with these thoughts early one morning as the others slept around the embers of our smoldering fire. I sat cross-legged on a stretch of sandy beach by the river watching the sky turn pink and orange as the sun rose. I could count on one hand the number of times I rose early enough to see the sunrise before I came here. Now, I was in the audience for the show every morning.

A crisp wind blew, and the tops of distant trees swayed gently. Birds woke and began babbling at each other. The land and trees around me were so alive; they had a pulse and I felt the thrum of it inside me beating in time with my heart. This country was wild and rugged and dangerous but beautiful in a way that all the clothes and expensive coiffures I once prized could never be.

"What's happening to me?" I murmured to the dark river water gurgling along a few feet away.

The scream of an eagle flying overhead, so majestic and fearless and free, gave me my answer.

On the morning of the fifth day after the battle of the butte, as we had taken to calling it, we rounded a bend in the river and saw clusters of buildings on the left bank of the river. Ribbons of smoke trailed into the sky from several of them. The settlement was too small to be called a town maybe, but I spotted a couple dozen homes.

I didn't see any kind of a dock, so I told Nick to take the boat in any place he thought best. He picked a spot where the bank sloped up a few feet, but the incline was gentle.

Once Nick helped Grace and me out of the boat, a black-haired man with weathered skin appeared, standing at the top of the rise with his arms folded over his chest. He had a stern expression.

"Where did you come from?" the man asked in a gravelly voice.

"Not really sure," I answered. "Do you have a radio or sat phone we could use?"

He studied us for several moments, as if trying to puzzle out a really hard crossword clue.

"Wait," he finally said, his face morphing into a surprised expression. "Are you—"

"Yeah, that's us," Grace said, cutting him off.

"Stay here!" the man shouted. Then he turned and ran.

I had a hundred questions for the guy, but he left before I could ask them. Had zombies overrun the cities? Did aliens invade Earth? What about planes? Were they still flying? The real question, though, was why did the world abandon us to die on the shores of Lake Makwa? I doubted he could tell us. I wasn't sure who could. We didn't always get answers for why shit happened.

Instead of asking any of my questions, I yelled after him, "Happy to meet you too!"

"Butthead!" Grace shouted.

Then we clamored up the shore to the top of the small rise, where we stood staring at a handful of people going about their business. An ATV passed by on a nearby dirt road, and the driver didn't even give us a glance as he drove by with one arm on his hip. A woman walked not far away, holding a child by the hand while her other hand squished an iPhone to her ear. She, too, paid us no mind either, dirty, bloody, and grimy as we were. Wait, they had cell phones out here?

People lived, struggled, and laughed. Life went on.

"I'm going to miss you guys," I said softly to Grace and Nick.

"What are you saying?" Grace shot back with an alarmed expression.

"Once I get my arm fixed, I'm coming back here. I think I finally know where I belong."

"But I just got you back," Grace objected, her voice quivering slightly.

"I'll be right here," I said in a totally pathetic imitation of E.T., and with a lopsided grin, I touched her forehead with my finger.

Nick chuckled and Grace shook her head at my monumental lameness before both pulled me in for a group hug. We squeezed each other, careful not to jostle our various injuries. We had faced down the great monster that lived in all of us and found out that the beast was part of who we were. It could make you strong or break you.

And so, on the banks of the Severn River, just below the arctic circle, our journey came to an end . . . and also to a beginning. But that was another story.

THE END

www.ingramcontent.com/pod-product-compliance
Lightning Source LLC
Chambersburg PA
CBHW021809110726
47902CB00006B/1715